MEN AND WIVES

BLOOMSBURY READER

Discover books by Ivy Compton-Burnett published by
Bloomsbury Reader at
www.bloomsbury.com/IvyCompton-Burnett

MEN AND WIVES

IVY COMPTON-BURNETT

BLOOMSBURY READER

LONDON · NEW DELHI · NEW YORK · SYDNEY

This edition published in 2012 by Bloomsbury Reader

Bloomsbury Reader is a division of Bloomsbury Publishing Plc,

50 Bedford Square, London WC1B 3DP

ISBN: 978 1 4482 0094 8
eISBN: 978 1 4482 0226 3

Visit www.bloomsburyreader.com to find out more about our authors and their books
You will find extracts, author interviews, author events and you can sign up for
newsletters to be the first to hear about our latest releases and special offers
Printed and bound by CPI Group (UK) Ltd, Croydon, CR0 4YY

Contents

Chapter I

"Well, Buttermere, this is a day that is good to live and breathe in, that makes a man feel in his prime. Standing here in front of my house, I feel as young as when I moved into it thirty years ago, in the year eighteen hundred and fifty-nine. What aged man would you take me to be, as I step as it were casually into your view?" Sir Godfrey Haslam stepped, though hardly in this manner, through the window of his dining-room, and stood to face or to pass his butler's scrutiny. "I'll wager not fifty-six. But that is what I am. Six-and-fifty the month before last. Well, what would you say, Buttermere?"

"Good-morning, Sir Godfrey," Buttermere said.

"Three years and ten months under sixty! What some people would call an elderly man. Well, in later middle life would be the general verdict. But I don't feel anywhere near so far run down my course. I hope every man of that age feels as I do. I hope you do, Buttermere?"

"My circumstances have been at variance, Sir Godfrey," said Buttermere, continuing the duties that had brought him to what he was.

"Shine or shade seems to tip the scales one way or the other," said Sir Godfrey, frowning at the delicate balance of his life. "Well, I daresay it is the same with most of us. Up and down."

Buttermere stood with his back to the light, in illustration of his own experience.

Sir Godfrey Haslam, a fair, solid man, with kind, shallow eyes, indefinite Saxon features, and a genial and casual bearing, turned to the window and surveyed the English meadow and moorland that he had chosen, since he had had to choose, for the setting of his days. His butler, a man of the same build and age, with a large, hairless face and head, and a small group of features roughly arranged towards the centre of the former, could only give a glance in the same direction, and put more energy into his present employment of drawing breath. Both men looked as if they had led an easy life, the master, as was natural, as if he had led the easier.

"I feel a different man when the sun is at work. I feel proud of my home, of my wife, of my sons and my daughter, my menservants and my maidservants, and the stranger that is within my gate. I take a satisfaction in my possessions." The speaker's glance at his portraits confirmed his contented spirit, as his father, when causing them to be made, had relied upon his own experience that early struggling leads to ultimate success. "And in my dear old parents who look down on me from their frames, as if they were glad to see me set up in a different way from themselves. Ah, I remember their gladness. Nothing to be ashamed of in my heritage, Buttermere, in a useful little fortune and title earned by providing people with things they need, by putting at their hand what sufficed unto them. I should blush for myself if I blushed for it."

"Yes, Sir Godfrey," said Buttermere in a voice of rejoinder.

"You see I talk to you as a friend, Buttermere," said Sir

Godfrey, sensing that this tone was called for. "Twenty-five years you have been about us, and that gives a man a right to be treated as a friend, doesn't it?"

"Thank you, Sir Godfrey," Buttermere said, in a manner that did not testify to these dealings.

"I believe you would prefer a stand-offish aristocrat for a master," said Sir Godfrey, taking no credit for the soundness of his belief.

"I am satisfied, thank you, Sir Godfrey."

"Anyone down yet?" said the master, with an expression of pricked-up ears.

"Her ladyship is on the way, Sir Godfrey."

"Oh, her ladyship is first this morning," said Sir Godfrey going to the door with a firm tread and a suggestion of outstretched arms. "Well, my Harriet, well, my dear! And how did you sleep?"

"You know I do not sleep in these days, Godfrey. It is monotonous for you always to ask the question, and for me always to answer it."

Lady Haslam came into the room with a dragging step, a short, dark woman, with worn, firm features, a heavy jaw and unhappy brown eyes, looking much older than her husband, although of his age.

"Oh, but I meant, how much sleep did you get? I meant, did you have any sort of night at all? You know what was in my mind, as well as I know myself."

"Yes, I know, my dear."

"Oh, come, come, my dear girl. You must have some kind of rest, or you couldn't be all day about with us all. You are never withdrawn for a moment. I mean, we never have to do without you. Don't make a point of misunderstanding me. Don't come downstairs with that express intention."

Harriet was of better family than Godfrey, and had brought a darker heritage in her older blood. She had worn early in nerves and brain, with others of an inbred race, and an intense religious and family life bore heavily on her feebleness.

When her children entered, she searched their faces with hungry eyes, and returned their greeting with a passionate embrace.

Her second son, Jermyn, was a serious young man of twenty-four, who combined in his looks the best points of both his parents, and whose Christian name had been given him because it was his mother's surname, a reason seemingly valid only for a younger son, since it had not been applied to his elder brother. Her daughter, Griselda, was a handsome, unstable-looking girl a year or two younger, whose wide grey eyes continually sought her mother's, and never seemed at rest. The youngest son, Gregory, was an overgrown, featureless youth of twenty, with prominent, colourless eyes and at first sight no expression. The eldest son observed a custom of being late.

"Well, we are all here," said Godfrey, with a note of anticipation. "You are all with us, Buttermere?"

"All but Cook, Sir Godfrey," said Buttermere, choosing to disclose that duty detained one member of the household, in spite of, or rather because of its being a daily circumstance.

"Oh, well, we are all here," said Godfrey, causing Griselda to smile at Jermyn. "The eleventh Chapter of Corinthians, the fourteenth verse!"

Godfrey came of dissenting stock, and was used to religious officiation on the part of the head of the house. He had taken his father's mantle on his own shoulders with a willingness that had grown to zeal. Harriet was religious enough to care only for the

4

fundamentals of her faith. She accepted and respected him in this character, setting it above his other side, in which preference she was joined by himself. He read in an emphatic, satisfied voice, which he raised and dropped without regard to the words, and then laid the book aside and fell on his knees, when his example was followed by his household.

"O Lord," he exclaimed, in tones of respect and admonition, that somehow indicated the words with capitals, "Thou seest us gathered before Thee at Thy altar, at the beginning of our day, a simple family seeking Thy grace to bring us through it, sinful indeed in word and thought, yet without sin in Thy sight. For faith can remove mountains, and that faith is ours. Keep our three sons, the young men going forth, rejoicing in their youth, to the daily temptations that are its joy and snare. Keep our daughter, the solace of our age, the companion of her father's prime; hold her in Thy keeping. Keep our servants, those who are with us to do Thy work of ministering. And those who need especial strength, to carry them over the ground trodden so often that it has become hard, who find a strain in the trivial round, the common task, give to these Thy protection for their frail and gallant spirit. Bless my wife and all of us, and bind us all together with the great, unbreakable bond of family love and fellowship."

To these and other injunctions, though not laid upon themselves, the family gave an ear, Harriet with simple acceptance of the sphere which showed her husband strong and wise. Harriet and Godfrey had questioned their religion as little as the accepted shape of the earth they trod.

The service concluded with the Lord's Prayer, in which the household spoke for themselves, Godfrey's tones being apparently designed to suppress the sudden arbitrariness. Buttermere's voice on the words, "as we forgive those who trespass against us," suggested the suppliant's general frame of mind.

"Well, now, breakfast!" said Godfrey, receiving his world on secular terms. "Now a good breakfast to make up for the bad night, Harriet. Don't stand about loafing, you two boys. Good-morning, all of you. How is Father's girl to-day?"

"Quite well," said Griselda, giving him a startled smile, and leaning towards her mother.

"Mother, how did you sleep?"

"Not at all, my sweet one. Never mind, as long as you slept well."

Griselda held her eyes down, and Jermyn strolled to the table.

"Well, bad news of the night?" he said with a deliberate ease.

"There is no news, dear, but not in the sense that no news is good news. It must certainly be no news to you by now, and you speak as if you were reconciled to it."

"Oh, now, Harriet, now you are making a mistake," said her husband in a manner of making a last effort before yielding to fate. "We keep all our sympathy for you, but, as you say, it is not news to us now. Nor is it to you, my poor girl. Gregory, don't stand there, kicking your feet like a child."

Gregory took his place by his mother, and looked into her face with simple affection.

"Well, how did you employ the night watches, since you had them at your disposal ?"

"In pacing up and down the corridors, my son," said his mother in a soothed and gentle tone, and with almost a light of humour in her eye over words ominous to any other ear. "I knew I shouldn't wake any of you. You all sleep so soundly." Even this was not a reproach to Gregory. "I don't feel so wrought up as I generally do after a night without sleep."

6

"Oh, come, come, that is a good word, Harriet. Come, that is a brave speech," cried Godfrey. "Now we shall have a better day. You will have a better day. You will be able to amuse yourself a little."

"Amuse myself? Shall I, Godfrey? It has taken all my effort for years to get through the day, and to face the night, the night!" Harriet dropped her voice and bent her head as much in suffering as in the acting of exasperation, and Jermyn rose to the demand.

"What an offensive thing to say, Father! What worse insult than to be accused of amusing oneself? Amusing oneself, when life is but toil and duty!"

"I wish it were that for you, my son," said Harriet. "And for me, how I wish it were just that, just toil and duty!"

"That sounds to your credit. We are proud of you," said Griselda.

"Proud of her? Yes, we are," said Godfrey loudly. "We are proud of her for the high mettle that keeps her up and doing as if she had the toughness the rest of us have. Ah, we have cause for pride."

Harriet raised her eyes to her husband's in mingled affection and despair.

"Who is proud of whom?" said the eldest son of the house, a gaunt young man of twenty-eight, as much like his mother as was allowed by age and sex and human difference. "Good-morning to you all."

"Ah, good-morning, my dear boy," said Godfrey, leaning back with eyes full of affection, as his son disregarded the summons of Harriet's glance and went straight to his seat. "We wish you a good-morning indeed."

"Matthew," said his mother, "I don't know if it is anything to

7

you that you add to my burden; that you leave me morning by morning to feel you have had no part in our common preparation for our day?"

"Oh, prayers!" said Matthew. "They hardly seem to serve their purpose. I am not struck by the signs of preparation."

"No, that is how it must seem," said Harriet, turning her head. "I am a torment to you all, and a burden on your hours that you never escape ! But I am as much of a burden on my own, ten thousand times more of a burden. Griselda, my darling, don't look distressed; don't waste a thought on your harrowing old mother. Don't think of me. Be happy."

Griselda gave a response with her lips that did not develop into sound, and Matthew looked at her in gloomy compassion.

"How can her life be her own, when she is told that it is ? The two things are not compatible. None of our lives are our own."

"Some of them are more your own than I can feel they should be," said his mother in a different tone.

"You are speaking against me, and not to my face, Mother," said Jermyn. "That is a mean and unmannerly thing to do."

"I will say it to your face, my son. It is a sorrow to me that you and Matthew deal with your talents as if they were given you for your own use. I fear that may be your way of hiding them in the earth."

Harriet's ambition for Jermyn was a fellowship at Cambridge, his own that he should write original verse. Her desire for Matthew was a London practice in medicine, in which he was qualified, his aim for himself scientific research. Harriet's ambitions for her children were so confused with her religious zeal, that her natural sense of values hardly emerged. She was a slave to her feeling that ultimate good depended on effort for others and sacrifice of self. Moreover she alone in the house knew the common fate of such hopes of youth.

"We have a lot of beautiful things in the family," said Gregory in his dulcet tones. "Poetry and science and Griselda's looks and Father's seat on a horse. I hope I shall be generously proud. It is all wonderful."

"My darlings, it is," said Harriet in a deep, vibrant voice. "I should be a happy and grateful mother, and I am. How I should try to remember what I have! How I will try, if my weakness does not overtake me! I wonder if any of you can see me through it."

Buttermere opened the door and cut through his master's prompt and arduous words.

"Dr. Dufferin, Mr. Matthew!"

"Well, Doctor, how are you?" said Godfrey, who addressed and alluded to his friends according to their callings. "It is good of you to take us on your early ride. You will have some coffee with us before you drag this boy to his work. The young rascal is only just down."

"I have finished, thank you, Father," said Matthew, rising to accompany his friend.

"Now, now, don't mouth at me and argue," said Godfrey, in an easier tone than was warranted by his words. "Your mother wants a talk with the doctor, and if she wants it, she shall have it. The house is not yours. And if the talk is to be about you, be thankful that anyone wants to talk about you, that there are people who take an interest in you. Because you don't take much interest in anyone else."

Godfrey raised his voice to penetrate the door, and relapsed into mirth at the perception that half his speech was lost.

"Well, now, Doctor, here is my poor wife clucking on the bank, with her ducklings gone to water! Matthew is not starting on his profession, and Jermyn is not writing his what-do-you-call-it for his fellowship. They are deep in science and poetry and I don't know what. How should I know? I never did any of these things. It is not because of me that they do them."

"No, that is a just claim," said the guest. "Harriet must know that she is at the bottom of it. That makes her feel the responsibility."

Antony Dufferin was a dark, vigorous man of thirty-eight, with a broad, humorous nose, a covert quickness of eye, and to those who saw, a strong undercurrent of nervous and productive power. His career as a London physician had been broken by a marriage ending in scandal and divorce. He had not troubled to expose the truth, had given up his work with an easy heart, and settled in his native county near to the Haslams' place, to give his life to a corner of medical research. Matthew had chosen to work under him, rather than accept from his parents a London practice as a gift.

"Now, Doctor, I beseech you to bring home to my wife that she is building troubles out of air. She will give an ear to you, when she won't flicker an eyelid in my direction. I shouldn't think there are more prosperous people in the world than we are; I don't mean in any crude sense; I mean more fortunate in human affection, in family good fellowship, in the things that make life worth living. I should feel more fortunate still if my sons were laying the foundations for future usefulness."

"Research doesn't often promise usefulness," said Dufferin, "though you put it with a simplicity. But why shouldn't Matthew have an innocent occupation that he fancies himself? Other people don't give so much sign of thinking of him. His attitude is more benevolent than theirs."

"Yes, now, you are right, Doctor," said Godfrey. "Harriet, you see the force of his words. That is the thought that has been in my own mind, though I couldn't have put it better. I mean, we did well in asking him to sum things up for us."

"Matthew is serving himself first," said Harriet.

"Well, that is a true word of all of us," said Dufferin.

"Ah, so it is," said Godfrey with a chuckle. "I admit that I think of myself before anyone else comes into my head. I mean with a few exceptions, with the one exception of course; I am a married man." He looked towards the window, but Harriet did not glance at him.

"A doctor's life has great opportunities," she said. "We are serious people, Antony, and should take great pride in the serious success of our son."

"Plenty of preaching to be given in any life. People don't often want it, and they never take it. They don't even need it. If it was any good to them, they would be the first to give it to themselves. Matthew can use his own opportunities. He won't want a profession when he comes after his father here, and what he has chosen will take him to his end. Come and see me out, Haslam."

Godfrey followed his friend into the hall, and stood as if in doubt.

"What of my poor girl in there?" he said.

"I must be careful of my eyes. You see more with yours than you used. I see you have had to. I think it will be well enough, if she does not come under a real strain. I wouldn't answer for things then: this fighting with everything is strain enough. But I don't see how she can do that, with you all on the watch for her."

"No, no. We will all watch for her indeed," said Godfrey in a rather empty voice. "Matthew, here is the doctor waiting for you. Have you said good-bye to your mother, my boy?"

"No, there is no occasion, Father. I shall see her later in the day."

"But go in and say good-bye to her, my son," said Godfrey in a coaxing, deprecating tone. "Give her a word to take with her through the day. A word from you is a great stand-by for her. You know that."

"I haven't observed it," said Matthew, going down the steps. "Good-bye, Father."

"Good-bye, my boy, good-bye," said Godfrey, with cordial appreciation of this farewell. "My blessing goes with you."

Having uttered these last words in a tone too low to be heard, Godfrey retraced his steps to the dining-room, giving them especial force in case they should falter. Harriet was walking on the gravel outside the house, with Gregory holding her arm and stooping over her, and her face was happy and almost young.

Her husband threw back his shoulders and laid hold of the lapels of his coat, and walked about, swishing his feet on the carpet and breaking into snatches of talk and song. Buttermere entered and conveyed in silence his view of anyone engaged, or perhaps surprised in audible soliloquy.

"Well, Buttermere, so you have caught me in the act. You never talk to yourself, do you? You would be ashamed?"

Buttermere looked as if he could not but allow this to pass.

"You never do things you are ashamed of, do you, Buttermere?" said Godfrey, suggesting the truth, for Buttermere never talked to himself, did a woman's work as distinct from his own kindred duties, addressed his subordinates except with peremptory direction, or committed tangible dishonesty. Of taking pleasure in any human discomfiture, especially in that of the family he served, he was not ashamed, reserving this feeling for such things as threatened his manhood.

Gregory was pacing with his mother on the path.

"I am asking you a question I have never asked before. What

do you think about when you are treading the passages at night? Tell me at once and truly. Do you get into a habit of going over the same things ?"

"My darling, what do I think about? I ought not to tell you. I feel sometimes as if the curse were hanging over you, as if only your father were free of it. Yes, I go over the same things. That seems to be my weakness, almost my disease; I believe it is nearly that. I feel I must get something just as it was, and I don't quite reach it, and begin again; and each time something is missed, and never the same thing. And it goes on through the night; and I feel it hanging over me in the day; and the future stretches before me with all the nights. And when I differ from Matthew and Jermyn—and it is not what I want for them, Gregory, what they are doing—and when your father and I are not of one mind, I go over what they have suffered, and what remains in their thoughts. And I feel that if I could once come up with the thoughts, I should not mind what they were; that I could face them, if they were not hanging over me with threat; and they can never be overtaken. And I ought not to tell all this to you, who may be going to suffer it yourself. I never ought to have married, Gregory. But I am easier now you know it, and I am not living alone. It does not seem it ought to be what it is, and yet it is always the same. You could never understand, and yet there is nothing you cannot understand, my dear, dear boy."

"How clever of you it was to marry Father, when you were both of you as you were!"

"Well, my child, perhaps it was clever. Perhaps he was the right man for me, your dear, good father, my generous, forbearing husband. I may not be the right woman for anyone. But he is stronger than I am, just as he is weaker. I don't think it has hurt him, unless it is that I will not think so. I trust he is happy.

13

How I pray that he is! For I cannot help myself, Gregory."

"Oh, yes, he is happy, doing such lovely things, shooting and riding and reading prayers," said Gregory.

"Gregory, you know what our family service represents to your father and me, that it is the visible sign of the deepest things within us?"

"Yes. You are so fortunate to have them represented. Most of us don't get them attended to at all."

The mother was silent, a complex expression on her face.

"There are Jermyn and Griselda setting off for the moors," said Gregory.

"Come, come, my darlings," said Harriet in a passionate, crooning voice, beckoning with a large, maternal gesture. "Come and say good-bye to your mother. Go out into the sun and beauty, and leave uneasiness behind. It is I who have caused it. Leave me and be at peace."

The intenseness of Harriet's tone brought a change to her children's faces, and Gregory took his arm from hers and sauntered by her side with the eagerness fading from his eyes.

Godfrey, who tended to pair with Matthew, as Jermyn did with Griselda, and Harriet with Gregory, stepped out alone on to the gravel, shading his face.

"Well, my Harriet. Well, my dear, I heard you talking in a way that reminded me of our youth. I said to myself, 'Why, there is my Harriet chattering like a girl!' This is a brave morning for you."

"Godfrey," said Harriet, shrinking back in a manner that made her husband do the same, "I wish you would not comment upon any action of mine that happens to be natural. What would you do, if you could not be yourself for a moment without creating a storm of comment? How can I avoid being unlike other

14

people, if I am to produce stupefaction when I am as they are?"

"Oh, come, Harriet! Storm of comment! Why, what did I say but that you were talking like a girl? You would not expect me to be up in arms, if you said I was talking like a boy. You are not likely to say it to me. That would produce stupefaction, I can tell you."

"Godfrey," said Harriet, laying her hand on his arm, "I am not often myself in these days. Will you bear with me for the sake of those behind while we have a word about the future of our sons?"

"Bear with you? Bear with a word on the future of our sons?" said Godfrey, drawing her arm within his in well-thought-of emulation of Gregory. "I should like it above all things. A talk with you about our dear boys, who hold us together and prevent us from drifting apart; who make it worth while for us to hold together; who make our keeping together for our own sakes a good thing in itself! It is what I have been wanting without knowing what I wanted."

Godfrey, setting off at his wife's side, observed the sudden pallor of her face, and while keeping on the prudent side of comment upon it, was far from assigning himself as its cause.

Chapter II

"Words cannot do justice to my opinion of Gregory," said Jermyn, as he walked with his sister on the moors. "He seems to ask nothing but to curl up sleekly in other people's minds. I can almost hear him purring in Mother's. Beside him I am a monster of gross egoism."

"I hope I am too," said Griselda. "I think that is nicer for us."

"Matthew and I won't be useless to other people in the end. Far from it, if we are allowed the chance of being what we are. If we are driven to throw our powers into hackwork just when the early forces are in play, the spring might go for ever; it might simply break. You can't get too much into one youth."

"I shan't try to get anything into mine," said Griselda, with the humorous freedom she showed with her brothers. "I think my spring is too tender to be used at all. I daresay Gregory's is too."

"I was speaking in a serious spirit. We must do that for a second or two sometimes."

"Well, if we must," said Griselda. "Then you are in no danger from Father, and probably in none from Mother, though we tremble before signs that she is tempted to use her power. People can't have so much without its occurring to them to use it."

"I am protected by her weakness for seeing Father master in his own house."

"I had a feeling that you were safe. And you will be safer when you reach a more definite stage. Mother is simpler than she seems."

"You can't be as definite with poetry as if you were working with material things. It is simple indeed not to see that. The spirit comes and goes, as live things must. It is independent and ebbs and flows. At the moment it is on the ebb." Griselda nervously conquered a smile, and her brother continued with coldness. "You can't foretell your moods. All rare things are elusive. It is a condition of their being rare."

"Well, of course, those are not the words for Mother. She can observe that things are elusive without suspecting that they are rare, except in the sense that they are not to be depended on."

"You can't offer up poetry to order. You may laugh, but you can't gather up and put into form in a moment what has been stirring in your mind for years, what may have its roots right back in the deeps of childhood. Strange, strange, that human beings with centuries of thought behind them should think it were possible!"

"That is a hopeful view of Father's antecedents. The centuries behind him hold a good deal besides thought. We must take it into account."

"Of course it is my business to give him proof, and I am not far off it now. Things are rising and working and taking shape. A very few more months!"

"That is good hearing," said his sister. "A little family uplift would not come amiss. I don't see what we shall come to, if we don't have some soon. Matthew may not be able to wrest a secret

17

from the universe. We must rely on the one of you who can depend on himself."

"Each time I see the Hardistys' place," said Jermyn, as they came upon an eighteenth-century house, "I regret that we do not belong to what Buttermere properly calls the real gentry."

"We can't blame Buttermere for being ashamed of us," said Griselda. "We are at that particularly shameful stage when we understand it. Here is Sir Percy coming to meet us. He always does that when we arrive without being asked."

Sir Percy Hardisty, whom Buttermere described as a gentleman of the old order, had a shapeless, stooping figure, little, opaque green eyes, a boneless, spreading nose, an uncertain gait, and clothes of that peculiar shabbiness which rouses speculation upon the wearer's attitude to them. Sir Percy had no attitude to things of this kind, and Buttermere had summed up his own in the statement that his master, Sir Godfrey, owed more to himself; and there was truth as well as triumph in his perception that Sir Percy's corresponding debt was small.

"Well, well, this is a kindness to an old man," said Sir Percy, who was sixty-two and had for some years imposed this view of his age. "You have come to see me as well as the rest of us. It is a great favour to us all. Now tell me how your mother is this morning."

Sir Percy had a great affection and respect for Harriet. The feeling was shared by his wife, who was coming to join them, a sturdy old woman ten years older than her husband, with bright, steady eyes, a well-shaped head and a carefully innocent expression.

"It is an interesting time of the year, the time when our oldest shoes get really spoilt enough to be discarded. That is of no advantage to Percy. We say he is one of those people who can wear anything. I think he must be the only one who really wears it. I hope he hasn't been too certain of himself, and assumed you would stay to luncheon without being pressed."

"Why, they will have luncheon with us, Rachel. Luncheon must be on the table," said Sir Percy, looking perplexed.

"They are young and generous," said Lady Hardisty. "Come in, my dears, and begin at once having luncheon. It is worse to talk to hosts when you are not having it. You know I sit at the side of the table, so that people can see I do not shrink from sitting under my predecessor." Sir Percy fleetingly raised his eyes to the portrait of his first wife. "Everything has to be done to throw up the character of a woman in my position. You know I taught Milly and Polly to call me Mater, to show their real feeling of that kind was given to another long ago. I trained them myself in that for the sake of their loyalty. As Polly only knew her mother for an hour, her loyalty is a tribute to the dear child's constant nature, that it pays to foster."

Sir Percy paused in his carving, his knife and fork aloft and wide, and leant towards Jermyn.

"And how did you say your mother was?"

"Not up to a great deal," said Jermyn. "She does not sleep, and that makes the day rather much for her."

"Yes, yes. And your father?" said Sir Percy, laying down his tools. "He is perhaps not too much put about by it?"

"He is anxious about her in his own way. He tries not to let it get the better of him, for all our sakes."

"Oh, yes, yes. Not get the better of him," said Sir Percy, rising to yield his place to his wife, and stooping over Jermyn's chair with his hands upon it. "Then you can cheer me on the whole about everything?"

"Percy, you can't expect Jermyn to be a second mother to you

19

as I have been," said Rachel. "Poor little Grisel is looking at you as if she really were your mother. It is too much for them."

"And Matthew?" said Sir Percy, passing along the table with a hobbling step. "Matthew is still at his work, is he? He doesn't often come to see us all. And you, Jermyn, are still at poetry? Well, that leaves you more at ease; that is one thing about it; that is a great thing for your friends."

"Percy, of course Jermyn is not at ease. Do say less dreadful things," said Rachel.

"He is coming out as a full-fledged poet almost at once," said Griselda.

"A little later than that," said Jermyn.

"Ah, now, now," said Sir Percy, leaning back in his wife's chair, "that will be something for your mother. Because she must want a little cheering sometimes, with all of it, with your work and Matthew's. Of course I know it has to be done, that it is a great thing that you can do it. Both of you, too; it is a great thing; but still your mother, you know. Now, Rachel, I must insist upon relieving you."

"No, my dear. You must learn to think of others."

"Well, now, poetry, Jermyn," resumed Sir Percy. "Do people ever make anything out of it, as far as you know?"

"Well, I hope I shall make a few hundreds a year in the end. People don't often take it up as a life work. I shall have to be content with a very little for a long time, and to be a poor man at last."

"Well, now, and does that content you?" said Sir Percy. "That is what you want, is it? Well, of course, 'poets are not people we can understand. They would not be what they are if we could."

"No, they might as well be something else," said Rachel. "I wish I had ever been misunderstood. People so often give us our due, and that is bound to remind us of it."

"Of course my life work must involve many kinds of sacrifice, perhaps nearly all kinds," said Jermyn. "I am more than content."

"Oh, many kinds of sacrifice, nearly all kinds?" said Sir Percy, lifting his head. "Nearly all kinds? And you are content? More than content? And your poor mother does not like it? No, I am sure she would not."

"I think she will be reconciled to it, when she realises that any powers I have tend that way," said Jermyn. "She can hardly forbid my making sacrifices for my own sake. It is for nobody else's."

"Oh, for nobody else's?" said Sir Percy. "But what good is it then? I mean sacrifice not for someone else? I thought sacrifice— I mean sacrifice for your own sake, isn't that a little fanatical, Jermyn? I don't think that is what your mother means, when she is herself just a thought serious-minded, you know."

"No, no. She does not mean that. She thinks I am a pompous, sluggish young jackanapes," said Jermyn.

"Yes, but, now, what about what your mother thinks?" said Sir Percy coaxingly. "I don't mean what we know hasn't entered her mind. But isn't there something in it? Because all this sacrifice for nobody! Well, you know. Now why not think of your mother and father, instead of sacrifice for people outside, for nobody at all?"

"Griselda, it is too considerate to make us think it is a laughing matter," said Rachel. "I do appreciate it, and Percy would if he could."

"I shall have to sacrifice my mother's satisfaction with the other things," said Jermyn. "It is the sacrifice I shall like least to make."

"Oh, well, sacrifice," said Sir Percy, accepting persistence in

21

this line. "Well, so you must have it, Jermyn. Well, well, there seem to me to be better things. And your mother's satisfaction. Well, sacrifice has to be sacrifice; I see that it does. But you must have your way, and join the martyrs, the poets, take what seems to you the right course. Why, there are the girls, Rachel. There are Mellicent and Polly, back from their picnic in time to get something besides their sandwiches. Sandwiches are not very much."

"They are nothing. Nobody can eat them," said Rachel. "Well, my dears. Give your sandwiches to Merton for the fowls."

"We have finished them, Mater," said the younger girl.

"I thought that was why places were so untidy after picnics, that people took sandwiches and could not eat them. I don't understand why so much is left, if they can be used. Mellicent, you must make up to Jermyn for being told that poetry is not worth a sacrifice, that his mother ought not to be sacrificed to it, when of course she ought. It is trying in such subtle ways to be told that you must not sacrifice your mother."

Mellicent Hardisty was a contented young woman of twenty-six, very like and nearly as plain as her father, except that her eyes, as small and pale as his, were alive and clear. Jermyn's face lit up at her coming with welcome for a congenial presence. Polly at nineteen was a simpler version of the portrait that hung before her father's eyes. Her changing, unfinished face seemed to say that it would be equal to her mother's, if as much were done for it. Sir Percy's portraits were not on a level with Sir Godfrey's, and much had been done.

"Well, now, I am going to get up and go," said Sir Percy, carefully adapting his actions to his words. "And you know an old friend meant nothing, Jermyn, about things beyond his scope. It is for you and Mellicent to teach me; it is for me to learn. Now Griselda and Polly will chatter in the garden, and their voices will come in to Rachel and me, and be all the poetry we shall want. And you and Milly will settle it all, because these things involve too much." Sir Percy's voice died away on a murmur as he disappeared. "Yes, they involve a great deal in many ways."

"Mellicent, what heavy work is made for a poor young man who wants to justify his own sorry little tastes!"

"That doesn't sound as if it mattered much."

"Well, his own deep, serious tastes, then. And why shouldn't I mean that after all?"

"No reason at all. It is all or nothing with people with these things. But for most people it is nothing. We have to remember that."

"It is not the moment for remembering it, when you feel yourself on the verge of accomplishment."

"That is great news," said Mellicent. "We can't help getting a tendency to wait and see."

"I should say not," said Jermyn. "To think of the stuff that comes out!"

"People talk as if that showed the thing was easy. Really it shows it is too hard for most of us. It is not to be wondered at that gifts are rare."

"No, no, it is not," said Jermyn, his voice rising. "It is a great piece of fortune to be above most men, for those that are."

"It is a good thing to feel you are that. I don't think a strong conviction is ever based on nothing."

"Well, yours will be the first opinion I shall want, when the verses are ready for the human eye."

"We only really want one opinion."

"I know you have written yourself, Mellicent. And your writing has my gravest respect; and I am not given to easy praise of the artist."

"The other kind of praise is the thing," said Mellicent. "Here is Griselda, threatening to take you home."

"Jermyn, we shall soon have had a day of happiness. Lady Hardisty is sending us back in the carriage in the hope of saving us. And it is our duty to relieve Gregory."

"Does Gregory want to be relieved?" asked Polly.

"Yes. He is on duty with Mother," said Griselda.

"On duty?" said Polly with her eyes wide.

"We haven't your easy life, Polly," said Jermyn.

Polly wore a look of living sympathy as her friends drove away.

"Don't Jermyn and Griselda and Gregory much like being at home?"

"Their mother's nerves must be a cloud over everything," said Mellicent. "They were in real alarm at the thought of not being back in time."

"But they will be in time, now they have the carriage," said Polly, springing to take her father's arm.

Sir Percy looked down on his younger child with an emotion that forced its way to his eyes. He believed that his joy in life had ended with the death of her mother nineteen years before, and the conviction was the chief ground of his self-esteem, a feeling that had never had a strong foundation. If he had realised that a little later his contentment had begun, it would have failed to survive; and his second wife, knowing its right to its life, left the truth in silence.

When Jermyn and Griselda reached their home, Buttermere was stationed at the door of the house.

"Well, we are a little later than we expected," said Jermyn.

"Good-afternoon, sir," said Buttermere.

"Yes, yes, we have come home in the later half of the day. Is Mr. Gregory still with her ladyship?"

24

"Not after the first few hours, sir."

"How has her ladyship been spending the time?"

"Getting through it by herself in the garden, miss."

"Mr. Gregory is out, I suppose. How long has he been gone?"

"I cannot approximately say, miss."

"Mother, Mother, spare a glance for your children," called Jermyn, as Harriet came round the house from her garden. "We thought we should be at home before. How long has Gregory been gone?"

"Only about ten minutes, dear. I don't quite know what time it is. Have you noticed my borders this year?"

"Buttermere, what do you mean by giving a wrong impression?" said Jermyn, following the attendant into the hall.

Buttermere paused with the suggestion of a bow.

"Will you kindly answer me?"

"If you will kindly repeat your question, sir."

"I asked you why you could not speak the truth."

"I should be sorry ever to have done anything else, sir," said Buttermere sincerely.

"You knew Mr. Gregory had only just left her ladyship."

"I stated that he had been with her ladyship for the first few hours, sir. I was under the impression that you had not been gone for a longer period."

"You know quite well that you meant to mislead."

"I know only what I said, sir."

"Well, darlings, discussing your day?" said Harriet, with a nervous glance in the direction of Buttermere, whose disturbance always transferred itself to her. "Have you a morning's happiness to tell me of?"

"Yes, that is just what we have. Buttermere implied that we had deserted you for about twelve hours."

25

"Well, that would hardly have mattered, my son. There is no reason why you should be tied to me. If you are enjoying your day, that is all your mother asks. And Father is always ready to come to me, if we should need each other. I don't know why you should have two settled married people on your minds. It is we who should have you on ours, and so we have. But as it happens, Gregory and I have had a day together. He is just setting out to have tea with Mrs. Calkin. There he is, hurrying out of the house."

Chapter III

Gregory waved his hand to Harriet as he hastened down the drive. In placing high for himself the appeal of experienced women, he made no exception of his mother. His tastes were well met at the house to which he was bound.

His hostess was a massive widow of sixty, with hair brushed back from a solid brow, as if to reveal its proportions, and indeed with this purpose, and a broad-featured, honest, forbidding face, which changed with her every feeling. Her name of Agatha Calkin seemed to represent the two sides of her character. Her unmarried sister, Geraldine Dabis, who had taken the place of the younger for fifty-eight years, willingly for the last forty of them, was tall and thin and plain, and of a conscious elegance, with a habit of gesticulating with her long hands, and raising her voice to hold her position in talk. The youngest of the three, Kate Dabis, sister by half-blood to the other two, was an alert little woman of forty-six, with a dark, pleasant face, a quick, deep voice, and a studied kindliness and tolerance, which gained her less appreciation than if they had cost her nothing.

"You are all of you here. Not one of you ill or absent," said Gregory, his manner addressing each.

"Oh, I was ill the last time you came!" said Geraldine in her carrying tones.

"You are thinking of the day when I was at the committee," said Agatha, her voice of gentle comment holding its own.

"I am never the interesting one, never frail or public-spirited," said Kate.

"I hope you are not anxious about your mother at the moment?" said Agatha, seeming to broach a matter between herself and Gregory.

Geraldine leant forward.

"No, not more than usual. There is no definite reason for anxiety, or for expecting to be free of it."

"I think there is the especial something between you and your mother," said Agatha.

"We are great friends; I am always hanging on to apron-strings. People with apron-strings know so much."

"Oh, that is not the kind of thing we generally hear! It is a most refreshing point of view," exclaimed Geraldine, raising her hands and dropping them on to her lap. "What we generally have to face, is the view that women of our age are too out-of-date and outside the scheme of things to be taken into account! Mercifully it is chivalrously unspoken. That is one advantage of belonging to the fairer sex."

"Young people have not always much imagination," said Agatha.

"Or have they too much?" said Kate.

"No, not enough," said Gregory. "Well, they don't get anything, and serve them right."

"You must be a great comfort to your mother," said Agatha with quiet understanding. "I can follow so well the feeling between you, because of myself and my dear absent son."

"It is hardly an exact parallel," said Geraldine.

"I never think," continued Agatha, her eyes not diverted from their course, "that there is the same bond between mother and daughter. It never seems to me to be quite the same."

"There should be, there should be," said Kate.

"Now between father and daughter," said Agatha in full admission; "between father and daughter. Yes."

"Do you find that is so between your father and your sister?" asked Kate.

"Yes, in a way. He is bursting with pride in her. But his real crony is Matthew. Jermyn gets hold of Griselda."

"Ah, these young families! What complex and significant things!" said Kate, giving full due to what she had missed.

"The most complex, the most significant, the most deep-rooted in the world," said Agatha, giving it to what she had had. "The only thing is, when the break comes."

"Have you seen the Hardistys lately?" said Geraldine to Gregory, revealing that her attention was not commanded by this topic.

"Griselda and Jermyn had luncheon with them today. I am so enchanted by the difference between them and us. We have pulled up enough to make it really subtle. Have you compared their pictures and ours?"

"All my pictures were given to me by my dear husband," said Agatha, regarding walls that were a simple record of open-handedness; "given to me by him, one by one, as our life went on. Year by year we added to them together." She put on her glasses and surveyed them, and took up her needlework. "Yes."

"We ought to be thankful to them for ornamenting our home," said Geraldine. "I confess to a preference for bare walls myself. I sound very ungrateful. I know many people prefer a complicated effect."

"Oh, well, you have not the associations," said Agatha, her eyes down.

"Have you heard that Mr. Spong's wife is dead?" said Geraldine to Gregory.

"No, but I knew she was very ill," said Gregory.

"Yes," said Agatha. "Yes. She is gone. Last night at nine o'clock. They feared it. I heard from Mr. Spong to-day. He must have written almost immediately."

"Well, there were three of us to break it to. That accounts for our coming early on the list," said Geraldine.

"Ah, yes. Poor Mr. Spong!" said Agatha, shaking her work.

"Do put away that sewing, and give the whole of your mind to the talk," said Gregory. "I hate you to be only half attending."

Agatha laid the work aside, it seemed with some pleasure in submission to Gregory, drew off her glasses and faced her audience.

"Only last week I spent an hour with her. We had tea together on Thursday, just she and I. We had a very long talk. I am very glad I had it. I was very fond of her. Poor Lucy Spong! Yes, it is a terrible change for her husband. If anyone knows what that blank means, it is I."

She made as if to resume her work, but folded her hands as if finding unemployment in tune with her mood.

"It is said that these things fall to our lot," said Geraldine.

"Not everything to everyone," said Kate; "not this to us, not just this. Some of us may be better without the best and worst. We avoid one with the other."

"Yes, I think that is very true," said Agatha in a cordial tone.

"We are all built for different parts of the scheme."

"You think an easy emotional life is the best, Kate?" said Gregory.

"Not perhaps the best, but the most fitting for some of us," said Kate.

"I did not know we any of us ever had it," said Geraldine, glancing over the back of her chair. "We can never leave the other side with nothing to compensate. There must be both sides to all these emotional experiences."

"I am going to ask you all to excuse me, while I turn my back on you for a minute and write a word to Mr. Spong," said Agatha, who had considerately concealed that she was preoccupied. "I should not like him not to hear from me as promptly as he wrote. Then I will ask you to post it, Gregory."

She sat down at her desk, and took paper and pen, seeming conscious of eyes upon her. "It is a difficult letter to write on the spur of the moment. I don't know how one can avoid saying something that will jar. One can only do one's best." She wrote with a rapid hand, fastened the letter without glancing at it again, and handed it to her guest. "I have done as well as I could in a minute, and without any preparation. Thank you, Gregory."

"Ought we all three of us to write?" said Geraldine, leaning back.

"No. We will let Agatha represent. The easiest again," said Kate.

"I think it must always fall to one member of a family to act on certain occasions," said Agatha.

"The pains and privileges of the eldest!" said Geraldine.

"Poor Mr. Spong!" said Agatha, holding an open letter in her hand. "He is sadly cut up, I am afraid. I feel so much for him. He

31

knew I should, I think. I gather he guessed that, from his way of expressing himself." She turned the letter over. "'I know I can rely on an old friend's heart being with me.' 'My dear Mrs. Calkin'"—the impulse conquered that had hardly commended itself— "'My beloved wife passed peacefully away this evening at nine o'clock. I am writing first of all to you; and I know I can rely upon an old friend's heart being with me. I am a broken man. Yours in grief, and I am sure in gratitude, Dominic Spong.' Yes, poor Dominic Spong! Poor Dominic! I think of him by his name now he is in this trouble. I remember him as a boy, before he became the experienced lawyer he is now. Only forty-five and a widower! Well, it is not for us to interpret these things."

"I don't know whether he meant the letter for public recitation!" said Geraldine in an amused confidence to Gregory.

"Dominic Spong ought to be more than forty-five. He ought not to be a year younger than I am," said Kate.

"When you are so emphatically the baby of a household," said Geraldine.

"Ah, he will age quickly now," said Agatha, as though granting a tribute. "There are some things that do not leave us our youth."

"Some of us ought to be perennially young," said Kate.

"Well, I think you are younger," said Agatha, with definite concession. "That is one advantage that you have."

"I ought to be going back to Mother," said Gregory. "She has not heard about Mrs. Spong, and will want to write. Spong relies less on us than he does on you."

"It was simply in his mind that I have had the same loss," said Agatha.

"Have you read anything interesting lately, Gregory?" said Geraldine.

"No. No improper books have come my way. And I am too young to read anything suitable for me. If I don't have to hide my books from my mother, I can't take any interest in them."

"That is what you say," said Agatha, smiling into his face as she shook his hand. "I don't think you keep anything much from your mother. I don't see sons doing that, the sort I have any experience of. I don't fancy so."

Chapter IV

"Well, my dear Matthew, you have come back to your father!" said Godfrey, greeting his son after his absence of eight hours. "Now I am never the same man without my Matthew, never quite myself with my firstborn away from me. How has your day gone, my boy?"

"It has been very interesting, thank you, Father."

"It has been to your mind, has it? That is good news to me. Your research and all of it has been successful, has been what you call satisfactory? Because you don't set out to discover anything as a general thing. That is not exactly your purpose for your day?"

"No, Father," said Matthew, with his rough, deep laugh.

"Ah, now you're laughing at your father. That is what you do when I come out with one of my speeches. Well, I don't grudge you your crow over me. I am a proud man when I think of you and Jermyn. I don't regret that you took after your mother. You made the right choice."

"I am not so sure," said Matthew.

Godfrey, with a rather pathetic flush creeping over his face, strode on with his arm in his son's.

"Well, and what do you think of your mother lately, Matthew?"

"I don't think she is any better, Father."

"Not any better? You mean you regard her as ill? I have been intending to ask your serious opinion for a long time, but I haven't been able to bring myself to it. You think she is ill, my son?"

"I think she is threatened with mental illness. She might avoid it if she tried. But I cannot imagine her trying."

"Do you think she could try?" said Godfrey.

"That is at the bottom of things. You are on the point, Father."

"Ah, you see, I don't miss as much as you think. I am not blind where your mother is concerned, whatever else doesn't strike me as calling for notice. People are not always on the point about me. Whatever hint of a change comes over her, I am alive to it. In a moment my life is dark or light as the case may be. I speak the simple truth." Godfrey, though speaking what he said, came to as sudden a pause as if it were falsehood, as Harriet came from her garden into his sight.

"Pray don't stop, Godfrey. Don't pull yourself up as if you were doing something wrong in walking on the path with Matthew. Whatever is the harm in that? I hope if it were anything to be ashamed of, you would not do it."

"Oh, now, Harriet! Why, I have hardly seen you since the morning, and this is how I am greeted! You scarcely spoke a word to me at luncheon. Now, now, come, my dear girl."

Harriet stood with her face under a cloud.

"Well, Mother, you have spent a day out of doors?" said Matthew.

"Yes, my boy," said Harriet, raising her hands to his shoulders. "I have been feeling more my old self, and relied rather rashly on it, and let myself get over-tired. Have you had a satisfying day's work?"

"Yes, he has; I can tell you that, Harriet," said Godfrey eagerly. "He has had a day of great scientific interest, he tells me. He came home and came up to me quite full of it. Didn't you, Matthew?"

"I shouldn't put it quite in that way, Father," said Matthew, his face darkening in imitation of his mother's.

"Well, well, I will leave you to each other," said Godfrey, falling back on the only solution. "You will like to have a word together after your day apart. I was glad myself of my word with you, Matthew, and I'll wager that your mother will be. Ah, I know just how her heart yearns over you…"

"Here is Gregory coming out with a note," said Matthew, making a diversion in time.

"Ah, there is Gregory. Yes, it is Gregory," said Godfrey, shading his eyes. "Yes, he is bringing a note to us. Now I wonder what that can be. I don't know who should be sending us a note by hand at this hour. It quite beats me. I can't guess at all."

"We need not guess. We shall know in a moment," said Harriet, taking the note from Gregory, with her different smile for him. "Did you find this in the hall, my dear?"

"It has just been left. Buttermere was coming out with it. I think it must be from Mr. Spong. Mrs. Calkin told me that Mrs. Spong died last night. She had had a letter from him. No doubt this is to tell you the same thing."

"Yes, yes, that would be it," said Godfrey. "That is what it must be. Well, poor Lucy Spong! I was afraid of it. I had a misgiving, you know, when I heard that the illness was thought to be mortal. But one never knows. Many of us are alive to-day who have no right to be, and many of us will be dead to-morrow who haven't an inkling of it to-day."

"Godfrey, stop talking for a moment and let me read the note.

Yes, it is as Gregory says. It was last night at nine o'clock. These things are always a shock when they come. I must write to Mr. Spong."

"Yes, yes, you must, Harriet. That is what you must do. And you will do it well. Ah, you are the one to be set to a job of that description. It is a ticklish thing for some of us, but you will be up to it. Now, if I were to try to write that sort of letter, I should get a pen and ink, and I should sit down, and I should fidget and fume, and I should be thinking all the right things in my heart, I daresay, but as for getting them down …"

"Godfrey, are you not ever going to stop?" said Harriet, smiling, but her hands to her head.

"Oh, yes, yes, my dear; I was only saying a word about your being so up to this sort of thing, even above other things. Yes, we must leave it to you to write. Well, shall I have a look at Spong's letter? Yes, poor Spong! It will be a great loss to him, the greatest loss a man can suffer. When the end comes, then is the time to see that loss is not all gain."

" 'My dear Lady Haslam' "—Godfrey held the letter at arm's length, and, less delayed by scruples than Agatha, read in a full, deep monotone—" 'My beloved wife passed peacefully away yesterday evening at nine o'clock. I feel as I write to you, that I may depend upon the sympathy of true friends. I am a broken man. Yours most sincerely, Dominic Spong.' Yes, yes, poor Spong! He is a broken man. Well, I am sure I should be in his place. All the little jars and differences he had with his wife will come back to him and crush him to the ground. The great loss he has sustained will sweep over him." Godfrey's eyes went down as if in sympathy with his metaphor. "I am glad he finds us true friends; I shouldn't like to fail him at this moment. You will say a word from me in your letter, my dear?"

"Yes, I will write it from us both," said his wife.

Gregory followed his mother into the house.

"Father is a delicate piece of work," he said, bringing his face down to hers.

"Yes, dear," said Harriet, her voice trembling with different feelings. "I can't say I don't know what you mean. But it is better for you and me to look at his fine qualities, as he has so many. Your father is a good man, Gregory."

"I spend my whole life in contemplation of his fine qualities. Of course he is a good man," said Gregory.

"My dear, of course he is," said Harriet with instant self-reproach. "He is, indeed, my dear, generous husband. Try to let him see how you feel to him."

"Well, Buttermere," said Gregory, strolling into the dining-room, "so there you are, as always, at your duty?"

"I have not had great opportunity to sit down to-day, sir."

"And do you like sitting down?"

"I can do with a respite, sir."

"Yes, I suppose we all can."

"That is, we all could, sir."

"You did not know that Mrs. Spong was dead?"

"Yes, sir."

"Jermyn and Grisel!" Gregory called, as his brother and sister passed through the hall. "You did not know that Mrs. Spong died last night?"

"No," said the two together, while a nervous tendency to smile appeared on Griselda's face.

"Buttermere knew," said Gregory. "He takes great interest in his fellow creatures, don't you, Buttermere?"

"Well, not to say that, sir. Mrs. Spong was a Miss Dufferin, as I understood."

"You don't take any interest in Smithson, your lieutenant?" said Jermyn.

"I have seen no reason to remark any cause of interest in him, sir."

"No? Well, I believe neither have I," said Jermyn.

"Does it command your sympathy, that two of us have visited Sir Percy?" said Gregory.

"He is a gentleman I always like to have a glimpse of, sir."

"Do you like to have a glimpse of his clothes?" said Gregory.

"'Manners makyth man,' I believe, sir."

"Has Sir Percy any particular manners?" said Griselda.

"It is that point to which I was referring, miss," said Buttermere.

"Well, what do you think of the resurrection of my old suit?" said Godfrey, striding into the room. "Renovation I mean, of course, not resurrection. Do you think it does me for ordinary nights? Your mother was for sending it to the charity sale, but I said I could do better with it than that. I am not much of a one for clothes for myself; and my new suit would only get to be the same if I took it for every evening; and there should I be with nothing for an occasion when people expect you to lead the way, to be of those conforming to a standard. Don't gape and grin, Gregory. What do you think of it, Buttermere?"

"Her ladyship has gone into the drawing-room, Sir Godfrey."

"Oh yes, has she? Then we will go in. Don't sound the gong for a minute, Buttermere. Hold back until we have got across the hall. Don't hurry us into a nervous illness, I tell you. If her ladyship is in the drawing-room, we have to get in to her, haven't we? Didn't you say so yourself? Gregory, you little, unbelievable blackguard! That is a fit way to appear before ladies in the evening! I wonder Griselda can look at you; I can hardly look at you myself."

39

"Well, my three men and one girl," said Harriet, who was standing with Matthew on the hearth. "My Grisel is looking very sweet to-night. Gregory, I think that is going a little far."

"By taking no steps at all," said Jermyn.

"Yes, so I told him, Harriet. I hope you will keep your eyes off him. I have just begged Griselda to. Gregory, I ask you not to let this occur again. It implies an attitude to your mother that you do not intend. Why does not Buttermere sound that gong?" Godfrey retraced his steps and raised his voice. "Buttermere, sound the gong at once."

"I understood you wished it delayed, Sir Godfrey."

"You understood nothing of the sort. I told you to sound it when we were in the drawing-room. Do it this instant."

A subdued version of the usual summons gave the opposite quality to the master's steps.

"Buttermere, sound that gong in the proper manner immediately. And don't make that booming that will shatter the roof. Sound it as we always have it, or leave the house."

When a normal volume of sound had ensued, Godfrey followed his wife, settling his shoulders and resuming an easy expression.

"Well, Harriet, so you have written your letter to Spong," he said, as Buttermere pulled out his chair with an appearance of unusual interest. "I can tell that you have a little sense of accomplishment. And no wonder, I am sure. It does you good to have a little something to get through."

"My dear Godfrey, one small thing cannot fill a human being's horizon."

"Yes, well, but we are all concerned about poor Spong. I am afraid you have tired yourself, my dear."

"I don't know why. It is you who have put an unusual strain on yourself."

"Oh, what? An unusual strain on myself! That is what you call it, when I take it upon myself to see that things are going right for you all! I am not sure it is not a strain. Oh, well, have it that way. I have put a strain on myself. I never do anything, do I? Well, I do then. Who keeps the peace, and adapts himself first to one mood and then to anotner, and let's himself be passive or be active, or be taken up the wrong way or the right, just as it is all wanted? Who does it? I should like to ask. I don't know who else would do it. I don't indeed."

"Would you like Matthew or Buttermere to carve for you?" said Harriet.

"No, I shouldn't like Matthew or Buttermere to carve for me. And neither would any of you like it. It has been tried before, hasn't it? Matthew hacks the joint as if he were cutting a quarry in a cliff, and Buttermere gives little, lady's slices that are cold before they are seen, whether it it is the kind of meat to be cut thin or not, and takes a time about it that would see us all into our graves. And I am a fine carver!" The speaker withdrew for a moment from his task, and continued with his mouth opening wide. "I can carve any kind of joint as a gentleman should carve it. And it isn't everybody's job, I can tell you."

"Well, well, my dear, get on," said his wife.

"Get on! I have finished," said Godfrey grimly, laying down his implements and giving an adjusting touch to his own plate.

"A result worthy of a life-work," said Jermyn.

"Life-work! Yes, well, that may be what it all is," said his father. "Why, I was quite offended for a moment. I declare that I was. Well, how did you get on with your old ladies, Gregory?"

"We had a long talk," said Gregory in a serious tone.

"What did you talk about, darling?" said Harriet.

"Yes, that is what beats me," said Godfrey, taking something

41

from a handed dish. "It passes my understanding."

"We talked about you," said Gregory to his mother. "And about Spong and his wife. Agatha had just had her letter from him. She wrote her answer, and gave it to me to post. Kate was rather out of form in her talk to-day."

"Agatha! Kate!" said his father. "Well, I declare. Agatha, Kate! Do you call them that to their faces, may I ask?"

"Only Kate," said Gregory. "But I think of the others by their Christian names. Kate is a good deal younger than you are, Father."

"Well, that may be," said Godfrey. "But she put off her pinafore some time before you did."

"Twenty-six years," said Gregory in a satisfied tone.

"Twenty-six years!" said his father. "Agatha and Kate!"

"What have you said in your letter to Spong?" said Gregory to Harriet. "It is so subtle to write things that have no meaning."

"They were not without meaning to me, my dear. I said simply that my thoughts were with him in his trouble, as they were. There is no need to be subtle in saying the simple truth."

"Ah, it is your mother you take after in your knack with a pen, Jermyn," said Godfrey.

"Poor Mother is hoist with her own petard indeed," said Jermyn.

"I have always known that, my son," said Harriet. "There is nothing unnatural in your resembling one of your parents. I am only anxious that you should direct your talents towards a certain result."

"The higher the thing, the less certain the result must be," said Jermyn.

"Yes, there is something in that, Harriet," said Godfrey, looking up with a serious face from peeling some fruit.

"Perhaps you put your aims too high," said Harriet. "The years may slip away with nothing done."

> "'This high man, with a great thing to pursue,
>   Dies ere he knows it,'"

quoted Gregory.

"He may die in simple ignorance that he has done nothing," said Harriet.

"Ah, so he may," said Godfrey, dropping his fruit and recovering it.

"There is something to be said for doing that," said Griselda.

"We most of us do it," said Jermyn, looking out of the window.

"Well, Jermyn, and have you been out with your notebook to-day?" said his father, cordially proceeding with the subject.

"Not to-day. I have been with Griselda to luncheon with the Hardistys. But Mellicent and I had a talk that bore on my work."

"Oh, did you? Well, that is a mark to Mellicent. I daresay a woman would be an appreciator of poetry. Still, that is one to her."

Matthew gave a laugh.

"I don't know why you should all unite in efforts to jar upon me," Jermyn broke out. "I can't explain how I have called down on myself such endeavour to exasperate. I am sure it is natural that I should go and talk to a friend. It would not do to depend on my family."

"Oh, my boy, my dear boy!" expostulated Godfrey, leaning to touch his son's shoulder, while Harriet sat with her head bent, seeming to wrestle with her thoughts. "We are not trying to exasperate you. We would not do it for the world. We would rather be exasperated ourselves. We have the greatest respect for all

43

letters and science, and all the things that you and Matthew do. We know they are the greatest and the most to be respected things in the world. You have often told us so. And we know that that is the opinion of all thinking people. If you ever do anything with your poetry, there will be two proud people in the world, and those will be your mother and me. And if you do not, we shall be proud of you for having tried, prouder of you than if you had succeeded, knowing that there is more faith in honest doubt, more success in true failure, than in half the achievements we hear about. That is how we feel about it."

"You can't say it is not enough, Jermyn," said Griselda.

"Well, perhaps I am at the height of my honour now. They say these experiences fall short," said Jermyn.

"My dear, good, gifted boy!" said Harriet.

Chapter V

The rector of the Haslams' village, the Reverend Ernest Bellamy, seemed what he was, a man who had chosen the church because of its affinity to the stage in affording scope for dramatic gifts. He was a tall, dark, handsome man, with a suggestion of nervous energy and nervous weakness, who showed at forty how he had looked in his youth. As he stood at the house of his wife's mother, a modest dwelling in the neighbouring town, his movements betrayed that he was rallying his powers with a view to a scene to be enacted within. His mother-in-law came to the door herself, a small, energetic woman of sixty, with grey hair, high-boned features, and the kind of spareness and pallor that goes with strength.

"Well, Ernest, you are a living proof that absence makes the heart grow fond. I have never looked forward more to one of our stimulating wars with words. I always think that every mind, at whatever point it is situated in the mental scale, is the better for being laid on the whetstone and sharpened to its full keenness."

"I thank you for your welcome. I may not be undeserving of it, but it is nevertheless kind and just to give it," said Bellamy in a sonorous voice, as he followed her. "For you have not been blind to the truth."

"I hope truth is always apparent to me. It makes such a good vantage ground for surveying everything from the right angle," said Mrs. Christy, who suspected she had a remarkable brain, and found that her spontaneous conversation proved it beyond her hopes. "You and Camilla find my parlour constricted, but 'stone walls do not a prison make' to minds whose innocence takes them for an hermitage. I had almost taken refuge in some oft-quoted lines."

"It was as well you were prevented," said her daughter, looking up from her seat by the fire, a tall, fair woman of thirty, with the family resemblance to her mother, that may lie on the surface or very deep. "Those lines don't happen to serve as a refuge at the moment."

"Well, Camilla," said Bellamy, his eyes steady on his wife's face.

"I fear that lines rise to my mind at every juncture," said Mrs. Christy, moving her hand. "I must plead guilty to an ingrained habit."

"A harsh but just description," said Camilla.

"Well, quotation, description, analysis, anything is grist to my mill," said her mother, "provided it can take on literary clothing. That is my only stipulation."

"She is qualified to listen to you, then, Ernest," said Camilla, glancing at her husband's posture as at a time-worn torment. "You need someone with a catholic spirit. Tell her you are going to put it all on to me, if you are not ashamed of it in plain English. That is good enough literary clothing, and she can understand it, though she cannot speak it."

"Indeed it is good enough literary clothing!" said Mrs. Christy.

"My English is of the plainest. A few good words, a few expressions sanctified by long usage, welded easily into a cultivated whole!" She bethought herself to make a disclaiming gesture. "That should be the common standard in speech."

"Mrs. Christy, let us look at things," said Bellamy. "We have turned our eyes from them long enough, too long."

"Yes, well, people always find me such a help in setting matters on to their right basis. I put myself entirely into the place of the individual, and yet shed the light of my own view-point on the assembled facts, which is such an illuminating thing to do."

"Mother, do keep your hands still. You remind me of Miss Dabis. Ernest feels he has enough light in himself. It is his profession to let it shine before men."

"Camilla understands me. I am going to act according to that light. I am not a man to judge sternly a fellow-creature fallen by weakness, to learn no compassion from my own lack of strength. But on that very ground, neither am I a man who does not need support. God knows how I have craved for sympathy and been denied, how slow I have been in giving up faith and hope."

"Ernest, no one is asking you to hope for my sympathy," said Camilla, as though her impatience just allowed her to speak. "You know quite well that I am not able to give sympathy to you, that you don't command my sympathy. I am not imploring you to settle down with me again. The thought of it would be the end of us both. It is for that very reason that there is only one part for a man to play."

"You are asking me to give up my future and my hopes, when you have given me nothing. I am to consider you because you are a woman, to this extent. My feeling for women forbids me to sully the name I have a right to offer to another woman, unsullied."

47

"He is as polygamous as I am, Mother, except that 'to the pure all things are pure'. Well, Antony finds it all the same, and we can't expect a man to have a case trumped up against himself, who has spent his life preaching at other people. Poor Ernest!" Camilla threw herself against her husband. "I ought to have taught you that preaching is a game that two can play at. It is my fault that I have to be divorced and disgraced, and bring my mother's grey hairs with sorrow to the grave."

Bellamy stood aloof and silent, proof against the challenge he had taken so many times.

"Well, Mother, shall we break up the meeting? That must be Antony ringing the bell, another son coming to pay his respects to you! You will soon have quite a sizeable family if this goes on. You had better stay,. Ernest, and clasp the hand of your successor. It might be soothing to exchange a word of sympathy."

"Why, what is the matter with you both?" said Dufferin, addressing the women and not perceiving Bellamy.

"Mother is weeping about my being divorced. I am the one who ought to weep, but I am showing a criminal's courage."

"Why, what is there to weep about? It is my responsibility."

"You know it is not. You know you have done it all for Camilla's sake," said Mrs. Christy, weeping. "To think that this public dishonour is the end of my only child!"

"The public part won't take long," said Camilla. "The case against me will be too plain for that. And it is not the end, my poor mother; you let your hopes run wild."

"I don't dare to think what your father would have said."

"I don't know why, as he can't say it."

"Being actually divorced yourself!" said Mrs. Christy, brought to the final word.

"Well, she need never be that again," said Dufferin. "I have learnt the art, and if there is any more need of it, I will fall back on my acquirement."

"I don't know what people will say about her, or about you, or about any of it."

"I do. But it won't hurt any of us."

"You are not right. It will hurt you," said Mrs. Christy. "It is not true at all that that sort of thing does no harm to people."

"No. I have found that it does harm," said Dufferin. "Even Bellamy won't escape. It takes two to make a quarrel, when of course it does not. And a man should take everything upon himself, when there isn't anything for Bellamy to take."

"There is always enough for a man to take," said Camilla. "You know you have already taken it once. I shall soon be living with a man. I am all the woman that is necessary."

"A good definition," said Dufferin. "But doing a thing may make a man see the point of view of another who won't do it. Why shouldn't this one appear simply as he is? That is all he asks to do."

Bellamy stepped impressively into sight.

"Well, pretty good for a listener," said Camilla.

"I repudiate that word," said Bellamy.

"Yes, yes, you have every right to," said Dufferin. "She only meant that you overheard, and you don't deny you did that. Why that face of tragedy? We are doing all you want for you."

"I cannot forget my eleven years of spoiled life."

"Well, try to forget them, and don't spoil another minute. And I have nothing to do with ten and a half of those years. I have only known Camilla for seven months. I have done no harm to you."

"You could not know that," said Bellamy.

"Of course I knew it. Camilla was as clear about things as you were. It wasn't a case of the one in heaven and the other

49

somewhere else. It can't be very often."

"Well, this isn't leading us anywhere," said Camilla. "Mother, I had better get home before my partners for life have quarrelled about me too bitterly to bear me company for an hour. There are still some things to arrange in my present consort's house. And if I walk in the dusk alone, there may be further trouble; and the impression seems to be that I am giving enough. Which of your sons-in-law will you spare me as a protector? I leave the choice to you, as you seem to have an equal regard for them. I may be prejudiced in my judgment."

"I have to go home," said Bellamy. "We need not set the scandal on foot before the moment comes for it."

"We will defer people's satisfaction as long as we can," said Camilla. "I don't want to add to the pleasures of your flock. I have given them too much flannel and soup for them to deserve any more at my hands. Oh, yes, you paid for it, but I shall be paying for this. So honours are easy. I think I get the more expensive share. So I am to walk for the last time with you as your life-companion. Do you remember the first time? I have entirely forgotten it. Ernest, don't scowl at me like that; don't dare to. I have told you my nerves won't stand it. If we are to keep the peace until the truth is known, you must make my side of it possible. I can't be confronted with self-pity and self-righteousness and self-everything else."

"Good-bye, Mrs. Christy," said Bellamy, as though saying a significant word.

"Oh, my dear boy! How things have turned out! What am I saying? What am I to say?"

"Poor Mother, she goes to my heart," said Camilla. "A divorced daughter and a parlour full of sons-in-law! Poor Ernest, you go to my heart too."

"I am at last thinking in that way of myself."

"I am the last to dispute it," said Camilla, edging herself away with her elbow. "You have a natural gift for it. It is time you recognised where your talents lie, as they are rather specialised. But I shall have you on my mind, moping in that dank rectory alone. I could welcome my successor with open arms. I could throw myself on her neck and give her wifely directions about your health."

"You need not have me on your mind, Camilla. I can face having nothing. I am used to less."

"I don't know. There are not many things worse than nothing."

"Yes, many worse," said Bellamy.

"Oh, well, well, have it as you will. Many worse, then, many worse. We have had some desperate times together; we have had some shattering years. They have been the same to me as to you, though it has not struck you. How we have hated each other at times!"

"I think I have given you no reason to hate me, Camilla."

"You think that, do you? Well, that is reason enough. Oh, but you can't help it, my poor Ernest, mine no longer. Let us go our ways apart. We shall have to sort our worldly goods, and separate my own from those with which you me endowed, and endow me with no longer. 'Give a thing and take a thing is a wicked man's plaything.' What are you doing to-morrow?"

"I have Mrs. Spong's funeral in the early afternoon. Otherwise I am free."

"Oh yes. Funeral, funeral! Well, we have come to the funeral of our hopes of each other. I am not coming to Mrs. Spong's funeral; our own is enough. I have had my fill of funerals, and mothers' meetings and parishioners' teas. The funerals are the best; they do get rid of somebody. We emerge from them with

51

one parishioner less. They are better than the weddings, which promise us a further supply. Funerals have never failed us. Your flock behave at last with a decent self-effacement. The drawback is that they give you the opportunity of doing the opposite. I couldn't cloud my last days as your wife with the spectacle of you doing yourself justice at a funeral. It would destroy the sentimental attitude I am cultivating towards you. The funerals all stand out in my memory. They are like a string of pearls to me. I couldn't add another to them, with Mr. Spong as chief mourner. It would be a large, dark pearl in the front of the only string of pearls you ever gave me, and the little more would be too much."

Chapter VI

In most eyes Bellamy was justified in using his position at burials to do well by others and himself, and the combination was satisfying to Dominic Spong, as he stood, conspicuous and seemingly sunk in himself, at his wife's grave. He was a ponderous man about forty-five, with a massive body and face and head, a steady, prominent gaze and a somehow reproachful expression. His aspect to-day was of emotion unashamed. When Bellamy concluded with a depth of feeling and command of it, he stood for a moment as if unable to tear himself from the spot, and left it with a bearing unaffected by human presence.

"Spong, you will pass an hour with old friends this afternoon?" said Godfrey, intercepting him without appearance of approach, in deference to the occasion. "You will not deny me?"

Dominic stood as if his friend's proximity were gradually dawning on him.

"Sir Godfrey, I have no one but old friends to turn to from now onward. In your own kind words I will not deny you."

Dominic always addressed his two chief clients as Sir Godfrey and Sir Percy, while answering himself to his simple surname. It was as though he acknowledged his position of one employed.

"Thank you, Spong, thank you. My wife will be grateful to you for understanding her."

Dominic stood as if his balance were precarious, his hands, his handkerchief in one, just swaying, his eyes glimpsing the approach of Godfrey's carriage without recognition.

"Now, Spong, you will not refuse us what we ask of you?" said Sir Percy, suddenly at hand. "We shall be hurt if we do not see you at dinner this evening."

"Then, Sir Percy, you will see me at dinner. That is to say, if you have a welcome for a broken man?"

"Yes, yes, always a welcome for you," said Sir Percy, shufflling rapidly away.

Agatha Calkin took the widower's hand.

"I think you will grant us the privilege of a long friendship, and spend the evening with us, and share our simple evening meal? It will be very simple, if you will take us just as we are. We do not make differences for old friends."

"Mrs. Calkin, if I saw my way to accepting your kindness, I should be grateful to you for not making differences. As things are with me, I will ask your permission to come in to you between the hours of six and seven. It will be all that I can manage, or you bear with."

"Well, we must be content with what you feel you can give us. I know it needs resolution to come out at all. Believe me, we shall not think little of it."

"Now, Spong, now," said Godfrey, "the carriage is here. We shall get you home to us without your having even the effort of knowing it."

Dominic turned with a look of appreciation of this understanding, and walked slowly to the carriage, while Agatha stood

54

with an expression somehow taken aback by his having a prior engagement.

Harriet came into her hall to greet the guest.

"Mr. Spong, I hope that some day we shall be able to do something in return for this."

"Lady Haslam," said Dominic, who had a way of repeating the name of his companion as though in esteem or deference, "I cannot hope ever to see you in my present position. I will only thank you for proving indeed that you are not a fair weather friend."

"Ah, Spong, I hope you will never be in any doubt on that score," said his host.

"Sir Godfrey, I am not in doubt."

Dominic as he spoke was rising slowly to his feet, his eyes on the daughter of the house, whose hand he took with a smile that buried all personal feelings in a chivalry that came as a matter of course.

"You are well, Miss Griselda?" he said, in a manner implying that in spite of himself his interest was only conscientious.

"Yes, thank you; are you?" said Griselda, with the uneasiness of the occasion.

"I thank you, I am well," said Dominic, his stress on his thanks rather than his mere bodily health.

"I am dubious about this appearance of my three great sons," said Harriet. "They make us an overwhelming family party. Will you find them trying for you, Mr. Spong?"

"No," said Dominic, slowly shaking his head, and offering a hand and a smile to each young man in turn, as he remained in his chair. "No, it is not for me to find young people trying. The question is, Lady Haslam"—he turned with an air of sudden concern—"whether they will find my presence trying?"

"No, no, it is only you we are to think of," said Harriet.

"Because," said Dominic, leaning forward in gathering consternation, "I could not allow myself to be a damper on youthful spirits."

"Now, you need not give a thought to that, Spong," said Godfrey. "You can be at your ease about that side of things. They all want to think of nothing but how they can fit themselves in with your spirit of to-day. Am I not right, my sons?"

"Yes, certainly, Father," said Matthew, while Jermyn's glance at his sister resulted in a tremble of hysterical sound, and Dominic's half-smile told of a sympathy with her natural preoccupations, that would normally have resulted in a whole one.

"Well, now, Spong," said Godfrey, "and what will you be doing in these next months? I mean, how will you be managing in your spare time? You won't misunderstand an old friend's concern?"

"Sir Godfrey, I shall have my work. There is much in it happily that tends to the benefit of others, and so to the steadying of my own spirits. As for spare time, I must do my best to avoid it." He had the stoicism to smile.

"You are of a good heart and a good courage, Spong," said Geoffrey, content, as often, with an approach to scriptural phrase.

"Do you find that your research work continues to hold your interest, Matthew?" said Dominic, sinking himself in another.

"Yes, I do completely," said Matthew.

"You find it satisfying?" said Dominic, aware of Harriet's feeling, and ranged on the side of power.

"Yes," said Matthew. "It is like your work, and tends to the benefit of others; I should say to their ultimate benefit."

"Perhaps rather ultimate, Lady Haslam," said Dominic with

an arch smile at Harriet, his general subdued condition not extending to his intercourse with the young.

"The risk of achieving nothing may be involved in the effort to achieve something," said Harriet.

"Yes," said Dominic, his smile becoming tender.

"Well put, my dear, "said Godfrey, with a note of surprise.

"Do you find that you slip into the minds of your clients when you are dealing with them, or that you hate them?" Gregory asked him with gentle interest.

"I certainly do not find that I hate them, Gregory. Of course my work brings me into contact at times with the sordid side of humanity. But there is much to compensate, much beauty of character, much heroic effort, much sacrifice of self. All things come together in the life I have chosen."

"Isn't it very dreadful to see sacrifice of self?" said Griselda.

"Miss Griselda, sometimes very beautiful."

"It seems rather ruthless to be a satisfied spectator," said Jermyn.

"Well, Jermyn, and are you still wrapped up in your poetry?" said Dominic, reminded of Jermyn's tendencies by his own high words, and visiting his speech in his choice of phrase.

"Yes, wrapped up in it, absorbed in it, utterly engrossed in it to the exclusion of all juster claims."

"Oh, well, Jermyn, moderation in all things," said Dominic. "But it must be very beautiful, Jermyn, to go wandering about on the moors, notebook in hand, and jot down any little poetic thoughts"—Dominic made a waving movement with his hand— "that come to the mind with the beauty of everything around. To go roaming hither and thither, with nothing to do but let the fancies crowd through one's brain. If the real business of life had not claimed me, if I had not been vowed upon a somewhat "sterner altar, I should have been happy to take my share in the more graceful side of life."

"Original verse must make more demand than professional work," said Matthew, who did not cope with the problem of Dominic.

"Matthew means writing poetry seriously like a real poet," said Griselda.

"Miss Griselda, I was not speaking of writing poetry seriously like a real poet. I am not confusing myself with Tennyson," said Dominic, ending with mild laughter.

"Oh well, but Jermyn thinks of himself in that way. That is Jermyn's spirit," said Godfrey, not estimating his rashness. "He doesn't put himself down as some amateur poet, wandering about jotting things down, not Jermyn. He is to be one of those who are looked up to by future generations. And I for one believe that he will be."

"Ah, Jermyn, I have not been treating you with due respect. But, Jermyn, you will let an old friend say it? You must remember that to that position many are called, but few chosen."

"Yes, that is so indeed," said Jermyn, taken aback by this soundness.

Dominic rose as if his message were delivered.

"Lady Haslam, I have appreciated an hour that has brought home to me that family peace and unity still exist, in a world that I must not misjudge because it is emptied of them for me. I thank you."

"Now, Spong, give a thought to us sometimes," said Godfrey. "Come and spend a few hours at any moment, if you find your spirits sinking. We should take it as a kindness to us from you. We ask you to do us that kindness."

"Sir Godfrey, I have already done it to you. Miss Griselda, I thank you for enough in thanking you for your presence. And, Matthew, I hope you did not misunderstand me in my attitude towards your work. I have the greatest reverence for the things of the intellect. But pride of intellect is a different thing, and leads into many stony ways. Thank you, Matthew, for your hospitality this afternoon." Dominic's manner recognised Matthew as the eldest son. "And, Jermyn, I hope some day to join you in your ramblings, and enrich my own notebook with the reflections that come to us in our communion with Nature. And, Gregory, my boy, if I may still call you a boy, I will say to you that it is a pleasure still to have a boy to say good-bye to."

He went to the door, his back somehow conveying a feeling that he had shown himself rather conversible for his situation.

"Don't be in a hurry, Spong; we will have the carriage in a minute," said Godfrey.

"I have yet to respond, Sir Godfrey," said Dominic, turning mechanically, "to another offer of kindness. Mrs. Calkin prevailed upon me to spend an hour at her house, and the distance is too short for me to be dependent upon your consideration."

"Well, we will send the carriage to wait for you at her gate. Then we need not keep you at the moment, as her house is only half a mile away."

Dominic paused in a dazed manner, and passed from the house. When out of sight he steadied his gait, but imperceptibly, as if in deference to himself.

Agatha Calkin came to her door to welcome him. "We have a great appreciation of your feeling you could come to us this afternoon. I hope you found it fitted in with your visit to the Haslams. You have been spending a little while with them, have you not?"

"Mrs. Calkin, I am moved by the willingness, nay, the eager-ness, shown by my friends to bear with my company to-day. I was touched by your word, appreciation, as I came in."

"Well, come into the drawing-room and make yourself quite at home. My sisters are waiting for you, but I felt I must come and let you in myself."

"Mrs. Calkin, I trust I shall not discover myself ungrateful."

"I hope you will. Gratitude is a strain at any time, and just now would surely be your end," said Kate.

"You must expect us all to be grateful to you for not making yourself a burden," said Geraldine. "I have always been the most! impossible burden at my times of stress, utterly unable to raise myself from the depths."

"Miss Dabis, it has no doubt been much for a woman's strength."

"I have been saying that I felt I must go to the door to him myself," said Agatha.

Geraldine raised her eyebrows in perplexity over this advantage.

"I feel sure you could do with a second cup of tea, Mr. Spong," Agatha went on. "You will have to eat in the next few days by being taken unawares." She paused at his side after taking him his cup. "I can feel so especially for you in your great loss. It is not so many years since I had to face the same myself."

"Mrs. Calkin, I can only emulate your courage."

"I cannot offer any courage as an example," said Geraldine. "I can only remember writhing in darkness."

"There is the loss that no one knows who has not suffered it," said Agatha.

"All our troubles have been as nothing!" said Geraldine.

"No, no," said Agatha, "indeed not that. But not the one loss of all losses."

"It makes one more and more thankful one has not married," said Geraldine. "I have not realised quite how much reason I had for gratitude."

"Miss Dabis, it is not a reason for gratitude for someone else," said Dominic.

"As we are talking of marriage, can't we talk of the break-up of the Bellamys' marriage?" said Kate. "We are supposed to behave in a natural way with people in trouble, and it is very unnatural not to be talking of it."

"Miss Kate, do not let me prevent you," said Dominic earnestly.

"That is putting it in a much safer way. Agatha and Geraldine, do not let Mr. Spong and me prevent you."

"It is so strange to me," said Agatha, embarking simply on her own treatment of the subject, "that people who have had the great experience of coming together, and sharing the first deep events of married life, can break it all up as if it were a trivial, passing relationship. I have nothing in me that helps me to understand it."

"You can look at the things without you," said Geraldine. "There are plenty of illuminating illustrations about."

"Miss Dabis, I do not think there are plenty," said Dominic in a grieved and dubious tone.

"I was only thinking casually of the instances that rose to my mind," said Geraldine, her voice as casual as her thought.

"Was Lady Haslam upset by the news from the rectory?" said Agatha.

"I can hardly say," said Dominic. "I was not present at the breaking of it to her. She can scarcely not have been aware of it, but we did not carry on conversation on that line. I rose to go very soon. With your permission, Mrs. Calkin, I will now take my leave of you, with thanks to you for the words we have exchanged. Miss Dabis, Miss Kate, you will allow me to make my adieux." He seemed to find a fitness in the frivolous phrase. "I hope that when things are easier with me, I shall have the pleasure of welcoming you all under my roof, if you will tolerate my being, as I shall be, forced to dispense my hospitality myself."

"Can we tolerate it?" said Kate. "By himself he will not allow gossip; and how can we cope with circumstances we have never met? Most people insist on it."

"You will soon come up to Lady Hardisty, if you go on persevering in her line!" said Geraldine, with her eyebrows raised.

Kate looked kindly and uncomprehending, not ready to be drawn upon her emulation of Rachel, which had struck her as in its nature imperceptible.

"Poor man, he feels it very deeply," said Agatha, coming back into the room.

"He thought I did not feel it enough," said Kate.

"Well, anyhow he said so!" said Geraldine.

"We must not expect everyone to enter into everything," said Agatha. "That would not be possible. If Mr. Spong expects it, he is wrong. We must get to know that, those of us whose lives hold the Chapter not common to all. It is the price we pay for fuller experience. We must be content to pay it."

"We can be more content not to pay it," said Geraldine.

"I shall never get over being thought to behave with a want of taste and feeling," said Kate. "I shall harbour towards Mr. Spong the peculiar aversion we have towards those we have wronged." She glanced at her sister as she ended.

"Well, we can talk about the Bellamys now," said Geraldine,

with a faint air of hardly finding her sister's propensity worth considering. "I daresay Mr. Spong would have joined us, if we had persevered."

"No!" said Agatha. "No! There are some things that some of us can only bear a certain touch upon."

"I wonder how soon Mr. Spong will be looking about him for another partner," said Geraldine, reaching for a book. "I thought he already tended to a wandering eye."

"No. Not in this case. No!" said Agatha. "This is a case where devotion has gathered, risen to its height, and will hold to the end. He will go on his way alone. There are some of us for whom that path is laid out. Poor man! My thoughts will be with him to-night in his lonely home. They are with him now, as he goes his way towards it."

Dominic was going his way in the Haslams' carriage to the house of Sir Percy Hardisty.

"Ah, now, Spong, I take it as a kindness that you will try to feel at home with us to-night."

"Sir Percy, I can only thank you."

"You are saving us from feeling that our touch cannot be borne in trouble," said Rachel. "That would strike at the very foundations of our union. Will you not have something to drink, Mr. Spong? It is half an hour before dinner."

"It would strike, Lady Hardisty, at the foundation of our faith in many things," said Dominic, stretching backwards to a table in compliance with the degree of his interest. "The touch of certain people is the only thing that can be borne."

"Ah, now, forget it for the moment, Spong," said Sir Percy. "Don't be dwelling on it, my boy, to-night. I mean, dwell only on the bright side of it, on all of it; but don't be feeling alone among old friends."

"You may listen to Percy. He knows what can be done from experience," said Rachel.

"Sir Percy, I cannot feel alone amid so much kindness. I will simply feel that she who has left me is with me in spirit."

"Then you both will feel alike," said Rachel.

"You will not misunderstand me, Lady Hardisty," said Dominic, with a look of perplexity and a resonant utterance of the name, as if granting her full right to bear it, "when I say that to me any thought of a successor to my wife is sacrilege."

"Well, now, Spong," said Sir Percy, as if any subject were to bel preferred to the one that obtained, "how about this about the young Bellamys and Dufferin? Because we won't try you now by going on to ground that is your own. But that is one sort of business."

"Sir Percy, as family lawyer to all of them, I have been brought much into contact with the affair," said Dominic with an air of grave distaste. "I have done my best to advise each party for his or her individual good, but the upshot is, they are to all intents and purposes of one mind." He sank into dubious amusement.

"It is nice of them to agree under such a test," said Rachel. "We should never know people in ordinary life. Of course the whole of my life is a test. It is quite the best moment in Mr. Spong's life for us to have him with us, Percy."

"I am sorry for that poor woman, Mrs. Christy," said Dominic, with the dilation of his eyes that mention of a woman produced. "It is hard for her to have this trouble with her daughter. I have done all I can to show my sympathy towards her."

"Percy, we must see about showing sympathy," said Rachel, "if Mr. Spong doesn't mind our copying him."

"Lady Hardisty, indeed no," said Dominic.

"But the girl will divorce Bellamy, of course," said Sir Percy.

"No," said Dominic in a judicial tone, "apparently not. The fault is entirely on her side, and Bellamy appears to be anxious to keep any slur off himself. It would go hard with him in his profession to take any other course. And another point seems to be that he may marry again. And no breath of scandal has ever touched him, Sir Percy."

"I appreciate his taking thought for the successor," said Rachel.

"But would a woman like that sort of thing to be done about another woman?" said Sir Percy.

"Sir Percy, I am afraid you have very little idea of the attitude of the ladies to one another," said Dominic, with heaving shoulders.

"He only knows that of one lady to another," said Rachel, "and it has misled him."

"Well, but now, about Dufferin?" resumed Sir Percy. "A nice fellow, an able fellow, a man of family. What is he about, getting into muddles fitter for other people than for him? What does he get from making parsons afraid of slurs and all of it?"

"We are not able to limit our dealing to a world constituted just as we should like it, Sir Percy. We lawyers have to find that out."

"Well, well, but Bellamy's wife?" said Sir Percy. "Why shouldn't some other woman do for him?"

"Well, perhaps he thinks himself the judge of that," said Dominic, again with doubtful laughter. "Or, conceivably the lady constituted herself the judge. I shall be seeing Dufferin to-night, but possibly I could hardly venture to put that question to him!"

"To-night? Oh, to-night? You are to be with him to-night, Spong, about some of it? Well, now, wouldn't any other night have done for him?"

"Sir Percy," said Dominic, a flush creeping over his face, "the truth is, I could not bear the prospect of my own empty fireside. His being my neighbour in the town enables me to direct my steps homewards, without immediately taking the plunge that looms ahead of me." He ended with a considerate smile.

"Nor the prospect of our fireside either," said Rachel. "Of course the horror of the thought leaks out, Percy and me sitting opposite each other, with the shadows gathering and no memories in common, since old people live in their youth."

"You would be justified on your side, Lady Hardisty, in allowing a horror to leak out of any more of my company. I am conscious of showing the effort with which I respond to the kindness I would not be without. And such inconsistency demands banishment."

He rose smiling, and held out his hand, seeming to summon self-control to achieve a conventional bearing.

"Here is Polly, come in time to say good-bye," said Rachel. "Polly, you did not know that Dominic was here, did you?"

"I think, Lady Hardisty," said Dominic with a conscious smile, "that Miss Polly would be taken aback by the idea of such an elderly person as I must appear to her, being possessed of a Christian name, much more being called by it."

"Polly does not expect older people not to have names, or not to be called by them," said Rachel. "She knows they do not give up everything. And I thought you and Polly were the same age. That is the stage I have got to."

Dominic took his leave of Polly with a smile that did not comment on this, in deference to her point of view.

Sir Percy returned from attending him to the door.

"Well, now the poor fellow, Rachel! Does he have to be chasing about after everybody to-day?"

"I suppose he does; the urge of our natures is strong."

"Because I should have thought any kind of fireside was better than none."

"All kinds may be better still," said his wife.

Dominic was approaching the fourth fireside afforded him since his wife's burial.

"Well, Dufferin," he said, sinking down into a chair, "I have found my old friends very warm-hearted to a man in his first desolation. I have been deeply touched. I have had it brought home to me what kind hearts there are in the world."

"That is sometimes brought home. What would have been brought home to me, if I had been your shadow? They must have talked about something even to you."

"They spoke of you, Dufferin, with great respect and affection, and with deep concern for the position in which you find yourself. That is all I can say."

"You might have had better entertainment. You may have it soon. Camilla will be here in a moment, and you can see the play at first hand."

Dominic made a movement back into his chair, and his cigar wavered in his grasp.

"She won't hurt you," said Dufferin, giving him a glance. "You came, knowing that her mother's house was a hundred yards away. You may have come because you knew it. You wouldn't have been the first. And it is as good a reason as my being your wife's third cousin. There is her voice on the stairs."

Dominic flushed and laid his cigar aside.

"Antony, Mother thought it undignified of me to come. She can't understand that if we had relied upon her supervision, we could not have arrived where we are. If she had known Mr. Spong was to be our chaperon, she would have sped me with a light heart."

67

Dominic had drawn himself to his feet, offering this homage to womanhood in any condition.

"I believe Mr. Spong would insult me if I were a man."

"Mrs. Bellamy, you are not a man."

"The exactitude of the lawyer! No, keep your easy chair, Mr. Spong; you must be tired to death to-day. I will take my seat on Antony's knee."

Dominic glanced at Dufferin's position of hand and limb, just allowing himself to follow his experience.

"I don't believe Mr. Spong hates me after all," said Camilla, regarding him. "He can hate the sin but love the sinner."

"I hope, Mrs. Bellamy, that that is a true word spoken in jest."

Camilla leaned back and laughed.

"I think, Dufferin," said Dominic, gathering himself together as if he bethought himself, "that my presence here can be dispensed with during Mrs. Bellamy's visit."

"Oh, you think?" said Camilla. "Well, I should not act until you are sure. A lawyer knows it does not do to go on guess-work."

"What am I to understand from that?" said Dominic, smiling at Dufferin.

"That you are indispensable," said Camilla.

"Dufferin, am I to yield to pressure?" said Dominic.

"Oh, sit down, Spong," said Dufferin.

Dominic sat down.

Chapter VII

"Well, my dear Matthew, so you have given your support to our little service this morning. It isn't often that you hear your father doing what is in him to start the day for you all. I might be a cipher in the house in the morning for all you know of me. I was glad indeed to see you there. It gave me heart for what I was doing. I felt I did it better. Well, did you think anything of my way of getting along?"

"I can hardly give an opinion, Father. I am not present often enough to have a standard."

"Well, I hope you will be in the future. I trust it is the beginning of an era for your mother and me, when we see all our sons before us at the altar we raise in our house. For it is a right and seemly thing——"

"Godfrey, one moment while I ask you whether you will have tea or coffee," said his wife.

"——a right and seemly thing for young men and maidens, for old men, for men and children——"

"Godfrey, a word about which you will have!"

"Oh, well, tea or coffee then. Coffee, coffee!—a right and seemly thing for us all, lovely, of good repute——"

"Buttermere, take the dishes from Sir Godfrey and give them to Mr. Matthew."

"——lovely and pleasant in the sight of all who see it——" Godfrey raised his arms to facilitate the proceeding, lost the thread of his thought, glanced across at the dishes as they were discovered, and set to his conclusion as if his stages were complete. "For where two or three are gathered together——"

"My dear, there is a moment for everything. Just now we are having breakfast."

"Oh, my dear, what? Am I annoying you already? Well, I will stop talking and let us all sit in silence. I will not burden you with what is in my mind."

"You really were a long while saying it," said Harriet.

"Oh, a long while, was I? I suppose I may be permitted—— Well, I grant you I wasn't too quick about it, but I should have been quicker if I had been allowed my own pace. I hope you are not in for a bad day, Harriet."

"That is not a suitable thing to say to anyone who is not the victim of a recurring malady," said his wife in an acutely suffering tone. "Why should I be subject to insinuations that I am situated in some peculiar way? I hope you are not any of you in for a bad day."

"I fear we are, all of us," said Matthew.

"Oh well, you know, Harriet, you are prone to find things trying at times, more trying than most of us. Come, don't make a quarrel with me over that. You are not always at the top of your form, not always inclined to look at the bright side of everything. We don't any of us take it amiss. There now, I have told you we don't."

"You may spare yourself, Godfrey, I am clear that you find yourselves magnanimous and forbearing, and me a burden."

"Oh now, come, Harriet whatever is there magnanimous in steeling ourselves against what cannot be helped, against what comes from someone's being too sensitive to face things as tougher people face them?" Godfrey's voice naturally rose upon a successful note.

"You do well to stop, Godfrey. Your meaning is clear."

"Well, then, everything is all right if my meaning is clear. There is an end of the matter in that case."

"Then let us turn to something else. You did not speak the word to Matthew I asked you to. It comes through to me that you did not. The burden of father and mother will again fall on me."

"Don't let it fall on anyone," said Jermyn. "Burdens make habits of falling."

"And let something pass that ought to be said, and something lapse that ought to be done," said his mother.

"That would be lovely," said Gregory.

"No, my son, it would be wrong," said Harriet in a voice that made her daughter start. "I had hoped my children had learnt so much from me."

"The heart grows sick with hope deferred," muttered Matthew.

"It does, my dear. I am a heartsick woman," said his mother. "That is a fitter term for me than any that have been used."

"I suppose I am the spur to your eloquence," said Matthew, "and a woman whose marriage has been less fortunate than yours. Camilla will only gain from being the helpless victim of your bitter spirit. I wonder if any woman's marriage has been more fortunate than yours. It amazes me that you can demand so much and give so little."

"Matthew, Matthew, my boy!" said Godfrey, with warning. "Of course I give everything to your mother that is in me. She

71

may demand the whole. You must understand that."

"I understand it," said his son. "She understands it too."

"Matthew," said Harriet, at once conscious and sincere in a broken cry, "has ever a loving mother heard such words from her son?"

"No, I should think not; there would hardly be need for them," said Matthew.

"Oh, Matthew, now, now. Harriet, don't bear too hard on the boy; don't lay so much on him. He is a highly strung lad and says things as they come to his mind. He is more your son than mine, as I have always said. I have always said that, Harriet. That is why I find him such a companion; he reminds me of you. Come, don't be so heavy on him. You ought to understand each other better."

"Has he any duty to me?" said Harriet. "Or is all the duty on my side?"

"Mothers have a good deal of it," said Jermyn. "That is why it is hard to be a mother."

"I should not have thought you would see it even in that spirit," said Harriet. "But, my dear, it is not a joke for me."

"No, but try to see it as a joke, Harriet," said her husband imploringly. "Try to take it with a sense of humour, because everything has its funny side, you know."

"Not so many things should have," said his wife.

"You complain of my writing poetry, Mother," said Jermyn. "You ought to be thankful I am not a writer of tragedies, as a son of yours."

"I should be thankful to see you really write anything, my son."

"Oh, now, Harriet, that is not a fair thing to say," said Godfrey, almost laughing. "You must not say things to the children to hit

72

and hurt them. It is not like you, my darling, not like the old self you used to be. No, our children will do their best, the most and the least they can do; and their parents' duty is to cheer and believe in them; that is their mother's part."

"Well, I don't know what Father expects me to do my best in," said Griselda to her mother, making an unseen movement with her hand.

"My darling child!" said her father, in simple acknowledgment of the effort.

"I don't know either, my dear," said Harriet, held by the exclamation from her natural maternal response. "It would be wasting words for me to tell you the turn I should like your life to take."

"No, no, leave the dear child alone, Harriet. Don't make her all upset and put out the first thing in the day. Let her have her breakfast in peace. Give one of them a chance of it. What if she does see a little of the rector? He isn't a man we need mind her being seen with, surely?"

"That is all you want for your only daughter, Godfrey?"

"No, no, not all I want for her. I don't want anything for her. I want her to stay at home and be with me. But a girl can't only look to her father and her family."

"Well, Father, Jermyn, Griselda and I have been through the trial by ordeal," said Matthew. "Is Gregory to escape as usual?"

"Oh, Gregory would rather go and talk to a strange old woman than spend an hour with his mother," said Harriet in a suddenly wailing tone.

Godfrey met the eyes of his two eldest sons, and Matthew rose to his feet.

"Mother, I don't know if you realise in what an inconceivably senseless way you are behaving. I can only hope you don't, for the sake of your respect for yourself, and our respect for you. Do you think it an advantage to estrange your husband and family, and go your way with nothing in your life but deeper sinking into selfish bitterness? We shall not alter our lives and our aims for the whims of one woman. You may have your opinions. We have ours. We show extreme forbearance to your weakness, as if you look at things straight, you cannot but see. You have an excellent husband, dutiful sons, and a daughter who could only be a pleasure to a woman with the feelings of a mother. We have not spoken before; I am not going to speak any longer now. But if you do not pull yourself up in time, you will find yourself one day a very lonely old woman."

He sat down, breathing hard, and his mother, who had heard him with her chin resting on her hand, answered in a low tone of easy contempt, her eyes going slowly to him from lowered lids.

"So you have told us you are not going to speak any longer, Matthew. We might have been glad of that information before. As for my finding myself one day a very lonely old woman, I have found myself that for a long time." Her eyelids fell lower and her lip shook.

Godfrey looked at her with a stricken expression, and made a movement to rise, but checked himself to consider, and the hesitation did its work.

"I have an excellent husband and dutiful sons! A husband who will not abate one jot the things that are my daily torment; sons who pursue their selfish aims without a thought of my bitter suffering; an eldest son who can speak to his mother as Matthew has spoken to me; who can brutally and publicly expose her weaknesses, or what he considers to be such, hers, who has never exposed his, give simple praise to himself for an egotism no one but himself has mistaken for anything better, demand more from

74

her who has taken nothing and given all! That is what I have in my husband and sons."

There was silence.

"Have you anything more to say, Matthew? Because do not let me force you to stop."

"No, I have said what I meant, Mother. I stopped of my own accord."

"Ah, you cannot even grant me that, Matthew?" said Harriet with deliberate sadness. "You must stop of your own accord. Well, have it your own way then. Allow me nothing. You stopped of your own accord. You had done what you set out to do; you had given me the wound that you thought would cow me into submission, through my terror lest the knife be turned in it again. You hoped to add that terror to my burdens. When you had done it, you stopped of your own accord."

"No, no, Harriet, I can't have it left like that," said Godfrey in a despairing tone. "I can't have it quite in that way. Because it was not just that, my dear. Your sense of fairness tells you so. Matthew may be young and hotheaded, and I am not defending his words. But he was generous in the main; he was honest in his heart. He was making an effort for others besides himself. He had to call up his courage to do it. He felt like a man, and tried to behave as he felt. He knew it was time you should be protected from yourself. He saw that you must not smash up our affection and our family life, for imagined reasons that do harm to yourself. No, no, Harriet." Godfrey put a summons into his voice, as his wife rose and left the table. "There is still a word to be said, still a word. Still a word, Harriet! You must allow me one moment; I don't deny you. I spend my life responding to your demands. You are fair, my dear. I ask you for a moment in return. I don't mean that I don't identify myself with you. You and I are one in every detail of our lives. Matthew was address-ing his words to both, and I was taking them to myself."

Godfrey broke off at the sharp closing of his wife's door, and sat back with an expression strange to his face.

"The End of Breakfast!" said Jermyn.

"And the beginning of what else?" said Matthew.

"It isn't possible that all our lives should take shape from one person's pattern," said Griselda with tears in her voice.

"Possible. I hope not often actual," said Jermyn. "The strug-gle to avoid it shows that it might happen."

"No, no, it shan't be possible, my Grisel," said Godfrey. "You shall have your life according to your own pattern. Your life is your own, my sweet. And as for my poor boys, sitting there not knowing what to say or think, I can assure them that things will be as if this had never happened. I can set their hearts at rest. You did well to rise up and endeavour to get things on to a better footing, Matthew. You meant well and did well. You bore yourself like a man. Your speech was masterly! And if it was a little young and emphatic, we can't expect old heads on young shoulders. Mother will realise it when she thinks it over. It comes to me that she will. If she gives her impartial thought to it, she might. Gregory, you might do what you can some time. You could try to find some moment. You know we have sometimes to rely on you."

"And this is the reassurance you promised us," said Gregory.

"Oh, well, yes, I did promise you," said his father. "Well, but I begin to feel a doubtfulness creeping over me. I begin to feel in a proper fright, and I don't disguise it,"

"It was better when you did disguise it," said Griselda.

"You gave up so soon," said Gregory.

"You have done well only to begin to feel it this minute," said Jermyn.

76

"Will all our life consist of it?" said Griselda.

"It cannot consist of it more than it has for some time," said Matthew.

"There is Mother coming downstairs!" said Gregory.

Harriet's footfall passed through the hall and out of the house.

"Can she be going to church alone?" said Griselda.

"It is not time," said Matthew.

"Oh, yes, of course it is Sunday," said Godfrey.

Buttermere approached to clear the table, seeing the continued presence of the family no challenge to his routine.

"Her ladyship has gone out, has she, Buttermere?"

"Yes, Sir Godfrey."

"Has she gone out long?"

"As you heard her this minute, Sir Godfrey."

"Did she say how long she would be away, or leave any message about our waiting for her?"

"I am not aware that she has exchanged words with anyone, since she suddenly left the table, Sir Godfrey."

The carriage came from the stables and went towards the gate.

"Oh, well, she has deserted us," said Jermyn.

"On Sunday, too," said Gregory.

Griselda laughed, and Buttermere's face fell at this proof that the trouble bore easy treatment.

Chapter VIII

Harriet drove to the town, and directed the coachman to stop at Dufferin's house. Dufferin heard her voice from an upper floor, and came from his working room to meet her. She looked up at his face, caught sight of another face behind it, and stood with a drooping head and deepened breath, as if taking on her shoulders a further burden.

"I am hardened to being eyed askance because I visit my future husband," exclaimed Camilla. "But the attitude is to be extended to chance encounters with somebody else's son. A leopard's spots cannot be changed, and in Lady Haslam's eyes they are contagious, and shameless exposure of them increases the danger."

"Well, as you tell me what I have come for, I will go on from your words," said Harriet. "You know that Matthew has lived in a world very different from yours, a world narrow and careful in your eyes, perhaps narrow and careful in itself. You understand what I am asking you?"

"To recognise that the narrow sphere has unfitted him for the wider one! His handicap is to command my protective tenderness, tenderness being the last feeling you would wish me to harbour towards him!"

"Yes, in one sense as you put it, my dear," said Harriet, with the maternal touch she had with young women. "I only mean that you are older than Matthew——"

"Oh, am I? Grey-haired and in the sere and yellow leaf! Well, it can't do Matthew any harm to be exposed to my experience. It is Gregory who has a fancy for the aged of my sex. Tell him there is a winning old lady with a welcome for him, if he should care to enrich his collection. Matthew will vouch for my being an interesting specimen."

"You are right that I am in your hands," said Harriet, accepting this word of her son. "As that is so, I must leave myself in them. Antony, since I have come on purpose, and not knowing she was here, Camilla will allow me to have a word with you alone."

Dufferin led her upstairs to his working room, his face grave.

Harriet turned to him with as complete a change of bearing as if she were unaware of what had passed, Dufferin looking as if he were prepared.

"Antony, this is my life, what people call by that name. The time when they rest from their life is the culminating part of mine. I live while they sleep, and I sleep for an hour when they are waking, and I hear them wake through my hour. I creep from my room, feeling that a sudden touch or sound would drive me mad, already mad with the terror of what may come. And it always comes. Godfrey or the children say some word, and I am beyond help. Poor Godfrey is the goad. I steel myself to meet him, but it is always the same. And I see my children's faces, and am urged by the hurt of them to go further, and driven on to the worst. I retrace my way in my mind, trying to grasp at what they remember; I almost overtake it and it goes; and each time I reach it less and less, until I hope to get only to a certain point and then less far; and my brain is numb."

Harriet's sureness through her groping thought gave a strong impression of her dark and definite experience. She took a breath, and went on in lucid words.

"And it must happen again. They are young, and are planning their lives for themselves in the way of the young. They need forbearance even from those who have strength for it, and I have no strength. I feel that anything less than perfection would break down my brain. And my poor ones do not reach it—how should they, being children of mine?—and the round begins. And the night comes again. And, what is the worst, I am estranging my husband, my dear, good husband, who has always been generous and just to me; who does not number his forbearances, who would love me now, if I could support his love, and who does not know that I still love him, though to see and hear him is anguish. May you never know what it is, Antony, to be tortured by those you love, tortured in innocence, for a conscious wrong would be a simple thing. Now I have to say to you that things are too much. For you, I have already said it. I have tried to stand against them, and my strength has failed. It will never return. My impulse to react is dead. I have come to throw myself on your mercy, on the human compassion I have felt you had, through all that has been said against you. I beseech you to grant me from your pity and the power your science gives, what will put in my hands the means of escape. I know I am asking a thing forbidden to one of my beliefs. To me it is forbidden. But my power to help myself is gone, and I believe I shall be judged as helpless."

Dufferin had heard her in silence, and stood with his eyes on her face.

"What are you asking me?" he said.

"What you know I have asked you. What I shall ask you again

and again with my eyes, if I dare not ask it with my lips, until you grant it. I am imploring that of you, Antony."

Dufferin remained with his brows knit, and Harriet waited willingly, for him to take the necessary counsel with himself. He turned his gaze on her face again, and she lifted her eyes to his, to let him see what was to be seen. By the way his own eyes fell she knew that he had seen it, and again waited.

"Well, and you say you have no self-control," said Dufferin.

"No, I have none, Antony," said Harriet, and at the sound in her voice he spoke.

"Look here, I will give you this. You give me no choice. No, that is not true. Every man has a choice. I choose to give you this."

He unlocked a closet, and gave a bottle containing a tablet, into Harriet's hand. "An hour or two after you have swallowed that, you will sink into a sleep, into the sleep you mean. You have it in your hands. But you will not use it. You are a person of too much quality to leave it to somebody else to feel he helped you to that. But if you should ever take it, and regret it the next moment, as I know you are human enough and woman enough to do, take that moment to send for my help."

He turned and fastened the door of the closet, and Harriet stood with the bottle in her hand, and a great security in her face. As they went downstairs she turned to him with a natural voice and smile.

"Mrs. Christy has come to shepherd her lamb," she said.

"Why, Lady Haslam, when I came to recover my truant, I did not expect a definite reward for my duty. It is the drawback of our little town, that while we have plenty of society among ourselves in our Cranford-like way, few towns more, I should think, we do not often see our friends from the wider sphere. We

81

go in for depth rather than breadth of intercourse. Of the two I give the palm to depth, but it is refreshing to feel we are debarred from nothing under the pleasant head of fellowship."

"Poor Mother! What depths of middle-class yearning you reveal!" said Camilla.

"I have come to take you home, you fly-away girl. Lady Haslam will blame me for all your wildness. I ought always to have kept a firmer hand on you."

"I am not in the town so very seldom. You must let me come and see you," said Harriet, who never showed social or moral aloofness. "I am fond of our little town."

"I am so glad you agree with me in recognising its appeal. So many of my friends accuse me of eccentricity in electing to live in it."

"They could hardly accuse you of poverty in being forced to," said her daughter.

"Its old-world charm, its hints of memory and atmosphere, it echoes of the older, graver things of the past! I was under the spell in a moment. I confess it without any beating about the bush."

"You don't manage that," said Camilla.

"And these revelations that the restored church has made to our enchanted scrutiny! The shaping of those old lineaments, so quaint and strong, so almost threatening to our modern eyes! It goes to confirm my original view. I almost feel I was a person gifted with vision."

"I must make a point of seeing them," said Harriet.

"No, don't make a point of being threatened by those gargoyles, dear Lady Haslam," said Camilla. "They are so rude and useless. They haven't even threatened Mother out of the town."

"Don't you like the town, my dear? Do you mean you want a larger town? I love the country myself."

"Lady Haslam, the country throws so much counterweight into the scales. It offers such an unfailing appeal to our aesthetic side. The sobering tints of the autumn, the high lights of the spring, even the hard austerity of winter with its promise of what is to come! The call of Nature has always struck me as the deepest and truest summons that we have."

"I hope I shall stay in the country all my life," said Harriet. "I think I may say that I shall. I feel sometimes that my sons should try their wings further afield."

"I have such an admiration for your sons, and their disinterested subordination of themselves to their ideals. Matthew sacrificing London success to the austerer claims of essential science, so much more abstract, and fraught with so much less worldly reward! And Jermyn finding the service to his Muse ample exchange for academic laurels! I often think that, if any mother has true pride in her children, you must be that mother, Lady Haslam."

"You feel the force of contrast," said Camilla.

"I think an ordinary pride does an ordinary mother as well," said Harriet, as she took her leave.

"Mother, what a spectacle you make of yourself!" said Camilla. "You remind me of a dog waiting to snap, when you stand there panting to put in your words."

"Camilla, how can you speak in such a way? Lady Haslam and I would have so much in common, if we could see more of each other. You heard her say she must come and see me. Your talking like that only shows how little observation you have."

"I observed her. She is a high-minded old tyrant. I quite adore her. But it is no part of my duty to do her bidding."

Chapter IX

Harriet was in her seat at the table when her family came in to luncheon after church. Her eyes seemed to pierce at once to the truth, that the religious observance was a basis for their meeting with herself. Jermyn began to speak as he entered the room.

"Well, Bellamy was in great form this morning, Mother. He showed himself prodigal of his histrionic powers. It is well enough for Bellamy, who simply concentrates on making the best of himself, but less satisfying for anyone else. We had only to sit and feel nothing in comparison."

"Ah, my dear boys! You were there all together with your father," said Godfrey, walking in a subdued manner to his seat.

"Was it a good sermon?" said Harriet in a colourless tone.

"The best we have had for a long time. We had a word with Bellamy afterwards. He is coming in to tea," said Gregory.

"Yes, he said he would come in," said Griselda, striking her knee with her hand.

"It is a trying time for him just now," said Harriet.

"Yes, yes, it is, Harriet," said Godfrey, with a tentative eye and eager corroboration. "It is a thing that might be too hard for any man, before which the stoutest heart might flinch." He paused as though uncertain of his ground.

"I saw Camilla this morning," said Harriet, her manner forbidding comment. "I drove into the town to call on Antony; I wanted a word with him about my sleeplessness; and she had come in to see him. It is plain how hopeless she and Mr. Bellamy must have been as husband and wife."

"I don't know that she and the doctor will be any better," said Godfrey. "I am sorry she is dragging the doctor in her wake, that he is down again. Ah, Harriet, you were right to show a neutral feeling there. You are above looking down on your fellows. People will take their cue from you. You have done good to a friend."

"Antony has done all he can for me," said Harriet.

"Camilla could never have satified Bellamy," said Matthew. "For one thing her eyes would not always have been turned on him."

"And why have opportunities if you waste them?" said Jermyn.

"It does seem an odd profession for a man," said Godfrey, his tone encouraged by his knowledge of his wife's dislike of ritual rather than by his own training on this line, "to be twisting and turning and dressing himself up. I don't know why we can listen to him better for that."

"We can look at him better," said Gregory. "It is helpful to see him in different aspects. What other profession could he have, that would show him to such advantage? On the stage he would have to be disguised, and that would be unbearable."

"He makes me envious," said Jermyn, "and takes off my thoughts, so that I hardly remember where I am."

"Oh, you think Bellamy a very handsome man?" said his father after a pause. "You think he is what a man should be? He is your type? Well, you know, I think I prefer something a little

85

more solid, myself, something a little less effective and highly toned. A thought more weight and simplicity. Oh so you are all laughing, are you? You think I am talking about myself. Well, I am not; I am doing nothing of the kind." Godfrey drew his napkin over an unsteady mouth. "What are we coming to, if we can't say a word about a man's type, without being taken to be referring to our own? You were talking about yourself then, Jermyn, when you said that Bellamy made you envious. Well, he doesn't make me envious; that is one thing."

"Of course I was talking about myself," said Jermyn. "I hoped I had a better brain, and could make a concession in the matter of appearance."

"Oh, that is what you thought!" said his father. "Well, I am sure there is nothing I need mind. Oh, why Harriet, it is worth while making a butt of myself to see you laugh, my dear."

"It is always worth while to display ourselves at our highest and best," said Gregory.

"You are showing off, Father," said Matthew. "You and Bellamy are a pair."

"Oh, well, I wasn't presuming to identify myself with him, such a fine fellow as you think him!" said Godfrey.

"Mother, you had better go and rest," said Griselda. "You might get to sleep for an hour before Ernest comes."

"Yes, darling, you shall do what you like with me. I will come and do as I am told. I feel I might sleep myself."

"Well, I am thankful that that luncheon is over," said Godfrey, putting his hands behind his head, and surveying his sons in recognition of an occasion for letting forth his thoughts on equal terms. "Upon my word I was in a panic all through church. I didn't hear a word of the sermon, not a syllable. I kept on being afraid I should be asked about it at luncheon; ha, ha, I did.

Through all Bellamy's antics I was going over the scene, and totting up the reckoning, until I was fit to swoon. Ah, I am not so unlike your mother as she thinks. I understand what a storm of nerves is as well as anyone. It doesn't make it any better that it has to be bottled up. I was in a cold sweat when I came into this room, and faced your mother at this table. If ever a man walked up to the cannon's mouth, I did then. And all of you at my side, my poor boys, not guessing what was ahead! And my poor girl upstairs now, doing what she can! Ah, well, I daresay it has been for the best. It may have done its work, what we have faced. For it was not your mother who faced the most. I declare I had been accusing myself of arrant cowardice, and of behaving to a woman as no man should, and no gentleman could, and that woman my wife; and of encouraging you to do the same! It has been something to go through. Well, I think I will lose myself here, without troubling to get into the library; the library is right across the hall. You can tell me when the rector is due to arrive; Ernest, I suppose we shall have to call him, as Grisel seems to be tending in his direction. Yes, I will let myself go off as I am; I don't care what Buttermere thinks."

Godfrey put the paper over his face, and Buttermere, entering, gave a start, and tiptoed round the table with elaborate quiet.

"If Father did care what Buttermere thinks, he would go through a good deal," said Jermyn, as they went to the library.

"And he speaks of himself as already refined by suffering," said Gregory.

"I wish I could get not to care. I am terribly ashamed of Father before Buttermere," said Jermyn.

"Well, shall we lose ourselves or not?" said Gregory.

"Let us rather find ourselves," said Matthew. "We don't often get the chance of both our parents' absence."

"Matthew, you should say behind people's backs what you would say to their faces," said Gregory.

"Father sets us the example," said Matthew.

"In a fundamental way he does," said Gregory. "Well, Grisel, is all well upstairs?"

"So well that it makes me nervous about the reaction."

"Are we all to begin to be nervous again?" said Matthew.

"It is best not to break the habit," said Griselda. "It should become second nature."

"Do we ever break it?" said Matthew.

"Well, that comes well from you," said Jermyn. "You broke it at breakfast this morning:, we had cause to observe."

"I wonder if I did," said Matthew. "Perhaps I was in the furthest stage of it. Extremes meet."

"Well, then, they met," said Griselda.

"I am not now quite clear what Matthew has done," said Gregory.

"His best," said Jermyn.

"No one can do more," said Gregory.

"Not more than he did, certainly," said Griselda.

"I can't even now believe I did it," said Matthew.

"Shall we go back and realise it?" said Jermyn.

"No, not worth it," said Matthew.

"Extremes met!" said Gregory.

"I feel that virtue has gone out of me," said Matthew.

"Well, a good deal did get out," said Griselda.

"Virtue too," said Gregory. "No wonder Mother could not bear it."

"I wonder if I shall be made to pay," said Matthew.

"I wonder," said Jermyn. "Let us put it to the vote."

"What are you putting to the vote?" said Harriet, coming into the room.

"We are voting——" said Jermyn.

"About Matthew's future," said Gregory. "Will Matthew's efforts win reward or not?"

"I cannot say," said Harriet, looking at Matthew.

There was a silence.

"Didn't you get off to sleep, Mother?" said Griselda.

"Darling, you see I did not," said Harriet, stroking her cheek. "I could hardly have got off to sleep, and awakened, and got on my dress, and done my hair, and come down to you here, all in the space of these few minutes, could I?"

"You have been upstairs half an hour," said Matthew.

"Not since Griselda left me," said Harriet in a barely articulate tone, as if the words were hardly worth enunciating. "And even if it were half an hour, that is not long for all I said, is it?" She advanced slowly across the room.

"Our vote is decided," said Jermyn in a low tone to Griselda.

Griselda gave a startled laugh, and her mother looked at her with appraising indulgence, and turned to survey the shelves.

"Well, shall we have our weekly reading? Or are you all settled with books of your own?"

"Don't say things on purpose to make us feel awkward," said Jermyn. "You can see we are all idling about, doing nothing."

"And after all you have just come from your bed," said Matthew.

"Well, as we have all been resting together, let us all begin to read together. I wonder if Matthew would like to keep awake all night with me," said Harriet in a light tone.

"Here is a lovely book!" said Gregory. *"Lives of Mothers of Great Men.* When Matthew and Jermyn are great, I shall write your life,

Mother. I shall have that sort of position in the family. 'Gregory Haslam was not without his share of the family gifts.' I shall be the 'not without'. I ought to be collecting material. 'On Sunday afternoons her sons gathered round her.' I shan't make mention of Griselda; a daughter weakens it. Daughters don't have to owe everything to their mothers. I suppose they don't owe it to anybody. It would have to be their fathers, which is absurd."

"You begin reading, Matthew," said Harriet, showing her readiness to place an injunction on her eldest son.

When Bellamy arrived, he stood for a moment regarding the family group; and Godfrey came up behind him and caught his expression.

"Well, now, Rector, you don't often glimpse a scene of this kind. This sort of tableau doesn't come your way. It is a pretty sight, a mother with her ducklings round her, even when the ducklings are getting to be drakes. A sight that never loses its human appeal."

"Ducklings! Human appeal," said Gregory.

"You know I don't understand what it is to find my home looking as if a hearth were part of it," said Bellamy. "Home life ceased for me when I lost my mother. It makes it all the better to have a glimpse of it now."

He turned his smile on Harriet, who was regarding him with hospitable kindness.

"Well, come into the drawing-room and have some tea," said Godfrey. "We will all have tea together, a family party round the fire."

"Now that will be the nicest thing in the world for me," said Bellamy.

"Yes, I thought that was the sort of thing you would fancy, Rector," said his host, leading the way in this undoubting spirit.

"We were all very jealous of the figure you made in the pulpit this morning, Bellamy," said Jermyn.

"I declare that they were. I give my word that that is so, Rector, Bellamy, Ernest," cried Godfrey. "They kept on and on about it, the impression you made, the appearance you had, and all of it, until I felt the feeblest little figure beside you. I assure you I did."

"Oh, well, a little flattery doesn't come amiss. It won't count much in the welter of other things," said Bellamy. "All that seems to matter, Lady Haslam"—he looked at Harriet and spoke in a deep, sweet, hopeless tone—"is whether a man is prepared to make a complete sacrifice of himself to a woman. His future, his profession, his fair name, his chance of happiness with another woman, that woman's chance of happiness with him is all to go. And I can never take to this view of woman as a prettier, lighter, lower being, with whom men cannot live on terms of give and take. I don't mean that a man can't throw a cricket ball farther than a woman, or a woman watch by a sick-bed better than a man."

"It is surely something to be prettier and lighter, and to watch by a sick-bed better," said Matthew.

"Matthew," said Bellamy with affection on the Christian name, "I am not suggesting that we should not appreciate women, but that we should not look down on them."

"It is surely impossible to avoid doing both," said Matthew.

"Yes, well, there is something in that, Matthew," said Godfrey with amused rumination. "Of course that is what we do do, how we look at them, if we come to think of it."

"Godfrey, cannot you fetch me Griselda's cup?" said Harriet.

"Yes, yes. Why, Griselda, you are wanting some more tea?" said Godfrey, attaining the cup without rising. "Well, a man can reach farther than a woman, can't he?'"

Chapter X

"Well, fine feathers make fine birds, we all know. I don't need to be told that, so you needn't be in a hurry to snap it out at me. But I don't look so little of a fellow, when I have as much done for me as some men take for granted. I only do it for myself for an occasion, not being much concerned with the effect I produce. It doesn't happen to be one of my interests. Do you see I have my newest suit on, my very last? Would any of you have noticed it? Some men don't give the feathers the foundation. Well, my Grisel, what do you think of your father?"

"You don't need to feel any more pride," said his daughter.

"Oh, well, it was the suit I was thinking of. I was meaning to send it back to be altered, but I don't think there is much wrong with it. I suspected a little something on the shoulder, and I was working myself up into a mood. But I don't fancy there is great room for improvement. What do you say, Jermyn?"

"You must not expect more than the most even from your privy expert," said Jermyn.

"No, no, I must not. You say the word, Jermyn. And I think it is due to a middle-aged man to have a little more afforded to him than to youngsters. They have youth on their side. Not that the extra years always take from a man's general impression; far from it; that is quite a fallacy. Now do you think I had better wear these studs or not?"

"I like the plain ones better," said Griselda.

"Yes, so do I; I do too. Your taste is mine, Griselda. We don't care to see tricking out on a man, either of us. You think people will take it in that the plain ones are put on on purpose. And the effect is not too studied either, the effect of being nothing in a sense. I will change them here, and put the others on the chimney-piece, behind the clock. No one will see them, and they will be quite safe. Now do you think there is anything wrong with your father?"

"It is Grisel's appearance we should be concerned with," said Jermyn.

"And not that of four hulking males in a uniform," said Matthew.

"You are unjust to Father. That is not the number of males in his mind," said Griselda.

"No, no, but Grisel's appearance. That goes without saying," said Godfrey, settling his cuff with his eyes upon it. "That doesn't need any confirmation, the impression my girl will make. It is an old fogey like myself who has to bestir himself lest people should shudder to look at him. I don't see why they should be struck amiss by me to-night. Do any of you?"

"You are deciding the question for yourself," said Griselda, as her father adjusted his neck in his collar, but in the direction of a glass.

"Oh, indeed, am I? You monkey of a girl! Gregory, what is your opinion of my new evening suit?"

"A better one than of its predecessor," said Gregory, hunching his shoulders. "I would rather anyone's mantle descended upon me than yours."

"Oh, my poor boy!" said his father, surveying him. "Well, it is a nice suit; it really is a passable thing. I rather fancied myself in it at one time. My one before last, isn't it? I don't really know why I gave it up, unless it was getting a little small for me. Though I don't know that it was. I don't think I have got any fatter these last few years. Does it strike any of you that I have?"

"You clearly discarded it on insufficient grounds," said Gregory.

"I don't like to see a middle-aged man too much of a scarecrow," Godfrey continued along his own line. "Harriet, my dear, a very quiet and impressive effect! I never saw you look more yourself."

"That is a chance I have not had," said Gregory. "No one ever saw me look more like Father."

"Well, you should not have left your own suit at Cambridge, my dear," said his mother. "You could not be seen in the old one you wear or should wear every night."

"Oh, that is what it is, Harriet?" cried Godfrey. "Here he has been bemoaning himself and playing the martyr because he was made to wear other people's old clothes! I hadn't a thought but what it was that. I declare I have been feeling quite a sense of guilt, for dressing myself up to the hilt, while he was left to appear in cast-offs. And really he has a whole collection of suits, more than I have, I daresay. Well, what a boy!"

"I will give this one back to you to-morrow," said Gregory.

"Oh, you will, will you? Well, you won't then. I have done with it; I have got too fat for it," said Godfrey, laughing.

"Sir Percy and Lady Hardisty!" said Buttermere. "Miss Hardisty!"

"Well, my dear Rachel," said Godfrey, "I have had it in my mind all day that you were to be with us to-night. If there is a thing I like to see, it is you and Harriet together."

"It does show up Harriet as in her prime," said Rachel.

"Mellicent, you and I will be absorbed in ourselves the whole evening," said Jermyn. "People cannot think less of us than they do."

"It is unfair of them," said Mellicent. "We could so easily think less of them. Their opinion makes an impression that remains."

"Harriet, my dear," said Sir Percy, stooping very low, "you can tell me that things are all right with you? There is nothing for me to be troubled about?"

"Mrs. Calkin, Miss Dabis, Miss Kate Dabis!" said Buttermere.

"Dear me, three whole women!" said Rachel. "The drawback to a party is that it makes you so ashamed of being a woman, and it is paltry to be ashamed of anything that is not really wrong. Look at dear Harriet, greeting them as if they were nothing to be ashamed of!"

"That is the essence of being a hostess," said Mellicent.

"It is too kind of you to have a welcome for our whole party, Lady Haslam," said Agatha.

"I really think it is," said Mellicent. "Mrs. Calkin is known to be honest."

"No one is all bad," said Rachel, "though I never know why that is so certain."

"We felt quite embarrassed by coming in, a group of widows and spinsters," said Geraldine. "It is too much even of a good thing, people might think."

"Why is it a good thing?" said Mellicent. "And why do what causes you embarrassment?"

"Hush, my dear. Geraldine really is embarrassed," said Rachel. "It must be trying to speak true words in jest. It is such a true saying that many are spoken."

"We cannot have too much of a good thing, Miss Dabis," said Godfrey. "We are grateful to you for giving it to us."

"We all came because we were asked," said Kate. "It is so satisfying to come to a party, that we just thanked and came."

"Mrs. Christy!" said Buttermere.

"We shall be educated the whole evening," said Jermyn.

"And amongst old-fashioned men who do not approve of women's higher education," said Mellicent. "For it will be higher, I am sure. Here is the reason for Camilla's not coming!"

"Mr. Bellamy!" said Buttermere.

"Oh, yes, the reason. Yes, yes," said Sir Percy.

"They say a parson counts as a woman, but we won't count him one to-night," said Rachel. "I am sure Harriet doesn't mean us to, and we should follow the lead of our hostess."

"He does make rather an effect, coming in," said Mellicent.

"Yes, an effect, yes. He has rather much manner, hasn't he?" said Sir Percy, peering forward.

"Well, Lady Haslam, I am late," said Bellamy. "And I was not delayed or called away, or anything useful. I am just shamefully and miserably late."

"You will take my wife in to dinner, will you, Rector?" said Godfrey.

"The last shall be first," said Bellamy, bringing his hands together.

"You are not quite the last," said Agatha, as though content to annul this quotation.

"No, but I am to be quite the first," said Bellamy.

"Mr. Spong!" said Buttermere.

"It is almost your turn to be ashamed, Father," said Mellicent. "We are all human beings together, but we are not all men together like you and Mr. Spong."

"Yes, yes, men together, fellow-guests," said Sir Percy, just rubbing his hands.

"Lady Haslam," Dominic said, "I am sensible of your peculiar kindness in bidding me to complete your party to-night. I am neither the man nor in the mood to enhance the spirits of the occasion, and friendship confers the most when it demands the least."

"Spong, will you take Mrs. Calkin in to dinner?" said Godfrey.

Dominic caused a smile of conscious privilege to alter his face.

"Mellicent, you will let Jermyn take Griselda as well as you?" said Harriet. "We are a man too few."

"You are double privileged, Jermyn," said Dominic. "We shall all be finding it in our hearts to envy you."

"That is not at all a pretty speech to make before your partner!" cried Geraldine, leaning to catch Dominic's eye, as she accepted Matthew's arm.

"I am confident," said Dominic, "that Mrs. Calkin understood me to refer to quantity rather than quality of companionship."

"Now, Rachel, you and I will lead the way," said Godfrey. "I said to Harriet that I would have you for a partner, whether you fell to my share or not. I don't care a jot about the etiquette of the thing."

"Do you mean that I am not the chief woman guest?" said Rachel. "I thought that was why I generally went in with you."

"Sir Godfrey and Lady Hardisty are such very old friends," said Agatha, proceeding with Dominic.

"Yes," said Dominic, looking down on her with protection. "There is something very beautiful in the spectacle of a tried intimacy. I think our good friends, the Haslams and the Hardistys, show us as striking an example as we could see."

97

"I have found them all such congenial intimates myself," said Agatha. "I have always in my mind the kindness of the whole group at the time when life was emptied for me. It is at those times that we find out the true value of friends."

"Mrs. Calkin, it is," said Dominic, with an impulse to pause which he checked for the sake of the procession. "I should not have thought two months ago, when the greatest of all losses fell also upon me, that I should ever again call myself a fortunate man. But in the proven worth of my fellows, I must thus describe myself."

"Well, now, let us take our seats," said Godfrey, walking round the table. "Let us sit where our names are. Myself at the top, Harriet at the bottom, and all of you in between. Now are we all settled?"

He paused and bent his head, unmindful of Bellamy's office, and caused Dominic to cast an arrested look at him and stand with his eyes held down well into the hum of talk.

"And now what kind of wine are we all to drink?" he said in a voice that seemed to counteract the foregoing solemnity. "Mrs. Calkin, we must persuade you to change your custom to-night."

"No, I won't have anything to drink, thank you."

"Mrs. Calkin, we are not, I hope, to take that statement literally," said Dominic, supplying her with water.

"Lemonade, madam?" said Buttermere at Agatha's elbow.

"Thank you," said Agatha with dubious eyes on her glass.

"I am afraid I have been rather precipitate," said Dominic, glancing over his shoulder with spreading colour.

"Lemonade, sir?" said Buttermere, indicating Agatha's glass to his subordinate, and seeming to suggest that he was probably right in his gauging of Dominic's habit.

"Thank you," said Dominic in a casual manner, turning at once to his neighbour.

"Come, Mrs. Christy, change your mind," said her host.

"No, indeed, I must stand up for my principles."

"Mrs. Christy, that is often a very hard thing to do," said Dominic.

"I hope not at this table; I trust not indeed," said Godfrey. "Our friends' principles are always respected here."

"Yes, Sir Godfrey," said Dominic with gratitude.

"I do not refuse wine on principle," said Agatha in a distinct voice. "I have no conscientious scruples against it. Often I enjoy a glass of wine. In fact I was brought up to take a little. But I find it works better in different ways not to be dependent on it."

"I am dependent on it, and cannot have it," said Geraldine, looking at the colour in her glass. "That is the sad effect on me of the same bringing up."

"Well, get as far as you can to-night, Miss Dabis," said Godfrey.

"Food and drink are the things worth living for," said Gregory.

"Lady Haslam," said Dominic, leaning towards Harriet, "I assume we are not to take this young gentleman's statement seriously."

"I don't know, the little good-for-nothing!" said Godfrey. "What he has to eat and drink and wear! That is what seems to matter to him."

"It is the whole of civilisation," said Gregory.

"Oh . . . oh!" said Dominic, laughing with his eyes still on his hostess.

"I think my boy considers anything before those things," said Agatha.

"Yes, Mrs. Calkin," said Dominic in a serious tone that seemed to offer compensation for his withdrawn attention, "I can believe those things are a matter of indifference to him."

"I would not say that," said Agatha, causing her partner's eyebrows slightly to rise. "He likes good things to eat and drink as well as anyone; he makes that clear when he comes home. Wine isn't a luxury with us then I can tell you. But they are not the first things in life to him. No."

"They must be in his heart," said Gregory.

"Oh, Lady Haslam!" said Dominic, with further merriment.

"Gregory, this foolish joke has gone on long enough," said his father, presumably not noticing its effect on his guest.

"Gregory has made a joke," said Matthew. "He is doing his best to make the party go."

"Now that is a thing I cannot do," said Godfrey. "If anyone asked me to make a joke now on the spur of the moment, I could not do it for my life."

"Well, we will ask you," said Geraldine.

"You have made your answer betimes, Sir Godfrey," said Dominic with a touch of apprehension, "and one which I make no doubt will have to do for many of us here."

"I always think there is so much involved in humour," said Mrs. Christy. "So many things flood the memory at the mere conception of it. I am such a votary of the comic muse. 'No,' I have said, when people have challenged me, 'I will not have comedy pushed into a back place.' I think tragedy and comedy are a greater, wider thing than tragedy by itself. And comedy is so often seen to have tragedy behind it."

"That is true. I think all my jesting about Percy's first marriage is seen in that way," said Rachel.

"I am not speaking of the oft-instanced order of so-called humour," continued Mrs. Christy. "I hold no brief for Jane Austen and her kind. Woman though I am, I want something more involved with the deeper truths and wider issues of life."

"Well, I don't set myself up to be a critic," said Godfrey in an aloof and contented tone.

"You don't need to set yourself up in any way," said Gregory. "You are too high."

"High enough to be one of Jane Austen's fathers," said Jermyn.

"Oh, am I? Well, what do you mean by that?" said Godfrey, in a suspicious but still incurious spirit.

"What do you think of Miss Jane Austen's books, Jermyn?" said Dominic—"if I may approach so great a man upon a comparatively flimsy subject."

"Our row of green books with the pattern on the backs, Rachel?" said Sir Percy with a sense of adequacy in conversation. "Very old-fashioned, aren't they?"

"What do the ladies think of the author, the authoress, for she is of their own sex?" said Dominic.

"I have a higher standard for greatness," said Agatha, "but I don't deny she has great qualities. I give her the word great in that sense."

"You put that very well, Mrs. Calkin," said Dominic. "I feel I must become acquainted with the fair writer."

"That is a great honour for her!" said Geraldine.

"Miss Dabis, I assure you I do not feel it so."

"What do you think, Mr. Bellamy?" said Harriet.

"I did think something at the time when I used to think. She has some inner light. To copy her is hopeless. I am on my knees."

"Mr. Bellamy hid himself somewhat under his cover of silence," said Dominic.

"I did not know you wrote yourself, Mr. Bellamy?" said Harriet.

"I write and I paint and I play and I act, and I don't do anything well enough to be worth while, and everything rather too well to give it up. I am a rolling stone, a proof that a little learning is a dangerous thing, that he does much who does a little well. I am an illustration of every warning proverb under the sun."

"It may be something to be that, Mr. Bellamy," said Dominic in a complimentary but indefinite spirit.

"But I do not like to live simply as a warning to others. I often wonder why I continue to live at all. I honour those people we never meet, who take the matter into their own hands. Of course we cannot come across them after they have taken that step."

Dominic's gaze swelled.

"Mr. Bellamy," he said, with a forced smile, "that is hardly a speech we expect from a clergyman."

"Any kind of speech does for a clergyman. He can't be turned out for his discourse, in the pulpit or elsewhere. In his case actions really speak louder than words. 'Be good, sweet man, and let who will be clever.'"

"I never see why we should not end our own lives if we wish to," said Jermyn.

"Perhaps people would not suffer as much or as long as we think," said Harriet, as if to herself.

"Harriet, my dear!" said Godfrey, while Dominic turned his eyes on his hostess in involuntary consternation.

"It shows a want of courage to end one's own life. I think that must be said," said Agatha with gentle tolerance towards any human proceeding.

"I think it needs too much courage. I should be too cowering a soul to attempt it," said Geraldine.

"We have not decided what courage is," said Kate.

"Now I don't understand this line of talk," said Godfrey. "Here we are, happy, prosperous people, with all the good things that life can give us! And we sit posing and pretending we want to die, when what we want is to go on living, and getting the best out of everything as we always have. It is no good to disguise it."

"But it is natural to want to disguise that, Godfrey," said Rachel.

"I meant, I am content to wait for my appointed time," said Godfrey.

"Well, now we know what you meant," said Rachel.

"I always think that discussion whether it is better to be alive or dead is so irrelevant," said Mrs. Christy, whose eyes had been darting from face to face. "Not only because we shall not be dead, but more truly living, so that the problem is non-existent; but because we shall go on developing our natures, and gaining more experience of the wonder of the universe, so that we shall not be dead, but more truly living." Her gesture assigned her repetition to word rather than thought.

"I knew it was better to be dead," said Bellamy.

"My dear husband is with me even more than he was in his lifetime," said Agatha. "I don't know if anything can be deduced from a truth under that head. For it is a truth."

"Mrs. Calkin, our time will come one day," said Dominc. "It makes it easier to look forward to that it has come for some of us."

"It adds to the inevitability of it," said Mellicent.

"And that hardly wants adding to, does it?" said Rachel. "It seems to be established."

"Lady Hardisty, we know not on what day nor at what hour," said Dominic, turning her words to true application.

"No, that is it. You really don't, when you are over seventy," said Rachel.

Dominic laughed before he knew it.

"Comedy has tragedy behind it," said Rachel.

"Why, Harriet, you are deserting us, are you?" said Godfrey in a loud, light tone that had an announcing quality.

"Now I am going to give my best to my own sex," said Rachel. "That is thought to be such a rare thing, and it is so much the easier. It is no wonder that women are jealous of other women, when they so often see them at their highest; and men have so much excuse for despising women."

"Can't I come with you?" said Gregory. "I am so young. I go with the women and children."

"No, sit down, little jackanapes," said Godfrey. "They don't want you. Why should they?"

"No, but I want them," said Gregory, holding on to the door. "I am such a boy."

"No, no, apron-strings," said his father.

"Gregory," said Dominic, coming forward judicially, "I make no doubt that we should many of us give the palm to the gentler company, but we must follow the dictates of convention."

"Mr. Spong is a very cultured man," said Rachel when they reached the drawing-room. "The contrast of Percy makes me notice it. Comparisons are only odious for one side."

"Yes, indeed they are," said Geraldine, laughing with full comprehension.

"I feel so sorry for poor Mr. Spong, now that he has lost his life-companion," said Agatha. "I think he must have such a lonely home to go back to."

"Especially with his predilection for fair society," said Geraldine.

"I understand so well the void there is in his life," concluded Agatha.

"Spinsters are not supposed to have any understanding of a void!" said Geraldine.

"My dear, it is much worse," said Rachel. "I am a spinster in essence myself, as I did not marry until I was over fifty. A spinster is supposed not only to have understanding of a void, but to have nothing but a void to understand. It is bravest to look at it straight."

"I don't find it much of an effort to show that courage," said Geraldine.

"Of course I see how civilised it is to be a spinster," said Rachel. "I shouldn't think savage countries have spinsters. I never know why marriage goes on in civilised countries, goes on openly. Think what would happen if it were really looked at, or regarded as impossible to look at. In the marriage service, where both are done, it does happen."

"It depends on one's attitude to responsibilities," said Agatha in a low, almost crooning voice. "Do we want fuller responsibilities, deeper happiness, heavier burdens? That is what it comes to."

"Of course we do," said Kate. "That is everything. And you are recognised as having it, which is better."

"Do you want to marry?" said Geraldine in an astonished tone.

"I think perhaps I ought to want it. I may be one of those people who ask too little for themselves. I am told that I lose myself in books, and losing oneself surely shows too little sense of importance."

"Oh, I admit I show that sort of self-effacement," said Geraldine.

"I make that admission, too, Miss Dabis," said Mrs. Christy, glancing at Harriet. "It is such an instinct with me as to be almost a necessity, to lose myself in the masters of bygone days, especially in those in affinity with myself. I think we owe such a debt to the minds that illumine the past."

"An hour with a book," murmured Gregory.

"Gregory, I did not know you were here," said Harriet.

"I told you I was going to be, Mother."

"Yes, he was quite open about it, Harriet," said Rachel. "I wish I had realised it. He couldn't do more than tell us. He did hear mention of the marriage service, but we could so easily have gone farther and quoted from it. Everyone knows the parts that would have served. He was so full of faith in us, and it is a pity to shake young confidence. But I think I did go farther than anyone else."

"Yes, you did," said Gregory, in a grateful tone.

'Now our opportunity has gone," said Rachel. "I hear the voices of the men. I shall have Gregory to tea, and Percy shall not be with me, only the girls."

"Well, here we are!" said Godfrey. "Gregory, you young scaramouch, we missed you almost at once, but we thought they would send you out if they did not want you. So you have been listening to the ladies' chit-chat, have you?"

"That is what it was," said Rachel, "and I am afraid he did listen."

"Only such a little while," said Gregory. "They have joined us so soon."

"Well, Gregory, we cannot allow you a monopoly of the fair companionship," said Dominic. "We elders must assert ourselves."

"I did not assert myself," said Gregory.

"No, he did not!" said Geraldine, looking round and laughing.

Dominic walked consciously across the floor. "Jermyn, I trust I shall not be thought guilty of monotony in my enquiries, but I find it in me to ask again after the progress of your flights of fancy. I trust my interest will be my excuse for my frequency in overstepping the boundary between your world and mine."

"Thanks very much. I have been going slowly of late. I hope my verse will see the light of day before long, and it is halting work getting anything into its final shape. One will have burnt one's boats after that."

"Well, Jermyn, I hope you will have burnt nothing more serious than a little midnight oil. But when you have finished your book—it is the same book, by the way, that you were engaged upon when last I conversed with you?"

"The very same, and not a book yet at all."

"When you have reached its conclusion, is it your plan to turn to the ambition which is perhaps your mother's as much as your own, and revert to the more exacting field of genuine scholarship?"

"My plan is what it has always been."

"Yes, but, Jermyn, have you considered that the giving of yourself at this period of your life is a serious proposition? That you will never again have the boundless energy, the power to recoup after strenuous effort, that will be yours for the next few years? Or, if I may adopt a somewhat personal note, the opportunity to fulfil at trifling cost to yourself the dearest wishes of her whom it must mean more than anything to you to gratify? It is only in youth that such opportunities come."

"I have considered it finally long ago. I hope my mother will find some satisfaction in any success that may be mine."

Dominic stood and drew a deep breath in rising above his feelings.

"Harriet, it is Matthew I want to have a word with this evening," said Sir Percy. "I haven't had a talk with him ever since I can remember. I don't like your boy, Matthew, to be such a stranger to me."

"He is more of a stranger to me," said Harriet, who was crossing the room and did not pause to reply.

Sir Percy became as one who had not spoken, and Harriet continued her way to her youngest son, who was sitting on the floor, leaning his head against Agatha.

"Gregory, are you coming to have a talk with your mother?"

Agatha looked up with an emotional change of face.

"It is a party, and we do not talk to our family," said Gregory.

Harriet went on with an even step to the hall, where she paused and lifted her hands to her head. Matthew had come out before her, and was reading a letter at the table.

"The post has come, has it, my dear?" said his mother.

"Yes, the post has come," said Matthew, speaking as if at the end of his endurance. "And I am reading a letter from Camilla. And I will read a letter when I choose, and where I choose, and from whom I choose."

Harriet recoiled with fear in her eyes, and in a moment went suddenly and swiftly up the stairs. Matthew returned to the drawing-room, where Dominic was engaging in talk with Mrs. Christy.

"You may consider, Mrs. Christy, my criticism misplaced in a guest in the house; but I find myself out of sympathy with the trend of modern conversation. Taking it as instanced by the bandying of words upon such a subject as taking our own lives, I venture that my host and hostess would be with me."

Mrs. Christy glanced about her, and offered the degree of response suitable to the conditions, by a gesture.

"I always think it is a proof of sex equality that women commit suicide as well as men," said Geraldine, sauntering up in boldness.

"I don't mind anything about suicide but leaving letters

afterwards," said Mellicent. "It is ill-conducted to write a letter, and go at once beyond the risk of an answer."

"And why even refer to it?" said Griselda. "It can't matter what we do, if it is reasonable to do that."

Dominic stood dubious before the result of his words.

"It is a satisfying subject," said Rachel. "It makes us feel we are talking about ourselves. We have the importance of making a decision and the credit of settling on the nobler side. And I feel so equal to other people, with suicide possible for them and not for me. I may not have less life before me than they have."

"I choose the nobler side!" cried Geraldine.

"The years are not too many, and there is a great deal to be done," said Agatha, setting out her own point of view. "Gregory, is that your mother calling you?"

Harriet's voice was coming from the staircase, unfamiliar, repressed, imploring, with at once a guarded and urgent sound.

"Gregory, Gregory! Come to me, come to me. I need you, I need you, my son."

"Whatever is it?" said Jermyn.

"Nothing. Mother! One of her moods," said Godfrey. "My wife does not sleep too well," he added to his guests. "It gives us all great concern. My youngest son has the best touch with her. She is right to call for him. We have to be content to serve her in different ways."

Chapter XI

Gregory had reached the floor above and was leading his mother back into her room.

"Gregory," she said in a rapid, breathless voice, clinging to his arm and keeping her eyes down, "I have done something I should not have done. I have taken what will do me harm, what will part me from you if it does its work. I cannot face it, now I come to it. I want to stay with you all. I must have my life; I am only fifty-six; I thought I was old. Do something to save me. Send for Antony this instant. In a second it may be too late."

"Do you mean you have swallowed something dangerous?" said her son.

"Yes, I have. I have taken something that is fatal, and its action must be stopped. Send for Antony, if you want to save your mother. You want to save me, don't you?"

"What is the thing to do at once? Have you taken the first precautions?"

"No, no, send for him, send for him," said Harriet. "I can't be left to manage this for myself, not this. I am in mortal danger, and I am alone, alone. How alone we are when we do it! I never knew. I wish I had known. Send for him, himself; that is what he said. I will do anything in the world you say, I will do it instantly—I want to do it, don't I?—if you will once do that."

Gregory rushed downstairs and into the drawing-room.

"Mother feels very ill! She wants Dufferin sent for this moment. She is very frightened. How can we get him at once?"

"Haslam, my horses are the fastest," said Sir Percy, suddenly seeming another man. "They are best in my own hands, and they should be ready, as this is our hour to leave. I will be back with Dufferin in the shortest possible time. Meanwhile we will leave you your house to yourselves. Rachel, you will stay; you may be of use."

"Sir Godfrey," said Dominic, "if words of sympathy could be of any avail, at this moment that has descended on you with crushing force and suddenness——"

"But they can't," said Rachel, making a way for the family to come together. "It is just as you were going to say. Truth often goes without saying. You must know that, as you speak so much truth."

"I feel so useless," said Mrs. Christy. "There is nothing more terrible than helplessness. If I could feel I had done some good, I could go with a light heart."

"Let Mr. Spong take you home, and go in that way," said Rachel. "Don't talk about helplessness when you can do so much. You are right that nothing would be more terrible. Mr. Spong, we may rely on you to see Mrs. Christy to her door?"

"Lady Hardisty, it will be a privilege," said Dominic, bowing in open recognition that his scheme of words must be lost.

"I think we shall do what good we can by not troubling anyone to say good-bye," said Agatha, moving to the door. "If there is anything in our power, we are in readiness."

"And in eagerness," said Geraldine, looking back.

111

"I will see you home. I will be as useful as Spong," said Bellamy.

"All kinds of people are the same at a time like this," said Mellicent, when she was alone with her stepmother.

"It is a good thing we are all helpful in trouble. I do admire human nature," said Rachel. "I wish they would send for me. Your father will come back, and find I am not indispensable. In a few minutes it will be too late."

"Can you guess at all what it is?" said Mellicent.

"No," said Rachel. "Something was said at dinner. No, it was nothing; the sound of her voice brought it back to me. It was nothing, my dear. I cannot guess at all."

Harriet faced her family standing in the open space of her room, with a countenance of grave resolve and her eyes fixed and calm. She saw at a glance, marking to herself that her brain still worked in its normal way, that Gregory had told the truth. She walked to meet her husband, and stood with her hands on his shoulders.

"Godfrey, my husband, if these should be our last moments together on earth, my word from my heart is that you have been utterly kind and good to me. It is the one word I could ever say. I give it to you to take with you, as the only thing that could be said to you by me."

Godfrey, who had been gazing into her face, made an effort to speak, and took her hand and held it.

Harriet left it in his, and turned to her children.

"My Matthew, my Jermyn, my Gregory, my little boys and my grown sons, I say to you that you have been at the root of all my happiness. I would have had nothing changed in any one of you, no word you have said to me, no look you have given me, no action you have taken for my sake or in spite of me." She put her gaze full on Matthew, to yield him the weight of her words, and giving her other hand to Gregory, to mark the open difference here, turned her eyes to her daughter.

"Griselda, my sweet one, the sweetest thing my life has held——" The mother's voice broke; she snatched her hands from her husband and son, and held out her arms to Griselda, who rushed into them weeping. Godfrey threw his arms round the two as they stood locked together. Jermyn looked dazed, Gregory broke into open crying, and Matthew stood with his eyes on his mother, as if dreading to see some change in her. Rachel hastened into the room, followed closely by Dufferin.

"It is nothing. It is nothing, I tell you. Stop this tragic acting, all of you. She has taken nothing that can harm her. Harriet, you are as normal as I thought! You took the tablet, and changed your mind. It would have been the wrong moment to change it if I had given you what you asked for. Of course I did not give it to you, when you came to me and explained you were not to be trusted with it. And I knew you didn't want it; and now you know yourself; so you won't come and ask for it again. Begging and crying for what you made that fuss about, when you thought you had it! I hope you see yourself as others see you. You can't cut much of a figure in your own eyes."

"Was there nothing harmful in what she took?" said Jermyn.

"Of course there was not. Should I give her what would harm her?" said Dufferin with guarded eyes on Harriet, who had sunk into a chair.

"I am thankful, I am thankful," said Harriet. "I could not face it when I had done it. I wanted to live."

"Well, you will know that another time," said Dufferin. "I knew it about you this time. We all understand it easily. It is more or less what we all want."

113

"And so are we all thankful, Doctor!" said Godfrey, speaking as if the breath in his voice were weak. "We are thankful to you from the bottom of our hearts for averting from us the great calamity that was threatening us."

"Nothing was threatening you. I have averted nothing. Harriet simply had an idea, that met the fate of many ideas and turned out to be of no good."

"Well, we are grateful for your wisdom in at once humouring my poor wife and saving her from herself. And she will thank you herself when she is up to it, and promise you that never again will she seek from you or anyone else what she sought from you the other day. For if you had yielded, and granted her the means of bringing on us all——Ah, we shudder at the thought."

"I have given you all a memory you should never have had," said Harriet in a faint voice.

"You would have given us a reality, as far as your thoughts of us went," said Jermyn.

"I fear my thoughts of anyone but myself went only a little way."

"Not a distance to be considered," said Matthew.

"Well, now, that was a moment to live through," said Godfrey, recovering his normal manner. "To think you had lost your wife, and because she didn't find life with you worth living! That is a thing most men live more years than I have without having to face. Well, we are over it now. Harriet won't forget again what she is to all of us. Because you forgot that, Harriet; you did, my dear."

"Yes, I did, Godfrey. I forgot it. I thought only of myself."

"That is not over-stating it," said Matthew.

"No, my dear," said his mother.

"I hope you are prepared to spare a thought in future for all of

114

us to share between us?" said Jermyn.

"Yes, I am, my son."

"You see, Harriet, they are all determined you shan't do a thing like that again!" said her husband with a note of triumph.

"Do you feel quite well now?" said Griselda, pressing up to her mother.

"Yes, quite, my darling."

"She is tired out," said Gregory, "and no wonder."

"She has done a very tiring thing," said Griselda, forcing a natural laugh.

"You see, Mother, this kind of thing would soon do for you what you find you do not want," said Matthew.

"Oh, now, leave that, Matthew," said Godfrey. "Yes, my Harriet, you must settle down to rest."

"It must be a strain, committing suicide," said Rachel, who had been silently watching the scene. "If people survived it more often, there would be more witnesses of how trying it is. We must take the ordinary line of reproach; nothing else would be flattering; and you do deserve flattery, Harriet, having faced death, and found it so uncongenial to face it, which makes it more heroic. You must give me a lesson in facing it, as for me it is getting imperative. I believe I shall die without facing it, and I would much rather face it without dying, as you have. I am letting my tongue run away with me, and it is not a suitable occasion, that of a friend's attempted suicide, but I am exhilarated at being your only guest to be in the heart of it all. You were still involved when Antony and I came in. It was noticeable."

"Yes, oh yes, I daresay it was," said Godfrey, giving a little laugh.

"Is Sir Percy in the house? Does he know it is all well?" said Gregory.

115

"Antony called to him over the stairs. He is waiting below with Mellicent," said Rachel. "I hate to think of their not knowing the best part; it seems selfish to keep it from them; but denying ourselves the relation of it will be atonement. Harriet took something by mistake and got a fright! And really she did so much more. She makes the greatest sacrifice of all. But people will not realise that the pleasure in being well-informed should be intellectual; they make it social. You can all go downstairs and say to Percy that I am staying here for the night, because I cannot be spared. Don't stand there, looking as if Harriet needed any of you, when she has me."

"Yes, she is right. We can all go," said Dufferin. "Matthew can bring me news of his mother in the morning."

"Harriet and I will have a talk before I see her into bed," said Rachel. "Our friendship is strengthened by our mutual interest in facing death. We will have a comfortable little chat about it. People will say it is braver to face life, so self-righteous and superficial. As if so many of them would be brave, nearly all of them! They talk as if nobody had ever known them. Harriet is quite an exception. Do go away, all of you. We don't want an audience for intimate feminine gossip."

"Oh, now, now, don't talk too much about it. Put it out of your minds once and for all," said Godfrey in an easy tone for an easy matter, going towards the door. "Help her to do that, Rachel, and we shall all be grateful to you. Good-night, my Harriet." He came back and embraced his wife. "Good-night in the ordinary, normal way. We are not going to make much of it. We know what is best for you better than that. Well, Doctor, if it were not for you, we should be a sorry family to-night."

"It would hardly be a natural thing to give a woman poison," said Matthew. "It would involve danger for the doctor as well as for the woman. I don't understand why Dufferin gave her anything at all."

"Because her reason might have failed if she had been denied," said Dufferin, in a low tone for Matthew's ear. "You know why now, and if you don't command yourself you will soon have something of the kind in your own experience. Camilla's belonging to me can't colour your outlook on every occasion."

"What, Matthew, what?" said his father, rising mechanically on each stair. "What tone are you taking, my boy? You used to be all agog if anyone said a word against the doctor, forgot to praise him up to the skies. And now you take us up when we express our gratitude for a great service he has done us! Why, you are all in a whirl, and no wonder. Dufferin will understand it."

"He is right. I needn't have given her anything, but I thought it best in a way," said Dufferin. "Well, Hardisty, you had a minute of suspense."

"We have been reminding ourselves that they also serve who only stand and wait," said Mellicent, "and have been at a loss to understand why."

"It was kind of you to call to us, Dufferin," said Sir Percy. "We thank you for it. We were uneasy, Mellicent and I, and Rachel was not with us; she was upstairs with all of you. Yes, our poor Harriet and trouble! They must be kept farther apart. Taking something by mistake and getting a fright! Something that did not matter. But if it had mattered! Rachel must speak to her about it. Is Rachel ready to be taken home?"

"She is doing us the kindness of remaining with us tonight," said Godfrey, "and we are accepting it gratefully, Hardisty. We are dependent upon it."

"Oh yes, Rachel is not coming then? Well, I will fetch her in the morning. I shall be wanting to know how it all is. But I shall not come in, you know. I shall stay outside, and Rachel will come out to me. Can I take you, Dufferin?"

Godfrey walked straight into the library and flung himself back in a chair.

"Well, what an experience! What an evening for us all! We couldn't have lived through it if we had been prepared for it beforehand. I should have fought clean shy of it; I make no bones about that. Gregory, my poor child, the worst of it fell on you. You have all had a rough-and-tumble time in your youth. I ought to have been able to save you, but the power was not in me; things have been too much. Griselda, my pretty one, you look all wan and worn out. Come to your father." Godfrey drew his daughter to his knee and played with her hand. "Well, that was a moment, when we realised the whole thing was moonshine! It was a reward for what we had been through, that relief! And your mother found it a relief too. Oh, yes, she did; there is no doubt about it. She didn't want to leave us all as much as she thought. She wasn't quite so near to the end of her tether."

"She found it more of a relief than anyone," said Jermyn.

"She didn't make any secret of it," said Matthew.

"That showed great quality," said Gregory.

"I declare for a second I thought it was all up," said his father. "I faced it for a moment. For a breathing space I knew what it was to be a widower. Ah, your mother did not know what she was putting before my eyes."

"She did. She gave all her attention to preparing our way," said Gregory. "No remorse."

"All the life she had left, to it!" said Griselda. "Fancy giving it to that! I always wondered if it were all true, the French Revolution and all of it. Now I know it is."

"People dying so mannerly!" said Gregory. "It is a great test."

118

"Yes, yes, it is, Gregory," said Godfrey. "Some people are equal to it. Your mother is one of them. She is a high-spirited, high-minded woman under the little foibles that make our life a burden, that cause us an anxiety that burdens our lives. You have hit the mark. But I think, for all that, her best moment was when Dufferin told her she had built the whole thing on air. I hold to that."

"The other moments would have been less satisfactory," said Griselda.

"My Grisel, you are feeling more cheerful!" said her father.

"I wish I were a girl, and could have a little attention," said Jermyn. "I feel I need it."

"Some comfort," said Gregory.

"So you do, my poor boys. So you do, my darl—my dear sons," said Godfrey. "I wish you were all of an age when I could pet and cosset you, and make up to you for what you have been through. But we shall pick ourselves up, and go forward as if it hadn't happened. It was only a mistake after all."

"It was not that, Father," said Matthew.

"Oh, well, well, it was regretted. And if that is not a mistake, what is?"

"The mistake was that the stuff was harmless," said Matthew.

"Very well, it was harmless, wasn't it?" said his father. "Why this arguing on an occasion like this? It doesn't really seem suitable. And we are tired out enough already."

"Well, I hardly am," said Rachel, coming into the room. "I still feel rather stimulated. I hope Percy felt it, that I could not go home with him. I have come to join you in disloyalty to Harriet. She would hardly expect to escape it. I have just been disloyal to her to her face. 'My dear,' I said, when she was afraid she would not sleep, 'it is not your fault that you are not in your last sleep. You do keep changing your mind. It is everything or nothing

119

with you.' But I think she will sleep; she is very tired. It takes a great deal to exhaust her enough, doesn't it?"

"She won't change her mind again, will she?" said Griselda.

"No, no, my child. She could not be up to so much."

"It cannot be called a heroic thing to do," said Matthew.

"I suppose it cannot be called that," said Rachel.

"No, no, don't you agree with him, Rachel. You stand up for my poor wife," said Godfrey, leaning back and relinquishing his daughter without sign of consulting her.

"It wasn't anything worse than a hastiness of spirit," said Jermyn.

"Yes, it was worse; it was deliberate," said Matthew.

"I wish we knew how she felt before she did it, the steps in her mind that led up to it," said Gregory.

"We mustn't want to go as far as she did," said Jermyn.

"Well, I hope there are some things you will stop short of," said Godfrey, opening his mouth in concession to the stage matters had reached.

"There are probably a good many," said Rachel.

"Yes, yes, there are, Rachel," said Godfrey, sitting forward. "You are right to make us see that Harriet was not to blame in what she did. She is a fine creature, making a fine effort against her weaknesses. Well, it is no good my sitting here, making an exhibition of myself. How you can all hold your heads up puzzles me. I will take myself off and leave you free of the sight of me. Harriet will sleep, Rachel, you say? Well, I shall sleep the better for knowing that. Oh, well, laugh then, all of you. Laugh. I am glad you have the heart for it; I have not. I am thankful you have something to laugh at, and glad if I have given it to you. Rachel, again I express to you my gratitude."

"Why is it more natural to be disloyal to your mother than

your father?" said Rachel. "It ought to be the other way round."

"He is more helpless," said Jermyn, "but it would be natural to take advantage of that."

"We can't explain chivalry," said Griselda. "It is a feeling I have never understood."

"Does it throw light on it that we could never show it to Mother?" said Gregory. "To think we shall have to meet her, when some of us must have been the cause!"

"Will she be able to meet us?" said Matthew.

"I suppose not, if she thinks of the past," said Griselda.

"We are all quite blameless," said Matthew.

"It is humbling to feel we are impossible without meaning to be," said Rachel. "Godfrey, why are you coming back when you had left us to be disloyal to you?"

"Oh, that is what you are doing, is it?" said Godfrey, crossing the room with his eyes on the chimney-piece, and his hand holding his coat together to cover some initial disarray. "Yes, here are my studs behind the clock! I remembered I had put them there. I was asking before dinner if I had better wear them, and Griselda voted for the plain ones, those I actually wore. I don't know if you noticed them; I expect you did not; that is the point of them, that they do not strike the eye. I thought she was right; I agreed with her; I don't care to see a man bedizened. What do you think?" Godfrey held the studs before his shirt, waiving compunction in the matter of its expanse. "I don't think they would have done me any good, do you? I think the effect was better without them, just careless enough. I think I shall have them made into something for Harriet. Though I don't know that I shall. I might come across some links to match them some time. One never knows what will turn up. There can be no harm in being all of a piece. Well, good-night again."

121

Chapter XII

"Well, mother found on second thoughts that we made life worth while for her," said Jermyn the next morning. "Let us hold on to that."

"We prove that she does the same for us by being here," said Griselda. "We can't have anything to complain of, clinging to life as we do. That is the real thing to face."

"Griselda, don't let your woman's courage do too much for you," said Jermyn.

"I hope she has not inherited that side of Mother," said Matthew.

"Things skip a generation," said Rachel.

"Courage does not take much account of other people," said Matthew.

"All qualities leave victims in their wake," said Rachel. "Look at truthfulness and justice."

"The reaction came sure enough," said Matthew.

"And truthfulness and justice have no reaction," said Rachel.

"Courage is the best of them," said Gregory.

"We are very satisfied with Mother," said Griselda.

"Are you, my darlings? Well, that is very kind, and I think in some ways fair of you," said Harriet, her voice revealing her presence. "That is a pleasant message from my children to set me off on my day."

"And, we hope, to bring you to the end of it," said Jermyn.

"My darling, your hoping it is what will bring me to it."

"We have one day secure before us," said Matthew.

"My boy, I must help you to forget it," said his mother.

"Harriet, your giving the whole of your attention to your children amounts to throwing up a guest's disadvantages," said Rachel. "You know you think childlessness a disadvantage."

"I should certainly be much the poorer for it."

"Much poorer is dreadful openness," said Rachel.

"You don't wish you had children, do you?" said Gregory to Rachel.

"I am not sure. People say you never die when you have descendants."

"That is true," said Harriet.

"Well, there wasn't much meaning in what you did then, my dear," said Rachel.

"There is Father's door. Ring the bell for the servants, Matthew," said Griselda.

"Does Godfrey have all the attendance?" said Rachel. "I did not know that a natural man existed in these days."

"We are summoning them to prayers," said Gregory.

"Our servants don't have that extra summons," said Rachel. "I don't mean we feel they get tired of being summoned; they must get a contempt for you if you consider them: it is contemptible to do things because you are forced to. And why shouldn't they object to being treated differently? They can see we don't consider each other. But Percy is not at his ease reading prayers, and not to be at ease is known to be such an unspeakable thing.

123

I could not bear the girls to lose their respect for their father. I am equally careful about their feelings to both their parents. Besides, we haven't anyone we need pray for, as you must have to pray for Buttermere."

Godfrey gained his seat with a glance around that seemed to be reassuring, and set to his office without dissipation of energy.

"O Lord, we are gathered together to greet Thee, thankful to Thee from our inmost soul for Thy mercy in averting from us the great ill, with which Thou wast pleased to threaten us. We have entered the valley of the shadow, with her who is nearest to our hearts, and we emerge with those same hearts filled with gratitude to Thee. Together with one voice we thank Thee, from the highest to the lowest, from myself to the least in my house, equally in Thy sight insomuch as the last is first; and likewise this our dear friend under our roof, to whom we have extended our hospitality in return for—whom Thou didst send to us, to support our steps from darkness. This is our brief word from all our hearts, brief in proportion to their fullness, to the fullness thereof."

As the family came to the table, Harriet smiled to herself.

"Harriet, my dear, you are better this morning. You are meaning to get on your feet again. You are plucking up spirit," cried her husband, beginning loudly and letting his voice die away.

"You did make me look a little ridiculous, Godfrey," said Rachel.

"My dear Rachel, I meant every word I said."

"I thought you hardly seemed to," said Rachel.

"Well, Rachel, you are not leaving us to-day, so I hope you don't think you are," said her host, doing himself definite justice.

"I would never go if it were not for the claims of my own life. I have never had such a full time. A dinner party generally goes by itself. Godfrey, do you prepare your prayers beforehand?"

124

"Rachel," said Godfrey, bringing his fist down on the table, "I give you my word that not a thought on the subject passes my mind until the moment when the words fall from my lips."

"You are not one of those people whose whole life is a prayer then?" said Rachel. "It is not nearly the whole of it."

"Well, it happens to be one of the things I do," said Godfrey modestly. "Harriet, try to manage a little more. Make an effort, my dear. You have been under a heavy strain, heavier than you can realise, as great as could befall a mortal woman."

"Her being mortal was the whole point of it," said Rachel. "Gregory, you are looking at me with eyes of real affection. I believe I am your favourite of all your old ladies."

"I declare, Rachel, you are younger than any one of them," said Godfrey. "Younger in spirit, I mean."

"I know that was your terrible meaning," said Rachel. "Here are the two eldest of the others coming up the drive! It must be to inquire for Harriet. How can we make her look as little foolish as possible?"

"I will tell the truth," said Harriet.

"Oh, no, my dear, I must protest against that," said her husband.

"I mean, I will say I took something I thought afterwards was harmful."

"That will do," said Rachel. "We thought you meant you could not tell a lie. That would be absurd after what you could do yesterday."

"Show the ladies in, show them in," said Godfrey to Buttermere, without waiting to be asked. "We have nothing to prevent us from seeing our friends this morning."

"Now, we already have a reply to our question!" said Agatha, advancing with her hand raised towards Harriet. "We have been

125

in such anxiety about you, that we felt we must come to inquire. And here you are, an answer in yourself!"

"She sounds quite reproachful!" said Geraldine.

"It is providential that Mother is an answer in herself," said Griselda to Jermyn. "Now perhaps they won't want any other answer."

"I feel so ashamed of giving everyone such a fright," said Harriet. "I swallowed something that I thought a moment later was something else, and got a shock, and I am afraid made a fuss. But it turned out that it was nothing."

"I am sure I should make a fuss in such circumstances," said Geraldine. "It seems to me that every quivering string within one would threaten to snap."

"You must have had some terrible moments," said Agatha to Godfrey.

"Terrible! That is the word, Mrs. Calkin, terrible. We thought for some moments—well, I won't tell you what we thought. But we had those moments. We lived through them. We have that behind us."

He put his hand on Harriet's shoulder, and she raised her hand to his.

"You have all had a sad experience for your ages," said Agatha, looking round.

"Yes, do give us some sympathy," said Jermyn. "Mother has nearly all of it, and Father any that is left."

"What was it that she took?" said Geraldine.

"Something marked poisonous, that was happily not poisonous at all," said Jermyn.

"Oh, what kind of thing?" said Geraldine.

"The sleeping tablet she was right to take, that had got into the wrong bottle," said Matthew. "She dispenses medicine to the maids. It is quite unnecessary to have such things about again."

"Quite, in that case," said Rachel. "Why did you have them, Harriet?"

"The servants can keep anything like that for themselves in future," said Godfrey.

"Then we shall be quite free from anxiety," said Rachel. "Nothing marked 'poisonous' within reach of the family."

"I admit I am in sympathy with your attitude," said Geraldine, chuckling in guilty fellow-feeling. "I fear I am a thorough-going conservative at heart."

"Well, we will not stay," said Agatha. "We shall carry away much easier minds than we brought with us."

"It is too kind of you, Mrs. Calkin," said Godfrey. "We appreciate it from the bottom of our hearts. We are unlike ourselves this morning, but we shall not forget it."

"I am sure you must be," said Agatha kindly, as she shook hands.

"You should protest that they are not. That is not at all the way to respond," said her sister.

Agatha stood with an aspect of practised patience.

"Are you coming in to see us this afternoon?" she said to Gregory.

"Yes, do, my dear," said Harriet, as Gregory glanced in her direction. "I shall be glad for you to have a change from me."

"Then I will come to tea, if I may," said Gregory.

"Harriet, I cannot understand why you feel that Matthew and Jermyn should not give themselves to creative work," said Rachel. "Think what they will accomplish in their lives, when they can do so much in a few minutes!"

"I am not going to feel it any longer. I will be simply thankful for them and for their gifts."

"You must have been thankful for those just now," said Rachel. "I should have been, in your place. I was in my own. But they must not stay and see you losing your personality before their eyes. And, Godfrey, don't stand there, brooding over Geraldine. You should keep your mind on wholesome things. And here is another inquirer coming to probe for the truth! Of course it is well worth probing for. I wonder if people would inquire for me, if I took a tablet from the wrong bottle—do remember it was that—or if they would think it natural to pass away at my age, or a mercy, or a happy release, or all for the best, or anything else that excuses survivors from grief. It is Ernest Bellamy! I should love to have him inquire for me, if any illness now might not be my last. I hope he did not see me looking out of the window, and being reminded of the dream of my youth. He must get so apt at recognising that expression."

"Now this is the sight of all sights I would choose to see!" said Bellamy in a grave, vibrating tone. "Fate deals with me this morning as I would choose."

"We are indebted to you, Rector," said Godfrey. "My poor wife gave us a terrible fright, and herself into the bargain. She didn't get out of it herself. She took what was really a sleeping tablet, that had got into a bottle marked 'dangerous', and we had some minutes before Dufferin arrived to put us out of our misery. Every moment of that time is imprinted on my brain, and will go down to the grave with me."

"I hope you are as ashamed of yourself as you ought to be," said Bellamy to Harriet.

"Yes, I am. I caused great suffering."

"To yourself as well as to others."

"Yes. She can feel that nobody went through what she did," said Rachel.

128

"Oh, I don't know about that, Rachel," said Godfrey.

"This is not a case where two people can be one flesh," said Matthew. "Mother has earned the doubtful distinction of suffering in utter loneliness."

"Matthew, would you rather have your mother harmed than yourself?" said his father in a tone high from incredulity.

"Of course he would," said Rachel. "That is the weak point about suicide, that no one feels the worst has happened."

"Well, well, we are not given the choice," said Godfrey.

"There would be very little gained by it," said Matthew.

"I wonder what we should think of anyone who rated himself below anyone else. Just as a matter of theory, I mean," said Godfrey, having disposed of the subject otherwise with advantage.

"It could never be a matter of anything else," said Matthew.

"Well, well, I have seen some fine things in my life," said Godfrey, his eyelids flickering.

"Can you tell us of a single one?" said Rachel.

"Oh, well, they are hardly things one speaks about."

"If they happened, you would never speak of anything else," said Griselda.

"Feelings can be too deep for words," said Godfrey.

"We must never talk again about those we had when Mother's moment came," said Jermyn.

"I think I have said least about mine," said Rachel. "Take Mr. Bellamy out to see the horses, Godfrey. There is no need to show any more solicitude for Harriet. Nothing really happened to her at all. A hostess always has a parting gossip with a guest, and she can simply do her duty. Now, Harriet, this is not a thing you can really be apathetic about."

"It is not much of a matter," said Harriet.

129

"It was a matter of life and death."

"Only my life or death. I made too much of it."

"You did, if that was your view. We got the impression that you felt quite definitely."

"I did at the moment, just at the moment," said Harriet in a dreamy tone.

"My dear, had you any excuse for putting yourself in the limelight, when you should have been throwing up your guests? You owe it to me to explain."

"I will perhaps tell Gregory some time," said Harriet, "but perhaps I shall not tell him."

Rachel looked at her in silence.

"Do you like the idea of Griselda's marrying Ernest Bellamy?"

"I must not dislike what my dear ones do. I have found I must not."

"No, that is true love," said Rachel.

"I am not sure," said Harriet, raising melancholy eyes.

"I am," said Rachel. "It is so untrue that we can love the sinner and hate the sin."

Harriet smiled.

"But I find it hard to wish my girl to marry a man who has divorced his wife," she said.

"Why, what better way could there be of dealing with her? It is as far as possible removed from Percy's way, which is the worst."

"She would only be living in the town; and Antony is a friend of ours. Griselda would often have to meet her."

"Only in the flesh," said Rachel. "That puts a woman at a disadvantage compared with oils, and the town is a fair distance compared with the dining-room."

"Well, I must let things go as they will. I have found I have not the strength for guidance."

130

"Harriet, things deserve a little spirit, that are worth committing suicide about. I begin to see there was no excuse for what you did."

"There was not. I hope I may be forgiven."

"I hardly see how you can be."

"I cannot forgive myself."

"Well, then you can understand it."

"God is good. He tempers judgment with mercy."

"Then perhaps it hardly matters. But it is difficult not to feel only judgment. God may be different, but I can't have mercy on a friend who keeps everything selfishly to herself."

"You don't know how little I want it all for myself."

"How can I, when you won't give a word of it away?"

"If I could make you understand, I would not."

"I really have cause for complaint," said Rachel. "Here is Percy come to fetch me! Camilla is sitting in the carriage with him, and he is letting Johnson drive, to give all his attention to her. No doubt she has come to inquire. She doesn't know how little good it is. What a primitive quality it is, that power over men! I do respect Camilla for it, and I rather respect Percy for responding to it. If I had had it, do you suppose I should have been a second wife? Camilla, I should be proud of you, if I were your mother."

"Mother is not the foremost among my proud, but other people make up for her, notably my husbands. My former husband was quite proud, and my future husband is prouder. Proud, prouder, proudest! There will have to be a third. We heard that you were clothed and in your right mind, Lady Haslam, but nothing would do for Mother but that I should come to inquire. So here I am, inquiring. Sir Percy gave me a lift, and I began to teach him the art of pride. I promised to sit by him on the way back. You won't mind, Lady Hardisty? It is his fault, not mine. People always ask me to sit by them again."

"Then I am glad Percy did," said Rachel. "It is so unfair to say that he is not like other people. Harriet, I try to forgive you for not treating me as a friend. I won't bring Percy in to be a witness of it; and making inquiries of you is simply a mockery. Come along, Camilla, and sit by Percy. Percy, Camilla is going to keep her promise."

"Oh, what?" said Sir Percy, getting to his feet in the carriage. "I did not see you in time to get out, my dear. Harriet is still all right? Ah, that is good to hear. No, I won't go in. She saw enough of me last night, and we must wait to see enough of her. Yes, I told Mrs. Bellamy we would take her home. We shall have the pleasure of Camilla's company on our way back, Rachel."

"There now, he has given me right away!" said Camilla. "I couldn't bring myself to warn him. The sight of his face would have been too much. But I expect you guessed I was romancing."

"No, my dear, it sounded to me so likely; but I am sorry you did not warn Percy; you will have to sit behind with me. Percy must not suspect; he would be too upset about failing a woman. I don't mean that he has failed in his heart; it was only because he was disturbed about Harriet. He will not another time. Gregory, go indoors and sit with your mother. She must not bear the miss of me by herself."

"I adore Lady Haslam," said Camilla, "though she by no means pays me back in kind. I surprise myself in returning good for evil."

"We all adore her in proportion to the good in us," said Rachel. "I saw there was much good in you, my dear; and I saw Percy seeing it in the carriage. She is most of all to me."

Gregory had gone to his mother and settled himself at her feet.

"Now tell me all about it," he said.

"About what, my son?"

"About all the things that made you do it. Tell me in plain, simple language so that I understand."

"If the feeling should come again," said his mother in a low, musing tone, "it would seem a hard thing to have failed to do it, when I had made up my mind. There was the making up my mind. But I have not felt since that I very much want to do it." She raised her eyes as if seeking explanation of her feelings.

"Will you promise to tell me, if you want to again?"

"I don't know if I ought. You are so young, my poor boy. I have already brought too much on you."

"Will you promise?" said Gregory.

"Yes, dear," said Harriet, in a voice that held no meaning.

"You don't break your promises, do you?" said Gregory, looking at her doubtfully.

"No, we don't break promises," said Harriet. "Here is your father."

"Well now, Harriet, here you are, sitting with your son!" said Godfrey, as though he spoke glad words. "Well, you are a heroine. I knew that the first time I saw you; I sensed the stuff you were made of. Well, Gregory, and how do you find your mother this morning?"

"Not very good at telling the truth about the darkness into which she descended."

"Ah, now, Gregory, we won't go into that," said his father with a movement of shuddering. "We will leave it to fade away. It is as if it had not happened. That is what it is to me, what it will be for all of us, for your mother first of all. She is right not to tell you; she makes the wise decision; we can trust her to make it. Now what you have to do is to help her to forget it, to sweep it right out of her mind, and the way to do that is to forget it yourself. Forget it, Gregory. Serve your mother by controlling yourself in that matter."

Harriet raised her eyes and rested them on her husband and son, as if weighing the difference between them.

"Forget it, Gregory, forget it," repeated Godfrey, turning himself on his heels with his hands in his pockets, and seeming to feel released from something normally involved in his wife's presence. "Forgetting it is the thing we have to remember."

Harriet gave a low laugh.

"Oh, that is what you are doing, Harriet!" said Godfrey, pausing on his heels, and bending from his waist towards his wife. "Laughing at your poor old husband, because he is advising what is best for you! And this boy aiding and abetting you! Well, what a wife and son to have! Wife and son to have—wife and son!" The speaker revolved in time to his refrain.

Harriet and Gregory laughed together, and Harriet continued her laughter as if she could not control it.

"Well, you are cheerful enough without me at the moment. I needn't stay to be made a stock of. Not but what I am glad to be anything for you, my dear. If you need me, send to where I am, the stables or the garden or the library, and I am with you."

"Places in the order of probability," said Gregory.

His mother laughed again, and her laughter seemed to hold and shake her.

"You had better come upstairs and lie down," said Gregory, holding out his hand. "It was very unwise to get up at all this morning. Some of us ought to have thought of it."

Harriet looked at the hand as if uncertain of its purpose,

deliberately placed hers in it, and rose. She stumbled as she went upstairs, and fell again into hysterical mirth. Gregory helped her on to her bed, and went to his father in the stables.

"I can't make Mother out this morning. Of course there must be some reaction from the strain of yesterday, but I don't understand her state. She is emotional in a way that is not like her, and seems to have no control of herself. I suppose it doesn't mean anything?"

"What it means, Gregory, is this," said his father, passing his hand down a horse. "It means that your mother is a wonderful woman, and has made up her mind to cease throwing a blight, to atone to us for what she has made us suffer. Ah, if there is anyone who appreciates your mother, it is I. If there is anyone whose bitterness is swallowed up in admiration, it is I, it is mine, it is I."

"Yes, but have you noticed her this morning?"

"I have not, Gregory, I have not. I have refrained from gratifying my curiosity, satisfying any particular anxiety on purpose. It seems to me a piece of consideration that we owe her."

"We owe her other things as well," said Gregory.

"We do, Gregory, we do. And whatever we owe her shall be given her in measure full to overflowing. My beauty, my lovely girl"—Godfrey was now addressing his mare—"you don't know what it is to be tossed and torn and have no peace, when you are doing your best for everyone, do you? No, and you shan't know it. I would rather I and everybody belonging to me knew it, than you, my pretty, my sweet."

"We don't often get so completely what we would choose."

"No, but she shall have it, she shall," said Godfrey, assuming a concentration similar to his own. "Everything she shall have that her master can give her."

"Your benevolence seems to be genuine, but not of wide application."

"Well, I have always been a soft-hearted fellow, Gregory," said Godfrey in a tone of disarming admission. "Any creature alive, man, woman, child, or beast, is certain of a response from me."

"I am sure of it," said Gregory.

"Ah, you are a good boy, Gregory, a kind son. Both your parents have reason to know it. Your father needs a little sympathy and understanding. He doesn't have much of a time as a whole, much as he has to be thankful for. It is amazing what a man can get used to, and sad in a way. I don't wish you my life, Gregory."

Gregory looked at his father with an affectionate smile coming over his face.

"I don't know which is the greater person, you or Mother."

"Ah, your mother is the greater, Gregory," said Godfrey, in full, melodious tones, not repudiating the adjective. "Never be in any doubt about that."

"Every now and then I do have a doubt about it."

"Well, don't, my boy," said Godfrey, sweeping his hand from his horse to his son. "Don't. Your father asks that of you." He turned and left the stable with an emphatic tread.

Chapter XIII

Harriet sent a message from her room that she would remain by herself, as she hoped to sleep. Towards evening Godfrey visited his wife, and they agreed that she should dine with her family. As the group awaited her in the drawing-room, Buttermere appeared.

"Have arrangements been made for bringing her ladyship downstairs, Sir Godfrey?"

"Bringing her ladyship downstairs? Whatever do you mean? Bringing her downstairs? Cannot she come downstairs?"

"Do you mean that she cannot walk by herself?" said Gregory, looking up quickly.

"I am not aware that she can, sir."

"Say what is in your mind, Buttermere," said Jermyn, leaning back and nervously tapping the table.

"I am under the impression that matters are as I have stated, sir."

"How was she when you saw her, Father?" said Matthew.

"I think very much as usual. She was lying on the bed as if she did not want to be disturbed. I disturbed her as little as possible. We exchanged a word, and I left her."

"Have you been told that she cannot walk by herself? And if so, who told you?" said Jermyn to the butler.

"I was given the information by Catherine, that that conclusion had been arrived at, sir."

Catherine was the housemaid who waited on Harriet, who cared for too little attendance to need a woman of her own. The father and sons exchanged a glance, and Jermyn and Gregory went to their mother's room. They found her sitting in an upright chair, with her elbows resting on the arms. The maid was moving about the room, worried and unwilling to leave her. She looked up with the expectant, acquiescent air of a child awaiting help.

"Why, cannot you come downstairs by yourself?" said Jermyn.

"She seems unsteady on her feet, sir," said the maid, "and she speaks much less than usual. She has only been really awake for about an hour since the morning. The upset of yesterday has been too much for her."

"Well, come along down to dinner, Mother," said Gregory.

Harriet raised her arms with a smile, for her sons to put their hands beneath them. She rose with their help, and moved downstairs between them, but gave no heed to her steps, and at every stumble fell into helpless emotion, and let them support her weight.

"Harriet, my dear girl, what is this?" said her husband, who was holding open the door of the dining-room.

Harriet gave another smile, and went with her head drooping forward to her seat, and taking it, looked in front of her. Gregory and Griselda watched her with startled eyes.

"What is wrong with her?" said Godfrey.

"I don't know. What you see. We know no more," said Jermyn. "Catherine says she has been asleep all day."

"I was not asleep," said his mother, just shaking her head.

138

"What were you doing then, my darling?" said Godfrey.

"Not asleep. Just on the bed," said Harriet, turning calm eyes upon him.

"Oh, yes, you have been in bed, haven't you?" said her husband.

"Not in bed. On the bed," said Harriet.

"I came in twice to look at you, but you did not see me," said Gregory.

"Yes, I saw you," said Harriet, smiling to herself. "I heard you, and then I saw you. You thought I did not see you." She gave another tremble of laughter that lingered as it died.

"She is not herself," said Matthew. "Are you not going to have any dinner, Mother?"

Harriet looked at him as if to speak, but remained with her expression fixed.

Godfrey got up and went to her side, and taking her soup, began to feed her with it. She opened her mouth for a while, and then stopped and gazed into space. Her husband, distraught and acting mechanically, took a spoonful of the soup himself, and Harriet turned and leaned towards him, unwilling to be supplanted.

"She is ill. We can't have Buttermere coming in," said Godfrey, continuing to move the spoon, and finding himself speaking as if his wife could not hear.

"Buttermere!" said Harriet, looking with the smile of a conspirator at her husband.

"We must carry her upstairs," said Matthew. "You and I are the strongest, Father."

"Yes, yes, you and I," said Godfrey, turning his arms as if finding relief in their competence. "Come, my darling, let us help you into this other chair. This will be better for carrying

139

you. Yes, you will be safe in this."

Harriet looked at the chair, and then at the table.

"We will have your dinner sent up to you," said Gregory.

"My dinner!" said Harriet, still looking at the table.

"She is hungry. She has had almost nothing since breakfast," said Jermyn.

"Hungry!" said Harriet, as if at once touched and amused by the idea.

"Yes, yes, my darling. We will get you upstairs, and Catherine will take care of you, and see you have what you need. You are not very well this evening. You will be better in your own room. You will be quite yourself in the morning."

Harriet smiled at the sensation of the chair, swayed her hands in time to its motion, and appeared regretful when she was set down. Godfrey saw her in bed, with her wants supplied, and returned to his children.

"Well, you have waited for me; that is good of you," he said in a lifeless tone. "You would not let your father have his dinner by himself. Mother seems to be getting on well with hers, considering. Well, I suppose we had better have Dufferin come and see her."

"It will be wiser to wait until to-morrow. He can judge better after the night. It is nothing urgent," said Matthew.

"You think it is nothing urgent, my boy? Not serious, do you mean? Well, you have the knowledge," said his father. "We will be guided by you. Have you anything to say about it yourself?"

"Nothing definite. Dufferin will know better. But I should think it may be serious. I meant it was not a case in which moments were significant."

Godfrey sat back in open depression.

"You had better have something to eat, Father," said Griselda.

"We don't want you ill as well as Mother."

"My dear child!" said Godfrey, rousing himself. "Well, I would a good deal rather be ill than have her ill. I can tell you that."

"You can't make the exchange. It would be a case of both of you," said Matthew.

"And there will be a greater strain on you than on anyone, if that is so," said Jermyn.

"Jermyn!" exclaimed his father, and changed his tone. "My dear boy, I don't throw doubt on your concern for a second. I know even from my own feelings how some people would be worked up. I mean I am an older and more stable man. All our feelings simply go without saying."

"Do you think she will sleep to-night, Matthew?" said Griselda.

"He cannot say, my dear. We can't any of us," said Godfrey. "But I shall be able to in the morning. I know that. I shall be in every hour to see."

Godfrey sent word on the morrow that prayers would not be held, implying that concentration appeared unthinkable. He came to the breakfast table later than usual, and in a more deliberate manner, preoccupied to the exclusion of daily custom.

"Well, does the opinion of all of you agree with mine this morning? I don't think there is much change. I can't say that I do."

"The absence of mind has become almost a trance," said Matthew. "She seemed to be sleeping most of the night. I went in at three and at five. Gregory and Griselda thought she had slept. Unless she was just lying in a coma, with closed eyes. What did you think?"

"Oh, well, I can hardly say. I was very exhausted," said his father, pulling back his chair with his eyes on it.

"What time in the night did you first see her?" said Matthew. "I met Gregory in her room at about three. I hadn't been in until then."

"Yes, yes, I think you are right. I don't think there is much difference between her state and a trance. A trance, a coma, a sort of stupor is what I should call it."

"I want to know how gradually the change came on."

"I can hardly say. I slept a very exhausted sleep. You think there is a definite change, then? That is what you would say?"

"Undoubtedly, by now. But I should like to tell Dufferin when it began. What was the earliest hour you saw her?"

"When I saw her just now, I thought there was a change certainly," said Godfrey.

Griselda let a sound of laughter escape.

"I wish I had the spirit to laugh," said her father, regarding her with knitted brows.

"I know how you must wish it," said Jermyn, "from being in the same situation. This is not an occasion when a night of unbroken rest makes for self-confidence in the morning."

"Oh, well, no, it is not. That is the truth about me," said Godfrey, his voice breaking out towards fullness. "I slept like a man recovering from sickness, and that in effect was what I was doing. The strain of submitting to this cannot be supported easily. Every ounce of my energy was drained out. I hadn't enough, after what I had been through, to raise my head from the pillow. It might have been me and not your mother in a trance, for all the difference there was."

"Unfortunately there was a fundamental difference," said Matthew.

"Unfortunately? Well, I don't know what you mean by that. I should have thought you would be glad to have one of your parents in a fit state. How would you like to face what is on us now, without me at the helm, or somewhere in the background where I could be relied upon?"

"As absolutely as anywhere," said Matthew.

"Yes, well, have it as you will. Somewhere in the background I said, didn't I? It is a good thing that some of us had a good night, and are not in a state of nerves this morning. Well, what arrangements are you going to make, Matthew, since you are at the helm, and not I?"

"I thought I would go after breakfast and bring Dufferin back."

"Yes, do, my dear boy. It is you at the helm indeed. If any two people can put things right for us, they are you and our friend, the doctor."

"We can only tell where they are wrong," said Matthew.

"Ah, well, that is half the battle," said his father, "to know where things are wrong. To set them right is a small step after that."

"We could do a great deal if that were so," said Matthew.

"You are really worried, my son?"

"Yes, I am, Father."

Godfrey rose and paced the room in simple, open dissatisfaction with fate. When the carriage returned, he gave a sigh that seemed to hold relief, since this feeling must now supervene.

"Well, whatever is coming upon us, we shall know it now. Our time of suspense is over. And suspense is the worst part. Reality is as nothing to it. We can feel the worst is behind."

He conducted Dufferin and Matthew to Harriet's room, and Griselda and the younger brothers remained below.

"Who would you rather was ill, Mother or Father?" said Gregory, setting himself to pass the time. "You would all rather

143

that Father was ill, and that you had a respite from Mother."

"That is near enough," said Jermyn.

"And I would rather it all came true of Father," said Gregory. "So Mother is first."

"There is Matthew's vote to be taken," said Griselda.

"Why does Matthew hate Mother?" said Gregory.

"Well, you must know, as you know all," said his brother.

"Because she does not admire him," said Gregory.

"She does not admire any of us," said Griselda.

"She does," said Gregory. "You and me. And Jermyn up to a point."

"She loves you the most," said Griselda.

"Love does not count like admiration," said Gregory. "She loves Matthew. Children hate parents who love and do not admire them."

"But not parents children?" said Griselda.

"Children never admire their parents," said Gregory. "Parents have nothing deeper than love."

"You admire Mother," said Jermyn.

"Yes, and sometimes Father," said Gregory. "But I am very unlike other people."

"Not as much as you think," said Jermyn.

"No, that could hardly be; but still very unlike," said Gregory. "So unlike that I have not found these moments like hours. They were not like hours. They are over. I have helped you through them."

The three men came from the room above, Godfrey walking first.

"Well, Doctor, we are here together prepared for what you have to say to us. We know that in the kindness of your heart you would spare us; but we ask you to tell us the truth, the whole truth, and nothing but the truth. Strong in the faith we share with her upstairs, we will bear ourselves worthily. You need not fear that the flicker of an eyelid will betray us."

"It is a mental breakdown," said Dufferin. "Her heredity is against her. She got by degrees into a nervous state, and it went from bad to worse, as you all know. The climax came when she made up her mind to end her life. The decision in itself must have been a terrible strain, and she was not in a condition to bear a strain. Very few lives include one on that scale. Then the shock of realising that she had done it, and could not face it, was too much for her mind. It was at once the last and the worst thing. We cannot know what that moment meant. It is not in us to guess what it was."

"Is there hope that she may get well?" said Griselda.

"Yes, great hope; I think it is almost a certainty. It will take time, possibly years, but I do not think it will be years. We will have her moved to a suitable place. It will be better for her, and fairer to her in the end. You will see that it will, when you have a chance to consider. The brain doctor will come down to-morrow, but he can only say the same."

"No, Doctor, no, I refuse to sanction it," said Godfrey. "I will countenance nothing that throws any doubt upon my confidence in you. I have in you great, complete and perfect faith. I will not be a party to any slur cast upon it."

"It is no slur; it is the usual thing. Brain disease is not what I do the most at. You can show your faith by giving me a free hand. The other man will come and tell you what I have."

"He will, Doctor," said Godfrey. "We shall not need to give him an ear, but you may do with us what you will. We bow to any decision of yours."

"Your mother is not suffering, you know," said Dufferin,

looking at Griselda's face. "She will not suffer in body or mind, even when she begins to recover, as I believe she will. She will not know in what way she has been ill, until she is well. Her suffering is past. You saw and talked to her after that."

"You give us comfort, Doctor," said Godfrey. "You speak to us heartening words. Your mission is to heal both bodies and minds. We are grateful to you for your healing of both."

"You are grateful rather soon," said Dufferin, taking his leave. "And I shall not heal Harriet. I can do nothing, but I hope time and her own power of recovery can."

"We hope it with you, Doctor. And if there is no foundation for the hope, we are still thankful to you for giving it to us. Well, my children, if it were not for you, I should be a lonely man to-day. We must brace ourselves to meet without flinching what is sent to try us like steel in the flame."

"It is hard on Mother to be used as fuel," said Jermyn.

"Ah, yes, and she did not flinch," said his father.

"She did, I am thankful to say. It would be an impossible memory if she had not," said Jermyn.

"She is the most fortunate of any of us at the moment," said Matthew.

"She is, Matthew. That is our comfort," said Godfrey.

"I think she is the least fortunate," said Griselda.

"You speak the truth, Griselda. You of all of us have dared to speak it," said her father. "My sons, we must not be behind. We must quit ourselves like men."

"How fearful if we should succeed!" said Gregory.

"Ah, we cannot judge by the surface. The heart knoweth its own bitterness," said Godfrey with simple understanding. "And there is a gleam of hope yet. The specialist is to come. We can't be certain that we shall not hear a better word. The bigger the man, the larger the view."

"You have decided after all to give him an ear?" said Matthew.

"Now why in the world take that tone?" said Godfrey, turning roundly on him. "Why should I hurt an old friend's feelings? For what reason in the world should I do that? Dufferin has been a good friend to us."

"No one can accuse you of ingratitude," said Gregory.

"No, no one can," said Godfrey with a sigh. "If there is anything I can do to serve anyone who has served my wife, that thing is done."

"What time does the specialist come to-morrow?" said Griselda.

"I do not know," said Godfrey. "I shall not need to discover. It will make no difference. Whatever time he comes I shall be waiting for him."

"So shall we all," said Matthew.

"Well, I didn't say you wouldn't. I should hope you would. It didn't occur to me that anything else would be possible."

"You made the statement about yourself," said his son.

"Well, so did you, didn't you? When are you going to stop insinuating, and throwing up yourself in the worst possible light? We know you are worked up and worried, my poor boy. You understand better than any of us the inner meaning of our trouble. I daresay we don't any of us face what you are facing. Ah, now, don't look as if you were misunderstood."

"I am not so easily understood," said Matthew in a gruff mutter. "No one else is thinking of letting this upheaval change his life. I got a glimpse of what Mother thought I ought to do, when I saw her lying ill. I see what she has always meant. I may go to London to get my life into shape there. She will come back and find her black sheep the whitest in the fold."

"My dear boy!" said Godfrey, approaching him with an uncertain step, that seemed to represent a doubt of hearing aright. "I don't know what to say. If my words did not fail me, my spirit would. Not many things could make up to me for your mother's illness; but it reconciles me to our parting, that you will be using the time to ensure her joyful return. And this is what you were thinking, when you seemed a thought strained and out of sorts! Your heart was full to bursting, and I hadn't an inkling of the depths within you. If anyone understands it now you have said a word, it is your father."

"I rather feel I put the last straw that day when I drove her away from breakfast," said Matthew, lifting his head and speaking more easily; "the day when she went to Dufferin to get what she thought she wanted. I did not know how ill she was, and it was I who should have known. I had better go and learn the things I ought to know. The other work comes later, if it comes at all."

"My boy, my heart at once aches and cries aloud. My tongue cleaves to my mouth and is silent. Here I have been going my unconscious way, with you at my side, heartsick, racked by remorse! I ought to have gauged your nature. You and I will go our way together."

Godfrey took Matthew's arm and led him from the room, addressing himself to his purpose in letter as well as in spirit.

Chapter XIV

"There, my dear one, there, my own, you are just going from one haven to another," said Godfrey, as he followed the chair that bore his wife, conscious but recognising no one, from his house. "We will soon have you home now, for it will be home where your husband sees you every day. No, it isn't good-bye. I shall be over to see you in the morning."

Godfrey bent over Harriet's hand, while her eyes rested vacantly on him, and turned at once to the house, openly giving no meaning to the empty parting; and the carriage containing Harriet, Gregory and a nurse, moved down the drive. The father went swiftly to the library and almost burst open the door.

"My poor child, my poor boys, I fear you are upset. You should not have been allowed to witness what you have. It is a ghastly thing for you to see your mother taken from her home in her helplessness. It may well make an impression that will go with you to your graves. I ought to have shut you up and taken it all on myself. And I put myself under it as far as I was able. I saw you safe in here, and gathered the whole thing on to my own shoulders. But we wish we had done more, the more we have done. I declare I could find it in me to blame myself."

"Would you see anyone, Sir Godfrey?" said Buttermere in a hushed tone, putting his head round the door instead of throwing it wide in his usual way. "Mr. Bellamy is coming up the drive."

"Yes, yes. Show him in. We have no secrets," said the master in a voice correspondingly clear. "We are quite prepared to see our friends. Griselda, it is only the rector. What are you running away for?"

"Mother seemed not to like me to see too much of him," said Griselda, pulling her hand from her father's and escaping from the room.

"Ah, her father has sympathy with her," said Godfrey, sighing. "That is to be the lie of things now, I see, this following her wishes. Well, I shall make it my life to do the same, until she comes back to us. And then we shall all do it doubly of course. Well, so here is the rector coming to see us! I suppose it is because of all this happening. How it has got about so soon puts me at a loss. Well, we have done nothing to be ashamed of. Few men have thought less of themselves than I have the last week. Well, Rector, you find us a broken family to-day. My wife has to spend a little while away from us. No doubt you have heard. The time may not be long, but we are finding it hard to begin it."

"Haslam, all theories of pastoral duty go to the winds, but my wish to see you as a friend has forced me to indulge myself. You know how I have looked up to your wife, how I have felt myself the weaker, smaller creature. You can't feel it more wrong than I do that I should be strong and useless while she is laid aside."

"My dear boy, we appreciate what you say. At this moment such words are as oil poured into our wounds. We do not hail you as useless while you can say them."

"It has come very heavy on all of them," said Bellamy, looking

150

round. "Is Griselda more upset than she has to be?"

"Ah, knocked utterly on the ground," said Godfrey in a deep tone. "Laid out so completely that she has to go to her room. We none of us feel a jot or a tittle compared with her. Well, in a sense a mother gives everything to her only girl."

"I will come to hear how she is to-morrow. And to-day I will thank you for letting me say my word, and cease to be. Matthew, you are the person I envy at the moment. You can do something. I wish I had a man's work in life."

"Ah, if anyone has that, it is that boy, Rector," said Godfrey with half-guilty confidence. "If I could tell you what he is setting before himself, your tears would mingle with mine."

"Then don't do it, for Bellamy's sake," muttered Matthew.

"Yes, and for your own sake, my boy," said Godfrey with tender extenuation. "You need not be uneasy. Your father will not betray you. You don't want an audience about just this, and just now. It is no wonder and an honour to you. I won't give your little secret away. It is too big to my mind for that. I will only say that I envy you. I wish there was some sacrifice I could make for your mother, that I could give up my aims and my hopes for her sake."

"Sir Percy and Lady Hardisty!" said Buttermere, in happy ignorance of the service he rendered, flinging open the door as though, if things were to be in this way, so they should be.

"Percy and Rachel? Must you be going, Rector? Now how has it got about to Percy and Rachel? It seems a thing has only to happen, to be at the four corners of the world. Good news does not fly so fast. If that has never been said, it ought to have been. It ought to be a saying. If I have made a saying, I have made one." Godfrey put his hand on Bellamy's arm in amends for his complication of thought at parting. "Here are Percy and

151

Rachel falling on us out of space! And call her Lady Hardisty, Gregory, if you please, and if you don't please, because I won't have anything else. I have been through too much to be put about by trifles. How are you, Rachel? How are you, Hardisty? This is good and kind."

"Haslam, my dear old friend!" said Sir Percy. "I had to see for myself how all of you were. You will understand me?"

"He really had to, Godfrey," said Rachel, "and you are not even trying to understand."

"Well, you can see for yourself, Hardisty. We are together, trying to support each other. It is no more than that."

"Of course not. That is doing justice to Harriet," said Rachel.

"My little Griselda?" said Sir Percy.

"I can hear her coming downstairs," said Rachel. "We are the only intruders she can face. Did the rest of you bear with Mr. Bellamy? She is the only one who has given us a true welcome. I will repay her by keeping the house for a few days. You can't learn to be father and mother in a moment, Godfrey. I must take Harriet's place."

"Rachel, that is a heartening word. That gives me courage. I was at my wits' end what to do for my poor children."

"I hoped you would make too much of it. People are known to exaggerate kindness in trouble, just when it seems they would think it only natural. It makes kindness such true economy that we have to take advantage of our friends' misfortunes. I have heard that at other times it is taken as a matter of course, but I hardly believe that can really happen. Percy, it is not you who is to take Harriet's place, and there must be someone to go on bringing up Polly. Mellicent has not recovered from being brought up herself. Just tell them how you respect them for having a real experience, and say good-bye."

"Ah, yes, a real experience; I cannot judge what it must be," said Sir Percy, withdrawing without imposing the effort of farewells.

"Be just to your early life, my dear," said his wife. "And this is a chance for you to go home and live in it again. You cannot call for me until after the working party."

"What working party?" said Godfrey.

"The working party that Harriet and Gregory give, to make brightness for Geraldine Dabis and to clothe the poor. Gregory calls people by their Christian names, and Harriet cuts out. I don't wonder it is Harriet who has had the breakdown. I cannot cut out. I don't mean I consider personal risks with Harriet ill, but I am very little fitted for real life. Geraldine would be so jealous if she knew. In other things I will take Harriet's place; there is nothing else real. Percy, if you go this moment, you won't coincide with Dominic Spong. I discern him with the long sight of old age. It is a great disadvantage to be old. How officious of him to come to condole! Doing a thing gives you so much under-standing of it. We won't say good-bye, my dear; it would look like thinking of ourselves."

"Say, rather, *au revoir* Lady Hardisty," said Dominic, appear-ing in Sir Percy's stead, and pausing by Rachel, with his eyes averted in delicacy from the family. "Meeting you here lifts a great load off my mind. Sir Godfrey, at the risk of appearing obtrusive, I am inflicting my presence, feeling that if in anyone's heart a corresponding chord is touched, it is in mine."

"You are good, Spong, you are good. We should be badly off if it were not for the thought of our friends."

"Without being presumptuous enough to take my stand in that capacity by the side of Lady Hardisty, I yet feel that a sympa-thetic word is due from one man to another at such a time. I do not forget, Sir Godfrey, your kindness to me, and not only yours, when my own hour came."

"Yes, yes, Spong, thank you, thank you. And I will depend on you to serve us further and share our family dinner to-night. You will not deny us, as Hardisty has done. Perhaps we could expect no more of him, after what he has left with us." Dominic turned a smile of full corroboration to Rachel. "But we will trust you to do better by us in yourself."

"Sir Godfrey, it is true that I can do nothing in these days except through that often unsatisfactory medium. But I fear I should be but a poor substitute for Sir Percy Hardisty."

"We are not talking about substitutes. We are asking, for yourself," said Godfrey.

"No, Sir Godfrey," said Dominic, shaking his head, as if he had shown too little reluctance for the hospitality. "I could not dream of intruding upon you on a night when you all must feel that only one presence could complete your family circle. I should be the last to consider myself the one equal to filling that place."

"That place is filled. I am here instead of Lady Haslam," said Rachel. "But won't you stay as a friend? I ask you as her deputy."

"Since you put it in that way, Lady Hardisty, I cannot do otherwise than acquiesce."

"Capital," said Godfrey.

"A great kindness on your part, and a privilege on mine, Sir Godfrey," said Dominic, substituting his own choice of fitting words.

"Well, we must get ready for dinner," said Rachel.

Dominic stepped towards her.

"Lady Hardisty, I have not the means of 'getting ready', as I came unexpectant of, and accordingly unprepared for the invitation; but if I may have the opportunity of what is termed a wash

154

and brush-up, I shall feel myself less unfitted for your presence."

"Matthew will take care of you. I am doing what his mother would wish, and not allowing his father to be used as a host to-night."

"I am more than reconciled to being handed over to the kindly offices of Matthew, our future host in this house, or I should rather say our present deputy host; for although I am a family lawyer, and as such concerned with future generations, I am not one to anticipate the cry: 'The King is dead. Long live the King.'"

"Why did you have Spong to dinner, and not Sir Percy?" Jermyn asked Rachel on the stairs.

"Because Mr. Spong came to dinner and Percy did not," said Rachel. "Gregory, call to Buttermere that we don't want anything extra to eat. I am sure Mr. Spong will not eat before Griselda and me, such a physical thing to do. I don't think I will take your mother's place as far as having the room opening out of your father's, Griselda. It isn't that I wouldn't do everything for him, but I have had so much of things consecrated to early romance."

"Well, we are not to be alone on this first night of our new life," said Godfrey, as they gathered in the drawing-room. "We are to have some compensation."

"I am sure, Sir Godfrey," said Dominic, "that neither Lady Hardisty nor I would see ourselves in that light."

"I have come on purpose to be seen in it," said Rachel. "You are fortunate to be a chance guest, Mr. Spong. It does seem more sensitive."

"Lady Hardisty, I was far from making that comparison. Now if Miss Griselda can bring herself to tolerate an escort so many

155

years her senior, I shall be happy to do my best to bridge the gulf between us."

In the dining-room there occurred some hesitation over Harriet's seat, which Buttermere, in the failure of definite directions, had deliberately placed.

"Sir Godfrey," said Dominic, standing to elucidate the position, "I think we are all agreed that that is a place we should prefer to see unoccupied."

"It is my duty to prevent that," said Rachel, taking the seat, and putting her fan on the table.

"Lady Hardisty, I appreciate your attitude. You are doing more," said Dominic, turning on her a gaze that seemed to swell for different reasons.

"I am doing nothing, but it is better for them all not to see the place empty."

"Lady Hardisty, mine was the simpler masculine view. I bow to a woman's deeper insight in these matters."

"Ah, you set us an example, Spong," said Godfrey, as his guest gave a sudden rapid murmur, checked his haste and openly rounded his utterance, and looked towards the window.

"That was far from my thoughts, Sir Godfrey."

"True. It was not the view he thought we should take of it," said Matthew.

"He showed true courage," said Jermyn.

"But he showed it so plainly," said Griselda. "That is hard on others."

"It had always been the custom of my wife and myself," Dominic was saying, "to begin and end a meal with blessing and thanksgiving. I admit it would materially lessen my enjoyment of a repast to feel that either was omitted."

"'Materially' is an excellent word," said Gregory. "Of course

156

it is wise not to omit them."

"I confess," said Dominic with a touch of asperity and suspicion, "that I never do omit them, whatever difficulties may be placed in my way."

"No difficulties are in your way here, Spong," said Godfrey. "And I think it is a very good plan to express our gratitude for what is given us, as though we were not ashamed of it. We have grace on formal occasions; I don't know why we gave it up amongst ourselves."

"Not because you were ashamed, if you have it before guests," said Rachel; "though they say that showing in true colours is especially hard in family life."

"It was nothing more than the change of fashion, I think," said Godfrey.

"It is hardly the sphere, Sir Godfrey, in which the dictates of Dame Fashion need be meticulously adhered to," said Dominic, as if his host's position were sufficiently established to allow of entertaining lightness.

"I don't see any sense in fashion if it is not adhered to," said Griselda.

"No, Miss Griselda, that is the view you would very naturally take."

"I wish I could use a word like 'meticulously' as a matter of course," said Gregory.

"Gregory," said Dominic, "may I ask why?"

"Because of the effect of modern reading," said Gregory.

"I felt that for a moment," said Rachel. "But that effect would not fit the atmosphere I try to create."

"I entirely concur, Lady Hardisty," said Dominic, "that that is not a department in which you need take any steps to emulate me."

Gregory and Griselda laughed.

"It appears, Sir Godfrey," said Dominic with a good-natured chuckle, "that these young people are engaged in holding up to ridicule such old fogeys as you and me. We must not include Lady Hardisty in that category."

"The young monkeys! I daresay they are," said Godfrey.

"We do not grudge them, Sir Godfrey, the relaxation proper to their years, even though it be at our expense. We know they do not forget the occasion which has given rise to the presence of Lady Hardisty and myself."

"I had hoped they had forgotten it for the moment," said Rachel. "They did their best to avoid it, poor children."

"I doubt if they would thank you for that appellation," said Dominic with a rather difficult smile. "We may be safe in gathering from experience of young people that it would not appeal to them."

"Don't take any notice of me," said Rachel. "I can't forget the occasion, and remembering occasions does not improve anyone. It is so considerate of people to forget them, and give up their credit for depth of nature for the sake of others."

"Whatever you do, Rachel, we are thankful to have you here to-night," said Godfrey. "We are so grateful for your presence that everything else is swallowed up in our gratitude."

Dominic looked as if he somehow suffered in comparison with Rachel, and was at a loss to explain it.

"Don't let my taking the working party be swallowed up," said Rachel. "It is really important to deprive the workers of the pleasure of Gregory's taking it alone. Why should they have pleasure when Harriet can't? They might even forget the occasion. Mr. Spong has put that into my head, and I could not bear it."

"I shouldn't be there, anyhow," said Gregory, in a quiet, open manner. "I shan't be seeing so much of Mrs. Calkin and her sisters now that Mother is ill. She was anxious for me to make friends of my own age, and I hope to get on to the lines she wanted, before she comes back."

"Yes, that is the lie of the land, Rachel!" said Godfrey, after a prolonged look, with eyebrows raised, at his youngest son. "Harriet's children can think of nothing but how they can serve her, and meet her when she returns, with their whole lives adapted to her desires. That is their aim and object. Here is Griselda scuttling away from the rector, scurrying like a hare at the word of approach, because he wasn't her mother's fancy for her! And Matthew is giving up his research, simply and finally giving it up without a look behind, because she believed that humdrum work, useful work in the world should be put before personal ambitions. His personal ambitions, poor, dear lad! And now here is Gregory, the last and the least, I mean our dear youngest boy, snapping his thumb at his old ladies, resolving to see no more of them, because it was a whim of his mother's, his mother knew in her wisdom that his contemporaries were better for him! If these are not children to be proud of, I don't know whose are. Would you not be proud of children of that stamp, Rachel?"

"Children of that stamp couldn't be mine, Godfrey. There is nothing of anything you mention in me to be inherited. For example I couldn't make friends of my contemporaries. They are failing too rapidly. I hate people whose golden bowls are broken."

"I think we need hardly suggest, Lady Hardisty, that Lady Haslam's case is of that nature," said Dominic looking bewildered.

"Well, Spong, and what do you think of these children of

159

mine, now that I have told you what I have of them?"

"Sir Godfrey," said Dominic, "I honour them. I honour the young men for the sacrifice that seems to me a tribute to their essential manliness, though many people might take the opposite view; and I am sure Miss Griselda is not behind them in the feminine sphere, which involves no less than their more conspicuous masculine one. Sir Godfrey, I honour your sons and your daughter."

"Well, what do you say to that, Rachel?" said Godfrey, with his lips unsteady.

"I say everything," said Rachel. "And I will take them all into the drawing-room with me. They can have nothing against the feminine sphere after what Mr. Spong has said about it."

"One moment, Sir Godfrey!" said Dominic, raising his hand, in appeal to his host rather than to the woman guest. "Is Jermyn to be exempt from the privilege of concession to his mother's wishes? I should esteem it as great a one to him as to his brothers."

"Oh, I daresay Jermyn will be following on; I can almost get it from the look in his eye," said the father, not at a loss. "I can vouch for it that Jermyn will not be far behind."

"I will not refuse the credit," said Jermyn. "I may do more spadework and less of my own vanities."

"And I will not refuse my whole-hearted approbation, Sir Godfrey," said Dominic, "and congratulation. Congratulation is the meed that I offer."

"Don't stand waiting for more flattery," said Rachel. "Come into the other room and shut both doors. Your father may not pull himself up in a moment. You have been through a great deal to-day, my dears. Things have been going from bad to worse. I have not taken a mother's place, and thrown myself

160

between you and evil."

"Mr. Spong won't stay the night, will he?" said Griselda.

"No, my child. I am the housekeeper, and I cannot manage it."

"It is a mercy you are with us," said Gregory.

"It is indeed. But ought you to express appreciation of old ladies, Gregory?"

"It is incredibly catholic of Father not to mind him," said Matthew.

"Well, he does praise all of you as much as he is told," said Rachel. "I was much less of a success at that. It is grudging and wasteful not to be able to praise people to their faces. Praising them behind their backs is pointless, keeping it all from them. I wish I were more like Mr. Spong."

"May I be permitted, Lady Hardisty, to turn the tables, and express myself desirous of bearing a greater resemblance to you?" said Dominic, coming in unexpectedly with Godfrey.

"That goes without saying for all of us," said Godfrey.

"Sir Godfrey, compliments do not come my way so often, that I can afford to ignore one that is forthcoming. And those we do not in theory have the advantage of, are the sweeter."

"Why have you come in at once like this?" said Matthew to his father.

"Oh, well, I found it too much, sitting in there with all there is weighing on me. You didn't any of you stay in there, did you? I couldn't stand it for a second, and there is the truth."

"Sir Godfrey, I think the moment has come for me to withdraw from your hospitality," said Dominic, as though suddenly finding he had failed in some function he had believed fulfilled. "It remains for me to thank you for your welcome, and betake myself to my own lonely fireside, there in your manner to brood

161

on what I have lost. My comfort must be that for you the loss is transient."

"Oh, thank you very much, Spong. And all my sympathy goes with you," said Godfrey, extending a hand, and dragging himself up after it a moment later. "Matthew will see you out. Matthew, you would like to see Mr. Spong to the carriage. We will have the carriage out for him. I declare I am at the end of my tether, and not a fit companion for a living soul."

"You really are not, Godfrey," said Rachel. "You are behaving more unworthily of Harriet than any of us."

"Oh, well, so I am. So I may be. My mind is too full of her for me to behave worthily of her. People can just reconcile themselves to it."

"Yes, so they can," said Rachel. "They soon break the habit of speaking of a friend as an excellent host."

"Why, has anyone ever said that of me?" said Godfrey, sitting up but relapsing. "Well, I am sure I don't care whether they have or not."

"Your mind is not quite full of Mother," said Gregory. "Self has crept in."

"Oh, well, has it?" said Godfrey. "Well, I should be a peculiar person if I hadn't some thought of myself in these days. Well, we will have poor old Spong to dinner again some time, and I will try to be more myself with him."

"'Poor old Spong'?" said Jermyn. "He is younger than you are, isn't he?"

"I don't know, I am sure," said his father. "I don't know anything about him."

"He looks it," said Rachel.

"Does he!" said Godfrey, sitting up again, and this time retaining his position. "Does Spong look younger than I do? Do I look older than Spong? Well, you know, I shouldn't have thought so. Well, I can't expect this state of things not to have its effect on me. I am not superhuman, if I have looked young for my age. You will soon have a pitiful old man for a father. You seem to think you have already. Well, I will go and get a night's rest, or I shall be a wreck by the morning. If I am, you won't hesitate to tell me. Ah, you will all be ready to pop it out. Rachel, I apologise for stiflying yawns in your face."

"That is an optimistic view of what you are doing," said Griselda.

"My dear little girl, you are brighter!" said Godfrey on his way to the door. "Having Rachel is doing you a world of good."

"I wonder why Father and Mother married," said Gregory.

"We can't explain these things," said Rachel. "I say that to myself when I look at my predecessor's portrait. Well, I do not; I see the whole explanation there. When are you going to take the photograph of your mother into the town to be enlarged?"

"I had thought of to-morrow," said Gregory. "Of taking it myself and giving it afterwards to Father. A surprise."

"It is a good idea to give it to Father. It will be a surprise," said Matthew. "We had better follow his example and go to rest. The day will start with the little service, and the strain falls least heavily on him."

Godfrey was the first to be in his place for this ceremony, and sat with his Bible open before him, parting his lips once or twice while the seats were taken. This was the only indication he gave of unusual force of conception, and he came to the table in a cold and absent manner.

"It was a subtle recognition of my filling Harriet's place to make no mention of me," said Rachel. "But was it wise not to ask for any guidance for the household? Won't they need it especially, with Harriet away?"

"I spoke simply the words that came from my heart."

"And no words for the household came into them?" said Rachel.

"Buttermere is listening," said Jermyn, as the door gently closed.

"Godfrey, you mustn't be so happy-go-lucky. You must think of Buttermere. And I have done the unmentionable thing. Well, one point about that is, that no one can speak about it."

"Oh, a little accident, Rachel. Buttermere will understand it."

"Buttermere is impossible. Looking and listening, of course, but understanding! And he will know now that we don't have anyone waiting in the room at home. He will guess that we are poor. And I have tried to cultivate that kind of shabbiness that may go with anything. It is only Percy to whom it comes naturally. And now Buttermere knows what it goes with."

"Ah, Rachel, I don't know how we should be feeling this morning by ourselves. We quail before the moment of your leaving us. Quail before it. That is the word, 'quail'."

"It is an excellent word," said Gregory.

"Well, it is the one that gives my meaning. Quail before it, blench, flinch. Blanch, cower, wince. Shrink! I tell you what I do quail before, Rachel, and that is the course my children are taking. I look forward to the day when I can take their mother by the hand, and point out the extent of her children's sacrifice. That day is as a beacon before me. I should like to hear you say a word about the matter, Rachel."

"I remember I failed you yesterday," said Rachel. "But I have not changed in the night."

"Ah, yes, that is how one feels. We must not speak about it. Tears would start to our eyes."

164

"And yet you wanted me to. And Buttermere would be looking. Parents will sacrifice anyone to their children."

"Oh, well, Rachel," said Godfrey. "Well, tell us how long Percy will spare you to us."

"Until after the working party. I have to explain that it won't be held again. I must be revenged on the women who work for Harriet's illness. All of them well and strong, and Harriet ill!"

"Well, they can't help it," said Godfrey.

"They can," said Rachel. "I am sure they take great care of themselves."

"Who will be coming to the working party?" said Jermyn.

"Gregory's three, to see Gregory; and my two girls because I bring them; and Mrs. Christy to work; and Camilla because it is a kind of outing, and because it gives an effect of boldness to go where she meets Mr. Bellamy, which after all is better than the usual effect of wistfulness. And some more who have only names."

"And who seem not to have even those," said Jermyn. "'From him who hath not shall be taken away, even that which he hath.'"

"Yes, so it shall," said Rachel. "I think the working party is all that Geraldine has. You will not come, Griselda, of course?"

"Ah, Rachel, no one but a woman can be a mother," said Godfrey.

"True," murmured Gregory.

"Isn't the working party necessary?" said Jermyn.

"Well, it is to clothe the poor," said Rachel. "Your mother had it, and we are giving it up. Things depend on the point of view. Remind me to be early, Godfrey, for fear Agatha gets into Harriet's place. I am afraid she thinks it is she and not I, who is next to Harriet."

165

Chapter XV

Agatha walked in an unconscious manner to Harriet's seat, drew up and smiled as an afterthought at its occupant, and putting her gloves on the adjoining chair, loosened her mantle and began to speak.

"It is heartrending tidings about poor Lady Haslam. I was afraid there might be more in it than appeared, when I saw her the other morning. I was in her house the day after the dinner, and she told me a little about herself. It all seems to have come on very suddenly."

"It may not have, if there was more in it than appeared," said Rachel. "I believe we all of us judged by appearances."

"What kind of symptoms did she have?" said Geraldine.

"I am sure Lady Haslam is not a person to have symptoms," said Kate. "We should all have symptoms before she would."

"She seems to have stolen a march on us," said Geraldine. "I plead guilty to being a victim of symptoms at times. We are not all of the fortunate, tough kind that give no trouble."

"Then you and Lady Haslam are alike at the moment," said Rachel.

"I feel there must be some fundamental connection!" said

Geraldine, revealing a complacence in the comparison.

"I hope I shall never give anyone any trouble," said Agatha.

"We shall regret you when you die!" said Geraldine. "That is one of the privileges of the eldest, to be regretted and not to have to regret."

"We cannot foretell the future," said Agatha. "It may bring us anything."

"Yes, even the death of Geraldine, as Agatha means," said Rachel.

"It must in the end," said Mellicent.

"I don't think Agatha meant in the end," said Rachel.

"Oh, no, she didn't!" said Polly, clasping her hands.

"You are staying in the house, are you not?" said Geraldine to Rachel.

"It must be a great thing for them to have you," said Agatha, granting completely the deserts of a peer.

"Was Lady Haslam able to leave directions before she went?" said Geraldine.

"I am sure the Ladies Hardisty and Haslam understand each other without words," said Kate.

"Lady Hardisty, we were so afraid we were late," said Mrs. Christy. "It is such a relief to find you have not begun. This is the last day we should wish to show ourselves unresponsive. I have been saying to Camilla that you are the only person I could bear to see in Lady Haslam's place. 'If Lady Hardisty can be Lady Haslam's deputy,' I said, 'I can go to the working party in the spirit of effort for those poorer than ourselves, that the latter instilled into us.'"

"Is there anybody poorer?" said Camilla. "We ought to keep the things we make."

"I wonder if we really do take so much interest in the poor," said Geraldine. "I try to think I do, but I have a suspicion that I feel them to be on quite a different plane."

"We shouldn't have working parties for people on the same plane," said Mellicent.

"I see we ought to give the party up," said Rachel.

"What about Lady Haslam's object in inaugurating it?" said Agatha.

"The best of us make mistakes," said Kate, sending the glance of a fellow to Rachel.

"We prove that Lady Haslam is one of the best by giving it up," said Rachel. "If we cling to it, it won't seem that she has made a mistake."

"We don't want to cling to it, I am sure," said Agatha. "We don't come to work for our own pleasure."

"Isn't it a pleasure to work for those poorer than ourselves?" said Rachel. "Lady Haslam really did make a mistake."

"Did I hear something about the eldest boy's going to London?" said Agatha, her tone holding retaliation rather than question.

"I cannot tell if you did," said Rachel.

"There is some special reason for his going, is there not?" said Agatha. "Something about remorse for his relations with his mother? A hint of it came through to me."

"Oh, then you did hear something?" said Rachel.

"I heard for certain that it was so. That there was something like a scene one morning, that ended in Lady Haslam's rushing out of the room. And an approach to remorse would follow that, it seems to me, when her illness came on so soon."

"But you would have been sure if you had heard that. Especially if you heard for certain."

"One does not give one's attention definitely to servants'

gossip. The Haslams are not very fortunate in that little respect, it seems. I often feel thankful I am not able to keep what is called a trained staff."

"A thankful spirit does help us through life's difficulties, though I have never thought of dealing with that one in that way. And of course you must know about sons leaving home."

"They do not always leave home for the same reasons. My boy left to make his career."

"That is why Matthew is leaving," said Rachel. "I remember now. So they do sometimes leave for the same reasons. I am glad it was not for your reason."

"Are we not going to begin working?" said Agatha.

"I don't know," said Rachel. "I noticed you didn't begin. I haven't been here very often. I am only here to-day to take Lady Haslam's place."

"That was hardly her spirit," said Agatha.

"I did not mean in spirit," said Rachel.

"At any rate you are in her seat," said Geraldine.

"Yes, that is what I said," said Rachel.

"Are the things we are doing in the drawer?" said Agatha.

"I will put them out, Lady Hardisty," said Mrs. Christy, directing her words in accordance with discipline, and hastening across the room. "I am a person who never minds what I do. Usefulness to my mind gives dignity to everything. I am at one with Lady Haslam there. Come and help me to give the things round, Camilla."

"No, I am a humble person; I won't share the dignity. Mine is the embroidered thing, Mother, not the petticoat. I don't feel any ambition to adhere to this apparel, in spite of my claim to it."

"Now I think that was such a good thought of Lady Haslam's, to have some of the things embroidered," said Mrs. Christy. "It shows a true sympathy with those less fortunate than ourselves, an understanding that they too may like a little touch of the beauty of life. There was something about the whole of her attitude with which I am so much in sympathy."

"Poor Mother, you do cling to your illusions," said her daughter.

"I direct that everything shall be embroidered," said Rachel.

"Even the aprons?" said Geraldine, holding one up.

"Aren't they always embroidered?" said Rachel. "How like Lady Haslam to right a wrong! Yes, they must all be done."

"These for standing at the wash-tub especially!" said Kate.

"Yes," said Rachel. "Washing is so hard on clothes."

"Is this thing finished, Mater?" said Polly, throwing a garment to her stepmother.

"Yes, my dear, except for the embroidery."

"I can't embroider," said Polly.

"But, my dear, you must. You are working for the poor."

"The cutting out of things is more our problem than embroidering them," said Agatha, adjusting her work.

"We must give that up, with Lady Haslam away," said Rachel. "Things can't be cut out now, only embroidered."

"They won't last us long on that basis," said Geraldine.

"Won't they last for ninety minutes?" said Rachel, looking at the clock.

"Are we not to have the working parties after to-day?" said Geraldine with eyebrows raised.

"We can't, with Lady Haslam ill," said Rachel.

"Of course not," said Kate.

"How about the people who need the things?" said Geraldine.

"They can make shift without them," said Camilla. "I have proved that it can be done."

170

"Ought we to think of the poor as needing things?" said Rachel. "Isn't that rather out of the spirit of embroidery?"

"I think this spirit of embroidery is a wrong one," said Agatha, seeming to call up her courage to speak. "There is nothing questionable in making necessary things for those who find them necessary. It is our duty to go on working as steadily as if Lady Haslam were with us. She is only a single member of our society, and as its founder would not wish us or allow us to think of her as anything else."

"Oh, don't do what she would not allow," said Rachel. "Whatever would be the good of my being here instead of her?"

"So we have to consider several things if we are to plan to continue," said Agatha.

"But we are not to continue!" said Geraldine, keeping her mouth open after her words.

"Not in Lady Haslam's house of course," said Agatha. "Lady Hardisty has one sincere supporter in me there. It would not be suitable, or congenial to any of us. We must wait to use her house again until she is in it. But in the meantime we should continue our efforts for those who are dependent upon them. I don't know if anyone will volunteer to hold the meetings? Of course there is the cutting out to be considered. Will anyone volunteer for one thing or both?"

"I think you and I are both too far away, Lady Hardisty," said Mrs. Christy.

"I felt we were somehow prevented," said Rachel.

"There are some of us nearer of course," said Agatha.

"Do you not cut out yourself, Mrs. Calkin?" said one of the members. "I am sure I remember seeing you."

"I have had to do so many things in my life, that I have not been able to do quite without it. And anything that I can do, is at the

171

service of the community of course. It goes without saying. But it is very likely that other people have had more experience."

"Surely it is not," said Rachel, "if you have not been able to do without it. Most people have definitely less in their lives. And if what you can do is at the service of the community, if that really goes without saying—it is the only instance of it I have met—surely the community had better behave naturally about it. Its going without saying will save them from embarrassing obligation. I wish services always went in that way."

"Well, we will see what other people say," said Agatha, with folded hands and an air of by no means hurrying the matter.

"We say we are most grateful," someone said.

"You need not be that, you see," said Rachel.

"You need not indeed," said Agatha.

"It seems to be our duty to do it, as there are three of us," said Geraldine.

"Qualities do run in families," said Rachel.

"Don't let there be three of us. Let us leave it all on Agatha," said Kate.

"You are a half-sister of course, my dear," said Rachel.

"We shall have to be there," said Geraldine almost absently.

"It is not at all necessary, if you do not wish to be," said Agatha. "In taking something upon myself, I am not involving anyone else. That would be a most unreasonable thing. Well, shall we say then a week to-day at my house at the same time, and tea as usual after the two hours' work? I don't think we can better Lady Haslam's custom."

"Yes, we will say that," said Rachel. "About myself, you know I can't cut out, and I am sure you felt it right to discourage me about embroidery, so I had better just come to tea."

"That will be very nice indeed, if we cannot have any more of you," said Agatha, in a cordial tone.

"It will be better than wasting you over the work," said Geraldine, going further. "Will Gregory come to tea as well?"

"I think perhaps he won't, as his mother cannot," said Rachel.

"I can quite understand that," said Agatha. "I know how my son would feel, if he had to see my place empty, Gregory will prefer to come and see us when we are alone. That will be what he has been accustomed to. He made that habit quite by himself. I shall be doubly anxious to do what I can for him now. I always say he is my boy, when my own is away."

"I wish I could be that, Mrs. Calkin," said the rector of the parish, looking round appealingly before he relinquished his hat to a willing hand. "I know you will say I am too old, and that you want Gregory for a boy and not me. And I am left to wish I could be a boy to someone."

"You are in too responsible a position," said Agatha.

"I wish that were true," said Bellamy, taking his cup, and a moment after giving a bright smile to the donor. "I would not mind not being a boy, if I could have a man's compensations. But a parson goes to a wedding and marries somebody else! He won't even be able to bury himself, though burying is his profession. He goes to a working party and does not do any work! He drinks the tea that somebody else has made." He held out his cup with another smile to a hand prepared to replenish it. "Well, I know what I shall do. I shall learn to sew."

"To cut out?" cried Geraldine.

"To cut out and to buttonhole and to featherstitch. That will be real work, and help to qualify me as a human being."

He turned from the hilarity that the idea of his sharing these human occupations produced in those engaged in them, and began to talk to Kate, whom he was inclined to make a friend.

"A clergyman is a clown, Miss Kate, and a deal less respectable a clown than one on the stage. That clown amuses people as a life work, and what more useful work could there be? A parson amuses people because he is a man among women. A man among men and a woman among women are natural. No one who thinks that women do not like being with women has any knowledge of life; and no one does think that a man does not like being with men. And a woman among men has pathos and human interest. But a man among women is simply—oh yes, I know I am this—the thread that goes through their lives. I would much rather be an ordinary man than a thread. A thread is such a good word for me."

"Especially as you are going to involve yourself in sewing!" cried Geraldine from a distance.

"I wish some woman would find a proper use for me as a thread. I might be used to sew up a gap in things for her. Do you think Griselda would ever use me, Miss Kate? Lady Haslam wanted a stronger thread for her, and one that had not been used before."

"It has to be a strong thread to be used twice," said Kate in a hearty tone.

Geraldine, who had been looking at Bellamy and her sister in surprise and almost consternation at their intimate colloquy, rose to her feet and broke the meeting.

Rachel met Godfrey in the hall.

"Well, did you make a success of the working party?"

"No," said Rachel.

"What went wrong?" said Godfrey.

"My personality," said Rachel. "It went to pieces. Agatha is next to Harriet after all. It is worse than that. She is instead of Harriet."

Chapter XVI

"Well, my dear boy, welcome, welcome," said Godfrey, entering his dining-room six months after his wife had left him. "The oftener we see you the more welcome you are."

"Then I must be very welcome by now," said Bellamy. "But not to Buttermere. He looked at me with a stony eye because he had to lay another place."

"Your place was laid as usual, sir," said Buttermere.

"Buttermere, you will soon be sorry for ungenerous words. When I have carried my princess to the parsonage, and we are happy and hospitable at our own board, you will find yourself sentimental that our places know us no more. Make the most of a Chapter that will soon be closed."

"It is needless to go further when everything has simply to be done, sir."

"We will, indeed, Ernest," said Godfrey, putting himself into a gap he was prepared to fill. "It has been one of the happiest Chapters in our lives. I would not ask for a happier, if I could be offered it. Of course there is always the one thing wanting. But we won't keep on dwelling on it. There seems to be something grasping, almost a thought ungenerous in harping on our right

175

to have things all our own way. We will leave that alone for a little while. But it has interrupted my welcome of you, and I wouldn't have had it fail for the world. I am as pleased to see you as any of my other children."

"Whose presence has been staled by custom," said Griselda.

"Ah, now, Grisel! What will you do with this girl, Ernest?" said Godfrey.

"Nothing. She will do everything with me."

"Ah, I'll be bound she will. They do everything with us at first. And afterwards of course, even more until the end."

"Well, it is the beginning we have before us as yet," said Bellamy.

"Yes, yes, we all get the beginning," said Godfrey. "Nothing that comes later can cheat us out of that."

"Is it permitted to ask how Griselda's mother is?" said Bellamy.

"My dear boy, I am grateful to answer that question, when it is asked in that spirit, and not as if I were somehow to blame for her being ill. I should be the last person, shouldn't I, to wish it? Some people give me an actual sense of discomfort for going on my way doing my best, instead of sitting about in sackcloth, in other words for following my wife's teaching instead of disregarding it. I am not saying which is the better course. I won't throw up the one I am taking. It is second best, I suppose they think."

"Well, Ernest is not among them. You may answer him," said Griselda.

"Yes, well, it is all as it must be, Ernest. I am not allowed to see my wife at the moment. Dufferin has forbidden it, and I am to take that as meaning she is better. That may be the meaning; other things would encourage me more. But I have put my best foot foremost, and looked people in the face, and please God I will continue as I have begun."

"I trust not alone for very much longer."

"I trust not, Ernest; but I don't see my way very clear before me. I have no great conviction to help me forward. Sometimes it is borne in upon me that it is just the beginning. Well, one thing is, that the certainty will creep on us unawares, and we shall be broken to the burden. But these are depressing words. We will give you no more of them. We will pass to brighter things. I find I can support this entertainment in aid of your church, settle the financial side of it, I mean."

"What a lovely meaning!" said Bellamy. "It is so uplifting not to be told that charity begins at home, as if that were a reason for its not continuing as far as the local church!"

"Yes, I find myself in a position to do so. I have seen Spong, and he makes it clear that that is the case. I should say, he lets it out because he can't help it, because I can see it for myself. I am getting an eye for business matters. However, we won't speak about Spong; he will be here for luncheon in a moment. He rather looked at me, old Spong, when I said I was to finance a play in support of a church. It seemed to him a contradiction in terms. The church part he swallowed pretty well; it was the play that stuck in his gullet. 'Ah, well, Spong,' I said, 'anything done for a good purpose is done for that end.' I quoted a bit out of your theories to him. And he said not another word. I think he saw my mind was made up. So things are shaping as you fancied them, Ernest?"

"All my life is perfect," said Bellamy. "Perhaps it is partly because I have a patron. I believe that parsons have always needed patrons."

"Oh well, my boy, patron! I don't know anything about that. You are to be my son, you know."

"Indeed I do know. All my life has been leading up to it. It is just the right finish to Griselda that she has parents worthy of her."

"Yes, yes, my boy, you think of both her parents, don't you?"

"It seems that there is to be a reversal of the old order of things, Sir Godfrey," said Dominic, coming smiling to the table, "and that it is no longer to be a question of children being worthy of their parents, but of parents adopting that relation to their children."

"Oh well, Spong, the old order passeth," said Godfrey, condoning general change.

"Ah, I am of those, Sir Godfrey, who view with a sentimental regret the passing of things established."

"Camilla, my dear!" said Godfrey. "We had given you up. How are you?"

"A thought shaken for the moment. Having brought a message from my lately intended husband to my now intended husband, I find myself confronted by my former husband as a fellow guest! And by our common legal adviser, who knows what would be called the unsavoury details of the case. I am sure I may depend upon Mr. Spong, and that the court is closed. Matthew, Antony is summoned to a patient and will not be working at his house to-day. He sent the message to Mother's door, as he knew I was coming here. He puts me to any use he can, now I am not to serve my former purpose. Ernest, it is utterly congenial to me to meet you as a brother. We exercise quite a choice of ways of becoming one flesh. Matthew, when you glower at me like that, I cease to be your future wife. I am your slave, I am a bondswoman, a squaw."

"I hope, Sir Godfrey," said Dominic, "that that is your eldest son's ideal in his life-companion."

"Well, haven't you come at all to see me, Camilla?" said

Godfrey, his eyes undetained by Dominic. "Haven't you a word for your future father-in-law? Don't you think I am any man at all beside Matthew?"

"Dear Sir Godfrey, I have come with the express purpose of feasting my eyes on you. I had to pass from alliance to alliance until I came to the one that provided me with you."

"Father, let Camilla begin her luncheon. She is behind already," said Matthew.

"Mother was convinced that being so late would destroy my character for ever. Being divorced was nothing to it. The second is less inconvenient for other people. It provides them with an excitement instead of a trial."

"We must call that a cynical speech," said Dominic, in a tone that seemed expressionless through doubt how to meet the speaker.

"I am known to be a cynic," said Camilla.

"Quite wrongly then," said Gregory.

"But it is wonderful to have brought that off," said Jermyn.

"Jermyn, am I to understand," said Dominic, "that it is your aim and object to be regarded as a cynic?"

"I am a very ordinary young man," said Jermyn.

"Jermyn, you cannot expect us to subscribe to that."

"No. Of course I should be aghast if you did."

"Sir Godfrey, frankness is not a quality in which the modern generation is lacking."

"I believe it is not. I am thankful to say I have found it is not," said Godfrey. "My children keep nothing from their father."

"You could not have a greater compliment," said Dominic.

"I could not. I value my sons' and daughter's confidence above everything. If there is any little thing I can do for them, I count myself already repaid."

"Matthew, have you yet discovered a house in which to embark upon your married life?" said Dominic, as if Godfrey's words set up this train of thought. "I apprehend that the scientific success which has in a measure attended your pursuit of it, disposes of the question of your extending your sphere. I do not use the qualifying words in any carping spirit. I know how seldom a quarry is sighted in your chosen field."

"We have been looking at some houses in the town," said Matthew. "My father is going to take one for me near my work."

"It strikes me, Matthew, as no doubt it strikes you, that you have a very generous parent."

"Now, now, I won't have a word of it, Spong!" said Godfrey, holding up his hand. "I declare, when I gradually realise how much there is in this literary and scientific work, I find myself standing hat in hand before my sons."

"That is not an attitude, Sir Godfrey, that was readily adopted by our own parents. Matthew"—Dominic seemed gravely to recollect himself—"I have not adequately expressed to you my congratulations upon this imminent change in your life. Married happiness is the highest that man is supposed to have."

"He is not supposed to have the other kind, is he?" said Camilla.

Dominic cast a fleeting glance at Camilla, and continued in the same tone. "I have myself been very happy. I can do no more than hope that your future holds for you what my past holds for me." Another glance at Camilla showed him struck by the unlikelihood.

"Thanks very much," said Matthew.

"I gather, Sir Godfrey," said Dominic, subsiding into amusement, "that the youth of the day has a tendency to be what we may call laconic."

"Mr. Spong grudges me a roof over my head," said Camilla. "He thinks I should be what I am, a woman of the streets. He should have more sympathy with his fallen sisters. I try to look on him as a man and a brother, and I have seen the reverse of a brotherly light in his eye. I believe I have seen it in more senses than one."

Dominic turned to Bellamy as if he had not heard these words, but with a faint air of sympathy arising from them.

"I understand, Mr. Bellamy, that you are inaugurating some dramatic proceedings on behalf of the restoration of your church. Ecclesiastical architecture is a subject which I have much at heart. May I congratulate you on the expectation of a sum adequate to your projects?"

"Yes, I think you may. My future father-in-law is adopting another satisfying relationship, and becoming fairy godmother. He is financing the affair, so that all the takings will be profit. And we are putting the sewing ladies on garments for the play instead of for the poor. So all things and people work together for good."

"It is for the same purpose indirectly," said Dominic in a rather wavering tone.

"Very indirectly," said Camilla. "The poor can't be clothed in ecclesiastical architecture."

"Mrs. Bellamy, it makes a patch of beauty in their lives."

"But not a patch of any kind on their garments."

Dominic fell into open mirth, and exchanged a glance with Godfrey, or rather conferred a glance upon him.

"I will be going, Haslam," said Bellamy. "And I won't come back to tea. I know you are expecting friends. If my fair parishioners find me a too familiar presence, my semblance of usefulness will be gone. Tell them from me that stitching has never to be done so thoroughly for fancy dress, so that they should be making speed."

"Sir Godfrey, am I to be the one burdened with that message?" said Dominic.

"Oh, come in to tea, Spong, come in to tea," said Godfrey, leaning back.

"Jermyn," said Dominic, turning smoothly from Godfrey, as if his words of himself had been by the way, "I have been gratified to hear that our long interest in you is to be crowned with result, that in other words you are about to have a bound volume of poems to your name. It must be a great pleasure, Jermyn, to repay your father in this way for the patience and faith with which he has awaited this fulfilment. May I offer you my sincere congratulations and my hopes that this book may shortly be followed by many others?"

"Thank you very much. The congratulations are perhaps premature, as you have not read the book."

"Many others! Shortly followed!" said Gregory.

"No, Jermyn," said Dominic, shaking his head, "I do not profess to be a judge of the poetic output. I am prepared to accept the verdict of the public, or at any rate of the critics of your work, which I make no doubt will be in your favour. I have a great belief in the uses of poetry in the amelioration of life; and whatever some may think of it as an aim for manhood, it is my own conviction that the ministers to our leisure are as deserving of gratitude as those who strive for us in sterner vein. I shall be happy to receive a copy, if you can conveniently spare one, and happier still if you will write me a friendly inscription on the fly-leaf."

"Thank you very much. But it won't be out for a couple of months," said Jermyn.

"Not for a couple of months? Is there some delay?"

"No. It will come out in about the usual time."

"It strikes me, Sir Godfrey, that the accusation of dilatoriness, usually brought against us lawyers, might with advantage, or at any rate with justice, be transferred to publishers. Jermyn will be well on the way with his second book before the world has a chance to acclaim his first."

"Oh, there is a lot behind it, Spong," said Godfrey.

"Will you make a good profit out of the book, Jermyn?" Camilla asked in innocence.

"No, none at all. Father is bringing it out for me this time. It is often done with the first book."

"Jermyn, is that so?" said Dominic.

"I believe so, especially in the case of poetry," said Jermyn.

"Then expense is to be involved, in addition to the time sacrificed?" said Dominic.

"Oh, no, Spong, you are not on it. I was not myself," said Godfrey, laughing.

Dominic rose and took his leave, an extra heaviness in his breathing betraying his present unavoidable attitude to the house.

"Oh, Spong is an old skinflint," said Godfrey rather uneasily. "I don't know if he thinks he is the head of this family, that he is in my place towards you all. Your mother left me in charge of everything, didn't she, not Spong? I don't know what we are coming to, if lawyers are to be father and mother and legal adviser all in one. Why, you look quite depressed, my poor boys, and I am not surprised. It is damping for you to have wet blankets thrown in your face."

"A nice, consistent metaphor!" said Gregory.

"Oh, well, is it? It was what I meant anyhow; it expressed my thought. Well, I am glad we are having friends this afternoon; it will help us to get the taste of Spong out of our mouths. He won't count for much among the rest, though he is dead sure to turn up. Not that I would choose to speak in that way of an old friend. I have an excuse. Poor old Spong! I believe we make a good deal of difference to him, and I am glad we do. Our friends have been very kind in flocking about us since we were left to ourselves. We hardly have a day alone."

The afternoon was to illustrate Godfrey's words.

"I think we are really here too often," said Agatha. "We might not have a home of our own."

"Oh, well, Mrs. Calkin, I know how you appreciate young life about you. With all this youth and promise in my house, I feel I cannot do otherwise than share it. You will find Gregory waiting for you over there, ready to give some time to you."

There was a change in Godfrey's touch as a host since Harriet had left him.

"It really seems unnecessary to shake hands," said Geraldine. "We shall quite forget that we are guests."

"Oh, well, Miss Dabis, as long as it makes a change for you."

Agatha moved on with a modified expression, passed by Gregory with a kindly, easy smile, and went up to Dominic.

"We have met here several times lately, have we not, Mr. Spong?"

"Yes, we have," said Dominic with grave appreciation.

"It seems an irony of fate that Lady Haslam should not be here to witness her children's developing lives, when she herself has laid the foundations of them."

"Mrs. Calkin, it is a circumstance that makes us simply stand still and say, 'God's ways are not as our ways.'"

"It has been such a relief to me that Sir Godfrey has been able to recover his spirits. I hardly dared to hope it would not be beyond him."

"It is a thing we must regard with the greatest thankfulness," said Dominic, just glancing at Godfrey and withdrawing his eyes. "And, Mrs. Calkin, there is one thing we have to remember. 'The heart knoweth its own bitterness.'"

"Indeed, we do have to remember it. There is no need to remind me of that," said Agatha in a changed, controlled tone. "I carry that with me, the essential knowledge of it. After what I have been through, that goes without saying."

There was a pause.

"Mrs. Calkin, you must allow me to thank you for your service to the youngest boy. As the lawyer, and I may say as the friend of the family, I feel personally grateful."

"I have tried to do what was in my power. It seemed the least I could attempt."

"It must be a wonderful thing," continued Dominic, "to take the mother's place to a youth on the verge of manhood."

"Yes, well, do you know," said Agatha, recovering on this sufficient ground, and seeming in honesty to make a reluctant admission, "I believe that is what I have done. He comes to me with his troubles and perplexities, as if he had never known any other guide. It is a great thing, as you say—I think one does the work better for realising it—to guide the footsteps of a young man at the dangerous place, and to feel that one is requiting in that way his generous trust. I say to myself when I see him coming in, so affectionate and full of appeal, 'Am I doing all that is in me to repay this young creature for what is so spontaneously given?'"

Dominic met this degree of evidence with a slow shake of his head.

"He is such a friendly boy, so disappointed if one of us is out," said Geraldine.

185

Dominic swayed from one sister to the other.

"A mother's experience must come through," said Agatha, "just because it must."

"These soothing illusions!" said Geraldine.

"Miss Dabis," said Dominic, in a manner concerned and taken aback, "no one has ever thrown doubt upon the truth that single women have opportunities as valuable and satisfying as those of their married sisters. I thought that was a certainty by this time established."

"Why, did anyone question it?" said Geraldine.

"They did when I was single," said Rachel, "before the certainty was established, you know."

"Lady Hardisty, I think you are in popular parlance pulling our leg," said Dominic. "And personally I cannot retaliate, as I could not be accused of either figuratively or literally performing that office for a lady."

"Griselda, pour out the tea," said Rachel, "and give Mr. Spong something to hand before he reveals his true nature. It is extraordinary how everyone has a true nature, even when you would not think it possible. I believe natures are truer in those cases."

"Ah, my little hostess, so you are looking after us all, are you?" said Godfrey, throwing one leg over the other.

"It is so painful to me to see this house without its mistress," said Agatha, taking her stand by Rachel and stirring her cup. "She is in my mind every moment I am here. That things have to go on, and do go on, is of course a ground for thankfulness, but their very going on causes something very near to a heartache."

"Very near," said Rachel. "That is an excellent way of putting it. We are reminded that things will go on after we are dead, that people will be happy, actually be that, when we are not anything.

And yet it would not do to have quite a heartache."

"I suppose we ought not to feel it. We can do nothing while we are here for those who have passed before."

"You were thinking what we could do for them before they passed, if we could prove we should never be happy afterwards?"

"They would not feel that, though we cannot suppress a tendency to feel it for them," said Agatha, and added half to herself:

"'Better by far you should forget and smile,
   Than that you should remember and be sad.'

I am convinced that that would be—that that is my dear husband's feeling towards my life."

"People improve so tremendously when they are dead," said Rachel. "We see they do when we compare our own feelings. Of course poets ought not to found their poems on their baser side. And they don't, do they?"

"It is Christina Rossetti, the great woman poet," said Agatha, looking in front of her.

"Well, poets generally write as if they were dead. You see she feels exactly like your husband. It is we normal people who have nearly a heartache because people do not remember and are not sad."

"It does almost amount to not remembering," said Agatha, her words seeming to break forth. "In this case the absent one may return, and see for herself how things have gone without her hand on the helm. It is a heart-piercing thought."

"You do make it seem that it all ought to be stopped. You couldn't prevent Gregory from attending the working party, could you? I have less influence over him."

"No. No. That is a thing I could not do. I am almost sure I could not. He comes entirely for his own satisfaction."

"Satisfaction! It has a dreadful sound. I do agree with you. But if nothing can be done!"

"It was actually in her own home that I meant. Somehow I cannot throw it off, that her being away should make so little difference. I could almost feel a little disappointed."

"Of course it is awful to see human happiness," said Rachel.

"I think you know that was not my meaning."

"That is what I always mean."

"It is not always safe to judge other people by ourselves."

"I have always found it absolutely reliable."

"I think you are in jest," said Agatha with a forbearing smile, "or at any rate between jest and earnest. Your sense of humour is too exuberant."

"Is it? I had hoped it was subtle."

"Well, at any rate it runs away with you."

"Runs away!" said Rachel. "It must be exuberant."

"Are you two quarrelling?" said Geraldine.

"No, it takes two to make a quarrel," said Rachel.

"Well, what are you so deep in discussing?"

"My sense of humour. Your sister is describing it."

"Oh, sense of humour! I agree it does not make one popular," said Geraldine.

"A sense of humour need not be unkind," said Agatha.

"Doesn't it have to be just a little?" said Rachel.

"One may point one's shafts without realising it," said Geraldine. "When one has a selection of them, it is difficult to remember which are the sharpened ones."

"All the great instances of humour are mingled with

tenderness and tolerance," said Agatha.

"Yes, that is what I meant. Only mingled with them. Just a little unkind," said Rachel.

"Could there be anything worse than tolerance?" said Mrs. Christy, moving her hand. "Actual opposition is a thing I have nothing against. I feel it is worthy of my retaliation, that it may even sharpen the retributory powers that must take their place among our gifts. But tolerance implies no worthiness on our own part, no capacity for engaging personally in the fray."

"I would certainly rather face an active enemy," said Kate.

"How can you know without experience?" said Rachel. "None of us has ever faced an active enemy."

"Oh, I have," said Agatha, looking out of the window.

"You don't mean me, do you?" said Rachel.

"No, but that shows you have been naughty," said Agatha, shaking her finger.

"I should sum it up, that I like to advance true friends, and beat down baffling foes!" said Geraldine, dropping her hand and her voice with a glance at Mrs. Christy. "I have no use for what is in between."

"There again, how can you tell without having tried?" said Rachel. "No one ever does advance a friend."

"Oh, surely," said Agatha. "I have seen many instances of it."

"I have never seen one," said Rachel. "No one has ever advanced anyone I have known."

"We must not take things too personally," said Agatha with smiling repetition.

"No, but personally enough," said Rachel. "We ought to have our share of the advancing."

"We may not all be easy to advance," said Jermyn. "We must make allowances."

189

"It is hard to make them for anything so bad as not advancing us," said Griselda.

"Well, can't you ladies spare a word for any of us?" said Godfrey. "If that is not a pretty speech, I don't know what you would have."

"Perhaps not an interruption to their very animated conversation, Sir Godfrey," said Dominic.

"We are discussing the advancement of friends," said Geraldine, turning immediately to them. "Lady Hardisty says no one ever does it. We will put it to the profounder masculine judgment."

"Well, well, people must see to their own advancement," said Sir Percy.

"Just as I said," said Rachel.

"They generally do their best," said Jermyn.

"And small blame to them," said Matthew.

"Matthew, no one would suggest," said Dominic, "that you and Jermyn are in any way deserving of censure for the efforts you have lately made for yourselves, with such success."

"The point is, do people make efforts for other people?" said Matthew.

"No, Matthew," said Dominic, shaking his head; "in the course of a life spent in association with people's relations to each other, I am bound to say I have seldom seen it."

"I have never seen it," said Rachel.

"Well, I have seen it," said Agatha. "I have come upon many instances of generous effort for others. Some of them I have even prompted myself, generally to meet with a ready response. I have great faith in the possibilities of human nature."

"You must have," said Rachel.

"Ah, you bring out the best in people, Mrs. Calkin," said Godfrey.

"Well, I have found it so," said Agatha.

"Fancy daring to prompt people to effort for others!" said Rachel. "We can't know what would happen if we explored unknown possibilities. Percy, we will go home. Buttermere is being prompted to too much effort for others. But I don't think it was in his sphere that Mrs. Calkin meant. She could hardly have got such wonderful results."

Agatha moved on to where Sir Percy stood by himself, to exchange a word before parting.

"Your wife and I have been talking about our feelings as guests in this house, without our hostess. I fancy she thought I made a little too much of them, and I am quite prepared to say that I did. It is such a clearly defined thing to me, the setting asunder of husband and wife. When you have once grasped it for yourself and in yourself, there it is once for all sharp-edged for you."

"Yes, yes, undoubtedly," said Sir Percy.

"I forgot for a moment that you had had the experience in your own earlier life," said Agatha, laying her hand on his arm. "There must be much remaining, whatever has supervened, to give you the sense of my words."

"Yes, yes, there has been everything, you know," said Sir Percy, looking at the hand.

"My husband and I just had the one experience together," said Agatha in a low, intoning voice. "We just shared the one with each other."

"Don't probe Percy about his first marriage, dear Mrs. Calkin," Rachel called from the door. "He feels too deeply about it for words, and I do all I can to make up for him. He will tell you about his second in return for what he has heard about yours."

"Well, my dears, so we are to have an evening to ourselves,"

191

said Godfrey. "We don't have that often in these days. People have rallied round us in a way that has warmed my heart; they have gathered to our fallen banner as one man. I shall thoroughly enjoy an evening with you alone. I shan't have the smallest regret or thought of dullness creeping in. And we shall soon be having this play to hearten us up and take our thoughts off ourselves. We need that in these days. I have protected you from danger of morbidity. I have seen fit to. It would have been your mother's wish; and knowing that I have done it, that has been enough. If I could tell her of your achievements, my cup would be full. I am convinced they would have her full sanction, if she returned to us whole in body and mind. But we must not expect complete fulfilment on this earth."

Chapter XVII

"Well, so the performance was a success, was it, Ernest?" said Godfrey, standing outside the playhouse which Bellamy had hired in the town, or more truly he had himself hired through Bellamy. "It has fulfilled your hopes? It was worth your while that I should do it, that has been enough. If I could tell her of what you wanted for them? I declare they showed up bravely. Their achievement was astounding. I congratulate myself on affording them their opportunity; I feel I can do it. And what I marvel at for myself, is how I have spent all my life disapproving of the stage. I stand here and wonder about it. I take myself to task. For a play seems to do more for you in the time than anything within my experience. I have been living in another world these last three hours. You may laugh at me, but it is the truth. Now I suggest you should all come back and spend the evening at my house. I hope it is not a matter for discussion. Rachel, I may depend upon you to second me?"

"You certainly may," said Rachel. "It goes entirely without saying."

"Now I am glad to have you say that, Rachel. It gives me genuine gratification. I feel that life still offers something to me, when I can hear such words from my friends. Now we will go to the carriages. There will be seats for the least. We will all settle in together and go home. I hope it is beginning to seem that to all of you."

"I think that is still an extravagant hope," said Jermyn.

"We don't sleep there yet!" said Geraldine.

"You are quite a lighthouse in our midst, Sir Godfrey," said Mrs. Christy.

"We are getting to make ourselves look very foolish," said Matthew. "We behave as if no one had meat and drink in his house but ourselves."

"Well, there won't be any need for anyone to have any soon," said Griselda. "There may not be any to be had."

"Well, well," said Godfrey, "I don't know that it is quite so much that we manage. But I am glad if we have made some little breaks for our friends. It seems to be a thing we can do. And we have a great deal done for us by them. Now let us disperse to the carriages. Mrs. Calkin, I must insist upon taking you."

"Sir Godfrey," said Dominic, speaking with serious insistence, "I must protest against again becoming a member of your party. I have too often inflicted the damper of my presence upon your spirited gatherings, and on this occasion I must ask your permission to decline."

"No, no, Spong, don't set that example," said Godfrey.

Dominic stood aloof and as if in thought.

"If I am to be taken as setting an example, and therefore precluding others from exercising their power of choice, I cannot regard myself as a free agent," he said, and stooped to enter a carriage.

"No, that is right, Spong. I knew you would make the right decision."

"I believe Mr. Spong got into this carriage because I was in it," said Camilla.

"Mrs. Bellamy, I am not so ungallant as to dispute such a suggestion."

"It seems inconsistent of Sir Godfrey not to put us all up," said Kate.

"Miss Dabis, we must not overreach," said Dominic gravely.

Camilla leant back in laughter.

"Miss Dabis," said Dominic, "I admit that my quickness was at fault. But I am sure we neither of us regret a blunder that gave us that peal of mirth."

"Mr. Spong does not dare to use my name," said Camilla; "he feels it is too temporary and precarious. He finds the whole question of my names is better passed over."

"Well, well, here we are!" came in Godfrey's voice from his carriage. "Here we are at our destined halting-place. I hope we shall none of us leave it until the hours are small."

"We are in the current phrase to make a night of it," said Dominic, as he emerged and stood to assist Camilla.

Buttermere was standing in the lighted doorway, and spoke to his master as he passed him.

"Dr. Dufferin is waiting to see you, Sir Godfrey. He did not know you were all out, and can come again to-morrow if you would prefer it."

"No, no, I will see him. I will go and find out if he is in any quandary, if I can settle up anything for him," said Godfrey, going with swinging arms to the library. "Into the drawing-room, all of you, and dispose yourselves at your ease. I hope you are that already; I think I may feel you are. Now, Antony, my boy, in what way can I serve you? Out with it, without any effort. You have done so many services to me and mine that I should be a curmudgeon indeed not to be eager to make a return. I am finding it a privilege to accede to many requests from my friends. It has been a consolation to me in my widower-hood; for that is what it seems to be coming to be. While I can do something for others, I count my days as not lost."

"That is what I have come to speak about. It is not to be widowerhood, Haslam. It is good news I have for you, the very best. I have prepared you in a measure, but I doubt if you have dared to take my meaning. I have kept you from Harriet lately because she was better, not worse, because she was getting well. I have put off the truth to save her the risk of a pressed recovery, and to save you both the memory of meetings while she was not herself. When she did not know you, it was different. Now she will be herself as soon as she is used to being so. She has been asking for you all."

"Doctor," said Godfrey, taking a step backwards, "you lift up my heart. I have been a dreary and lifeless man these last months. The gaiety of my life, its apparent variety, has gone on over an inner deadness. If I can see my wife at times, I shall feel there is a weekly or daily goal, as it may be granted. And in my gratitude for what is given, I shall not overstep and ask too much."

"It is better than that," said Dufferin. "You may ask what you will. You may make up your mind for the best. Harriet has only to bridge the gulf of her illness, and return to her place."

"No, no, Doctor," said Godfrey. "We will not keep you to that. You must not promise more than the most. You will not raise our hopes to dash them; we know you too well. We do not ask impossibilities even of you. That would be a risk we must not take. We do not blame you for the inevitability of that; it is not indeed to be set to your account. We do not forget ourselves, to grasp at the completion of our own life at the cost of hers. I speak for my children and myself. We will leave her where she is, watched over, contented, safe."

"She is none of those things any longer, and I could have no better news. It is well I should not be clear in a moment, but I may be clear now. Harriet can soon come home. She is herself."

"Is she asking to come home? Has it come into her mind? Has she spoken of it?"

"It has come into her mind, as she is herself. She has not said much of it. She takes it as going as a matter of course, as it goes."

"It does, Doctor, it does. That is how the matter stands. We take up our life again, our old life. We go forward into it, resolute, resigned, rejoicing from our hearts. I will go and break it to my children, announce to my guests and my children this coming of joy. I will give you your due. I will say that our debt is to you and to no other. You will come with me and hear your success described to our common friends. I feel I cannot keep it from them another moment."

"No, I will go home. You don't need me. I shall see you next when I take you to Harriet."

"My dear old friends," said Godfrey, throwing open the drawing-room door, "rejoice with me! My time of sufferance is past! My wife is to be amongst us, fully restored! The moment has come suddenly. It was thought that the strength for patience would not be ours. My heart is full to overflowing; my words falter. I do not ask for your sympathy. I know it is mine."

Godfrey's children were in a group about him.

"Is it certain? Did Antony tell you?" said Griselda.

"Quite certain, my daughter. I would not raise your hopes to destroy them."

"It must have been certain for some time, if it is so now," said Matthew. "No doubt it has been certain. No doubt."

"Did Antony tell you just now? Is it to be at once?" said Jermyn.

"It is to be at once, if Dufferin says it is to be at all," said Matthew. "The end of it all has come. The whole thing is over."

"Does Mother know about it?" said Gregory.

"My dear children," said Godfrey, "there is one answer to all your questions. 'Yes!' The Chapter of your orphanhood is closed. Your faithfulness and your courage are to have their reward. Our friends will forgive our blundering words of shock. For our hearts can harp only upon one note. They will bid us God-speed upon the road that is opening out to us, the road that is old to us and new."

"God-speed always goes with separation," said Rachel. "We will leave at once. I am full of selfish gladness for myself, Godfrey. That does not sound a credit to me, but such a credit to Harriet that I sacrifice myself to her, and put myself in a light especially becoming at the moment. Percy, don't say anything, if you cannot sacrifice yourself. Godfrey will understand that I have spoken for both."

"Yes, yes, for both. The old times again. Glad most of all for myself, most of all for you," said Sir Percy, hastening his words and his steps.

"Camilla, we will do as we would be done by," said Mrs. Christy. "At this moment of tense concentration we will not deal in the mere emptiness of words. Sir Godfrey, I stand amongst those whose instincts have been baulked of late of their truest fulfilment. They have repeatedly been baffled in the bent native to them. Lady Haslam cannot have a welcome more in touch with the atmosphere carried in her wake."

"I am sure she cannot; it would be too terrible at the moment," said Camilla, using a sweeping hand, and calling her own

198

valedictions from the doorway. "Good-bye, dear Sir Godfrey. Good-bye, my Matthew. I have hated your mother's not having the opportunity to forbid our engagement. She must try to make up for it now. I can't bear for her to be denied anything. Tell me if we are ever to meet again. Her wishes must come first."

"I must just shake hands with you, and say a word," said Agatha to her host. "I was saying only the other day, how sad it was to me to see this house without its mistress, to see things having to plough their way, as it were, rudderless. I was saying it here in this room, it seems only a moment ago. It does seem such a coincidence, almost as if coming events do cast their shadows before them, to some minds perhaps that have a bent towards the future. We are full of thanksgiving for you. You will let me say it for all three of us."

"It would never do for us all to say it at that length, when we were told to bid God-speed!" said Geraldine.

"It is allowable to be without words," said Kate in a low, deep tone, as she followed them.

"Sir Godfrey," said Dominic, "my fellow-guests have taken their stand upon the assumption that something may be said from the much welling up within us. I am aware that anything must strike you in the light of hopeless inadequacy, and I will not burden you with the feelings inevitably aroused in a heart which has beaten during these months in tune with yours. I will simply say that I am thankful to see restored to you that which I myself have lost." After his congratulation Dominic turned and stumbled with bent head from the room.

"May I stay a little while with Griselda? I promise I will not talk," said Bellamy.

"Yes, yes, do, my boy," said Godfrey, going to the fireplace. "Well, I think the play and everything went off well. My dear children!" He turned and held out his arms. "You don't know what to say, and I understand it. I hardly know myself. I am not surprised that you are dumb. I shall say to your mother, 'Your children stood in silence to hear the news of your return. Their hearts were too full for words.' And indeed it is too much to come at once. I felt it was. If I had known this evening that our lives were to need readjusting in a moment, I could not have welcomed my guests with the easy hospitality that I showed them. I do not think I fell short with them, either when I welcomed them in, or when I came in and gave them the tidings in my own way? That is a moment that would not have left your memories. But if anyone understands your being without words, it is I."

"That is generous of you, as you are so different," said Gregory.

"It is a wise and provident theory," said Griselda.

"Neither on this occasion nor on any other can we fall short," said Jermyn. "And the worst of reunions is the falling short. Reunions are perfect without it. Mother must feel that our tongue-tied welcome is a proof of our worth."

"We shall have to give an account of our stewardships," said Matthew.

"Matthew!" said his father on the moment. "Do you insinuate that everything has not gone on in your mother's absence as if she had been with us?"

"You were ready to fit on the cap," said Matthew.

"Indeed I was not. You read into others the fabrications of your own mind. I blush for you, Matthew. It almost seems that your own conscience is not clear."

"We shall go on our way without a shadow," said Gregory.

"My dear boy, you will," said Godfrey. "My dears, we have clung together during these last months. We shall hold as closely in the time of test that is ahead of us. For all changes bring demands. We shall be equal to them by aiding and abetting each other, by uniting to aid our lost one to regain her foothold. Ah, sickness laid her low. Our wife and mother will return to us, and in spite of our being left without her guidance, will not find us wanting."

"With the help of silence," said Jermyn.

"I am glad to hear that definitely, Father," said Matthew.

"I state it definitely, Matthew."

"I wish you were the parson instead of me, Haslam," said Bellamy.

"Well, I have had some little practice in speaking at times. You know I have a service every morning for my household. I think they have got to depend on it. Yes, well, we all do our little part. You must go, must you, Ernest? I will see you out."

"Mother will be back again," said Gregory, smiling to himself. "I have felt lately that she would."

"You have taken Dufferin's hints," said Jermyn. "The rest of us waited for the actual words. Certainty is the only thing that counts."

"Dufferin's hints counted," said Matthew. "That is why he used them with such care. He saw we needed to come by stages to certainty. We have not really taken the leap."

"This is the scene of our welcome of Mother's recovery," said Griselda. "They say that such scenes fall short in actual life, so we may perhaps feel that this is up to the average."

"Poor Father does not dare to return from the hall and settle down to the future," said Matthew.

"That means nothing," said his sister.

"It may mean more than that," said Matthew.

"Oh, Mother will come home more herself," said Jermyn.

"Anyhow she will come home," said Gregory. "It is no good to give any thought to the occasion. All our little private preparation will be wasted."

"I always wonder about this self of Mother's that we hear so much of," said Matthew. "We have never had a chance of seeing it. She may not have more than one self, any more than the rest of us have. And if she has not——"

He left the room as his father returned to it.

Chapter XVIII

"Come, my harriet, come, my girl, come to your home. Step across the threshold back into your old life. The other is nothing but a dream. There, you are back in your own nest. Your children are coming to welcome you, hurrying as fast as their limbs can carry them, to welcome their mother home! Yes, yes, kiss your mother, my sons. Give her a greeting as if she had only been away for a little time. That is all it is. Well, I see you all together again. I have looked for this moment as I have looked for no other in my life. I declare to you, Harriet, that if anyone had asked me what I would take to give it up, I should have said, 'Nothing'. Nothing would have induced me to relinquish what I have been living for for months. For it has been that, my dear; not a little while, as I said just now. You know that now, my brave girl. There is nothing you can't face."

"Well, my darlings, you have a welcome for me? You can give me that, though I have been away so long. It has been a long while. I have had to learn that lately. And you have known it all the time, my poor ones, known it as the days dragged by. Now you can have your mother's sympathy."

"Months of arrears of it," said Jermyn, keeping his arm

round his mother.

"You are right to get to work at once," said Griselda. "There is much to be done."

"We are going to have the whole made up," said Gregory. "We shall not rebate a jot of it."

"My darlings!" said Harriet, turning her eyes to her eldest son.

"Congratulations on being back, Mother," said Matthew. "It is a tremendous thing."

"Tremendous! Yes, that is the word tremendous," said Godfrey, his eyes resting for a moment on Matthew. "Tremendous. Matthew has it there."

"And I am to have another son and daughter to welcome me. I have come back richer by two more children. Father has given me the news, and he has asked them in a message from me to be with us to-night. That is to be my first pleasure. My darlings, I have come back to love and care for them. The truest welcome for those who love you, is your mother's."

"Camilla says she can't bear to think you have had no chance to disapprove of our engagement," said Matthew, making an effort just within his power.

"Ah, she is doing Matthew good, Harriet. You will see that she is," cried Godfrey, turning a glow of appreciation on his son.

"I trust they will do us credit to-night," said Griselda, who was holding her hands clenched. "If they fall short on one evening, what of the future?"

"The future is yours and theirs, my sweet one," said her mother. "I will go now and rest and change my things. What a pleasure, with my girl to help me! I must take pains to be at my best to-night. People who have had to wait for a mother-in-law must not be put off with anything, and neither must people who have had to wait for a mother. I must remember it, and go on remembering it. How I will!"

"Well, what do you think of it, Matthew?" said his father. "What do you say to the way things are turning out for us? She is a great, noble woman, your mother, a strong, fine creature with a great heart, when she is herself. That has been our little trouble, that she has not always been herself. That was why we found a sort of misgiving creeping over us. It was a fear lest she might not come back in her true colours. But she has come back in them, ready to give us of her best. A thorough breakdown has done her good; a suspension of energy was what she needed, what her system craved, my poor wife, your poor mother! I am ashamed of my petty, self-regarding qualms. I blush for my fears and finickings about what was in store for my precious self. As if it mattered, as long as she came back safe and sound! As if it was worth a brass farthing!"

"It was nothing to worry about, if your theories are true," said Matthew.

"Matthew, you do not take up a position of doubt! I can hardly believe it. It seems to me too far beneath you. Well, Griselda, you have come from your mother? You have had the post we should all have liked to fill. And you have filled it worthily, I make no doubt. Mother has found you a comfort. Ah, that is a thought we would share."

"She is going to rest and arrange her room. Catherine is with her. She seems wonderfully well. I have never seen her in such spirits."

"Ah, my poor child, you have never known your mother. But, please God, you will know her now. Our previous knowledge and love of her will be as nothing. I declare it will be something to see her greeting Ernest and Camilla. That has become a thing to look forward to."

"Dear Lady Haslam, it has been such a blight on my happiness, that you were not here to cloud it," cried Camilla, at the moment for Godfrey's anticipations to be realised. "I know so well that it ought to be clouded. Even a fresh piece of goods would not be worthy of Matthew—I know 'piece of goods' is how you think of me—and I am so shop-soiled. Mother was in such a fright at sending me here to-night, an article in its third season! She can feel for you in your bargain. She knows what it is."

"Well, I am soon to know it, and I hope I can help to make this season the last one. My dear, I have only one feeling for the woman who loves my son."

"There, you see, Camilla. You see how it is," said Godfrey. "Matthew's mother has simply the feeling for you that she has for all her children. She and I hold out our arms to you as a daughter, standing side by side, as we have not had the chance to stand these many months past.

"You look adorable, doing it. Matthew and I are the feeblest imitation of you."

"Well, you are not the only pair of lovers in the room."

"They are useful for showing you up," said Griselda. "I shall soon be seen in that office myself."

"Yes, we shall have another couple with us in a moment," said Godfrey, "another pair to show us up. I declare I almost feel that is what they do. Buttermere, you know that Mr. Bellamy is dining?"

"Everything is as usual, Sir Godfrey, except for the return of her ladyship."

"Ernest often comes in to dinner, does he?" said Harriet.

"Yes, yes, as often as Griselda wants him. Often is the word," said Godfrey. "I tell you we have been glad of a little outside society sometimes, Harriet. We didn't want to be left alone with our thoughts. That wouldn't always have done for us."

"My poor ones!" said Harriet.

Bellamy came in with his smile grave.

"I shall hold my head very high, Lady Haslam. I have had the most coveted thing in the neighbourhood, a glimpse of you. You will always be more valuable for your time away from us. It is hardly as it ought to be, as you did less than nothing for us by having it. I could not forgive it, if you were not going to give me Griselda in compensation."

"Yes, I am going to give her to you. I have come home to a larger family. And as my family is all the world to me, I cannot have too much of it."

"Won't you let me have just a little point in myself? I am sure Griselda thinks I have."

"Ah, you can't fish for compliments to-night from Griselda's mother," said Godfrey. "She is my province. We haven't any attention over for you."

"I find it hard to do my duty to Matthew, with the spectacle of his parents before me," said Camilla.

"Ah, we none of us have thoughts for anyone but you, Harriet," said Godfrey. "You see, Camilla is one of us there. Jermyn, I have not heard many words from you about your mother's return."

"That is not only brutal but unjust," said Jermyn. "You talk as if the others were engaged in continual oratory. And you promised us that silence should be the approved vehicle of our feelings."

"Harriet, you would have wept to see your children when I told them of your recovery. They stood as if petrified, their feelings passing their capacity and leaving them turned to stone. I had to hold myself. I could have fallen on their necks weeping."

"It was not a case of like parents, like children," said Griselda.

"And now you find fault with silence," said Gregory.

"Godfrey dear, it is almost too much for me," said Harriet, touching his arm.

"My darling, I am an idiot, I am without judgment. We will talk about our children's other side, the ambitions and successes you have come home to share with them."

"Indeed, you will not," said Jermyn. "Having borne one reference to myself, I will suffer no more. And our baser side would be even harder on Mother than the other."

"What is the good of referring to the better one, if you are going at once to counterbalance it?" said Matthew.

"Ah, my dear children, it was not that you had no words to speak. It was that your hearts were too full for words."

"Well, now, leave it at that, and don't contradict it again," said Griselda.

"How soon can I have my first little private talk with you, Mother?" said Gregory.

"When would you like it, my darling?"

"To-morrow after breakfast in the garden," said Gregory.

"You shall have it, my boy. We none of us grudge it to you," said his father. "We don't forget the old days, when you so often took that on yourself. Ah, you have established your right to it, Gregory."

"Is not the dinner rather tedious for you all?" said Harriet. "Isn't it longer than usual, Buttermere?"

"Not according to our recent custom, my lady."

"Oh, we have had an extra course or two sometimes lately, Harriet. We have had people in, Camilla and Ernest, you know. We have wanted a little cheering up. If you could have seen our faces the first nights we were without you! We didn't want the dinner prolonged then. Ah, well, you were spared that. That is one thing we can think of."

"Griselda gives me what I like best," said Bellamy. "She is getting into training for a spoiling wife."

"That is a change you will be glad of," said Camilla.

"My poor child! Her mother is at home with her now," said Harriet. "I shall be so thankful to take up my duties again. My children have not been fortunate in their mother. You shall all have what you like best in every way, all six of you, and without having to think of it yourselves. I shall be meeting Mr. Spong in a few days, and as soon as I know how matters stand, you shall all have everything your mother can give you."

"I hope it is not dangerous to be so fortunate," said Bellamy.

"Dangerous? Now, what do you mean, Ernest?" said Godfrey. "I tell you, Harriet, old Spong will be glad enough to see you. He doesn't think my business head a patch on yours. I assure you he doesn't. I might be an old dodderer, for all his view of me. You may believe me or not; it is the truth. He thinks I am not fit to spend a farthing. I might be the woman and you the man, for his opinion."

Chapter XIX

A few days later Dominic entered the house with a hushed tread, holding his bag as a secular object brought on a sacred occasion. He remained leaning over Harriet's hand in silence.

"Well, Spong, you see we are ourselves again," said Godfrey. "Our tide has turned. I know you will rejoice with us."

"Sir Godfrey," said Dominic, not yet exposing Harriet to the reality of speech, "I could ask for nothing that would occasion me greater personal gratitude. That is my feeling upon your reunion."

"Thank you, Spong. We were sure of your sympathy. And I wish your wife could be restored to you, as mine has been to me. It lessens my personal joy that you cannot have your share in it."

"Sir Godfrey, it does not lessen mine."

"Well, let us get our business behind. We shall be more ourselves when that is not hanging over us. We can't come together without these things having to be adjusted, more's the pity. You and I must take them off my wife in future, Spong. I grudge her attention to them. We have formed the habit of getting along together, and we must put what we have learnt into practice. We can't allow her a ruling hand where it is too much for her. We must remember what has happened once, and be on our guard."

"If I remember Lady Haslam aright," said Dominic, unfastening the tape of his papers with a humorously rueful air, "I hardly think she will want much taken off her in the line of business decisions. To use what is at best a colloquial expression, I should put her, of the two of you, as 'top dog' in that department."

"Well, well, but we must take care of her," said Godfrey. "Now, Harriet, my dear, is there anything you would like dwelt upon in those papers you have before you?"

"No, they are quite clear. I went through them last night," said Harriet. "They are in order and just as usual. The investments don't need altering. Mr. Spong has been very wise in the one or two changes he has made. After all, my time away has been only a matter of months. But I don't understand about our banking account; our joint account, Mr. Spong, that both my husband and I supply and draw upon. It is overdrawn to quite a large amount, a thing which has never happened. We have not the pass book here. There is just the record of the overdraft in your summing up. Is any of the income not paid in to the bank?"

"No," said Dominic in a considering voice, "everything has been paid in as usual. And the statement is up to date, brought indeed to completion for this interview."

"Then there must be some explanation. I shall no doubt see it presently."

"There would have been in some ways an unusual drain upon the account," said Dominic in tones withdrawn from comment. "There would be the advance to Messrs. Halibut and Froude for the publication of Jermyn's poems; and the expense of hiring the theatre and providing properties for the dramatic entertainment organised by Mr. Bellamy; and the purchase money of the lease of Matthew's house. Those items would appear on the debit side, and result probably in abnormal depletion." He looked towards the window.

"Oh, yes, yes, Harriet," said Godfrey. "Those are things I have done, certainly. I knew we should be of one mind about them. I was not able to consult you, so where I was convinced you would approve I followed my own line. It was imperative for Matthew to have a house near his work, and he couldn't afford to take one for himself, the dear boy! There will be no rent now that we have bought the lease; that was taken into account; and I considered it was about the standard you would wish. And Bellamy's play was, between ourselves, for Griselda's sake. The poor children were deprived of you, Harriet. I did something to make up to them."

"Oh, yes, yes, my dear. I have no doubt it was wise. I only wanted to understand. Mr. Spong is right that I have a business conscience."

"Yes, but, Harriet, these are hardly matters for you to worry your head about in these days," said her husband with resumed gravity. "You know we are to keep such decisions away from you. You are going to be wise. What you have to do is to let your heart thrill with pride over the achievements of your sons. Ah, when I took in what it all meant, my own heart thrilled with pride and humble thanksgiving. I felt that if I could only share it with you, my cup would be full. It is full now."

Dominic looked torn between his human and professional feelings.

"Yes, so is mine," said Harriet. "We should indeed be grateful for our sons and for ourselves. I suppose poor Jermyn could not get his poems accepted. Well, I know that means nothing. You were right to save him disappointment."

"Harriet," said Godfrey, "I could not have faced it for him! He might have faced it for himself, but I could not. There was an end of it."

"Well, I hope it may not be the beginning, Sir Godfrey," said Dominic. "Young gentlemen may be apt to take advantage of such a parental attitude. Now this other item, the expense for the play. Does Lady Haslam wish anything to be said about that?" He spoke with his head bent over a moving pencil, and a hovering smile.

"Well, my husband knows about it. He can tell me anything I need to be told," said Harriet. "Thank you, Mr. Spong, I see the overdraft is accounted for."

Dominic turned at once to succeeding matters, as if he had felt no intervening emotion, and the interview proceeded to its close.

"You will stay to luncheon, I hope, Mr. Spong?" said Harriet. "We are expecting Mrs. Calkin and Miss Dabis to join us. Our friends are very kind in hastening to welcome me home."

"If I were to be the only guest, I should hesitate, nay I should refuse, Lady Haslam, to impose my presence on a family so lately restored to itself. But as that is not to be the case, I will take my place with a pleasure that will chiefly consist in seeing you again presiding at your own board. With due respect to my other friends and clients, the greater satisfaction will swamp the less."

"Well, well, it is time to go in," said Godfrey. "We can put away all this. You would like to get the dust off your hands, Spong. Buttermere, Mr. Spong would like some hot water in the room off the hall."

Dominic followed the butler with an air of being both accustomed and entitled to such ministrations.

"The water is hot, sir," said Buttermere, standing by the open door, and producing the impression that for many people he would have turned the tap.

"Oh yes, yes, thank you, I can manage very well," said Dominic, hastening to forestall the services to which he was used.

"Luncheon will be served in a minute, sir," said Buttermere, glancing at the guest as he left him.

"This is a very well appointed house," said Dominic in an easy tone, as he came slowly to the table. "Mrs. Calkin, I have not had the privilege of meeting you since the occasion when we rejoiced that our hostess was to resume the place we associate with her hospitality. Miss Griselda, I may congratulate you on your transition to a less important seat. I claim to know you well enough to assume it is a matter for congratulation."

"Even with your experience as a lawyer," said Geraldine.

"Miss Dabis, I still have remaining to me some belief in the soundness of my fellow creatures."

"I shall not try to say how thankful I am to see you in your place again," said Agatha in a low tone to Harriet. "It is a thing that is simply better not attempted."

"I agree, Mrs. Calkin, that it would be to court certain failure," said Dominic, leaning forward earnestly.

"I suffered the last time I was here," Agatha continued to Harriet, "in seeing the superficial sameness and knowing the essential difference. There must be much that you have to put right, now you are in the general's place again. You have all my sympathy with the demands of your position."

"They have not begun to trouble me yet," said Harriet. "I have to resolve never to let them again. I am simply in great happiness in being in my home with my husband and children."

"Will you have the working party at your house again now?" said Geraldine. "It has been most exciting lately with the garments for the play. We have had all kinds of odd, agitating things to accomplish. I always seem to get masculine habiliments for my portion! I don't know why they should be assigned especially to me."

"It seems to be going too well where it is, for us to think of change," said Harriet. "I hope your sister can continue to hold it."

"Whatever is thought best by everyone, is what I should like," said Agatha.

"Then keep it, Mrs. Calkin, keep it," said Godfrey. "My wife must not do as much as she used. She will come in and join you sometimes."

"We have done what we could to fill your place to Gregory," said Agatha, turning to Harriet, as if modestly to change the subject. "He has been in, I think, whenever he has known I should be by myself. I hope you find he has not suffered as much as you feared?"

"I have not found yet how much any of them has suffered," said Harriet, sending her eyes round her children's faces, and keeping them on Gregory's. "I trust none of them too much; I think not. I know what kindness you have shown us."

"I hope you will let Gregory keep up his intercourse with us? I should be sad, really genuinely sad"—Agatha paused for impartial apportionment of feeling—"to see it broken. I feel there is something I can give him, that I think he will tell you I have given."

"He probably will not, as you have given it," said Harriet smiling. "And Gregory does what he chooses in his friendships. You have found that he does."

215

"No. No. I daresay he will not speak of it. I think you are subtler than I am there. I think he will not."

"Sir Percy and Lady Hardisty!" said Buttermere.

"Harriet, we have come without being asked, because you have not asked us. We should not do such a thing without a reason. We supposed our welcome went without saying, as that was the way it went. Yours goes so much without, that I should be nervous lest Percy should speak, if that was his tendency."

Rachel's voice grew hurried and helpless, and she withdrew her eyes from Harriet's face.

"Rachel!" said Godfrey. "After all you have done for us in Harriet's absence, it cannot be said in mere words that you should have been here to enhance her homecoming. But our thoughts have been so engrossed with her, that they have hardly got outside our four walls. Our other friends would not be with us to-day, if they had not thought of it themselves, if they had not shown us the same kindness that you are showing."

Dominic looked down at his bread and fingered it, and Agatha raised a face that cordially confirmed this account of her position.

"Percy has come to drive me over. He did not think he was wanted. Johnson is ill, and Percy will have sympathy with people he employs, though it spoils the old-world atmosphere that is the point of him. I have come to have coffee with you in your own room, Harriet. I have had my luncheon, so you cannot have the rest of yours. Percy had better have it; he wants it, as I hurried him over his."

"No, no, don't get up, my dear," said Sir Percy, as Griselda would have relieved him of the duties of her mother's place. "An old man can make himself useful. Mrs. Calkin, you will allow me? Mrs. Calkin, Buttermere."

"Well, come upstairs with me, Harriet. Percy will look after them all," said Rachel, moving and talking quickly to cover the meeting. "I shall be glad of some of your coffee. Our coffee is poison; cheap things are; I can't help the vulgarity of truth. I might have brought some of it for your guests. I can't conceive why you didn't think of it, instead of giving all your attention to yourself. Why, Harriet, my little one, what is it?"

Harriet had flung herself into Rachel's arms and broken into weeping.

"Haven't you really had the fit of crying that goes with coming home? I thought people just crossed the threshold and burst into tears. Of course I understand; it was Buttermere. Your emotions have had no outlet."

"Rachel, my husband and children! They can do without me. That is why I have not sent for you; I have not had the heart. I have come home to find they can live with me away."

"Of course they can. What else were they to do? You must not force people to do things, and then complain of their doing them."

"I should not mind it. They had to get used to my being away. They could not help it, though they did it easily. I should not even mind their going against what I wished for them, though it was almost from the moment I left them. Their lives are their own."

"It was not from that moment. You did not see that one," said Rachel. "And what is it you do mind?"

"I know the moment would have been one by itself," went on Harriet, raising her face and smiling sadly. "But it was followed by few others of its kind. It is not that I would think of it; it would only be thinking of myself. But I see them with new eyes, Rachel, my husband and children, whom I feel I have not dealt fairly by.

217

I understand it was because of me, because I tried them beyond their strength, that they broke away when I was gone."

"Well, if they had a reason, and one you can understand! And it sounds a dreadful thing for you to do, dear."

"Godfrey is led like a child," said Godfrey's wife. "I feel now that I always knew it. I would not mind his spending too much; he never had a business brain; and I can put things straight. But he gives up the whole trend of his life at the touch of a hand. I would not speak of his supporting what we have set ourselves against; things are not wrong because we are against them; we will say they are not wrong. But his whole attitude to serious things is blurred and easy. He has been made what he is, first by his parents, then by his wife, and now by his friends and his children."

"Poor Godfrey! You do all take advantage of him. We seem to be the only people who do not. I claim that he shows no trace of my influence or Percy's. But that is not what you mean."

"He shows very little of mine at the moment," continued Harriet with the same smile. "Of course he will come back to it, is coming back. But that is all the same thing. I hardly know what man he is in himself."

"I know exactly from hearing you describe him," said Rachel.

"I know now from hearing myself. And I should not complain; he has had to get to know me, my poor Godfrey. And so have my children, enough to feel they must make the most of being without me. They all made the most of it, all of them, Rachel! There is Gregory, my Gregory, my dearest thing on earth, who binds me to life——"

"No, that is an exaggeration, Harriet. You know he did not bind you to it, that nothing did."

"He is in the grip of that worn-out woman," said Harriet, with what for her was startling bitterness. "It is the wrong thing for him, and it may end anywhere."

"You know it may not. It can end nowhere. It can only end. It shows how little worn out you are, that you have not had to face that."

"Rachel, if I thought it was simple jealousy, I would put it from me. If I find it is that, I will put it from me. But it is not only that. I admit that I think the feeling Gregory has for middle-aged women, should be mine; that it should be both earned and given, but I ask nothing that is not mine. If he were to fall in love with Percy's Polly, I would simply rejoice."

"Well, he shall fall in love with her then," said Rachel. "So there is an end of Gregory, simple rejoicing. And there is an end of Griselda too, because of course she has to marry Ernest Bellamy; everyone would have to. I should have to myself, if I agreed with you that feelings between the young and old could lead anywhere. So we can go on to Matthew and Jermyn. They have not taken advantage of your being away; they used to try to research and write poetry under your eyes; and now they seem to have done it. You have come back to find them more than the same sons to you."

"They are the same in that they still put ambition for themselves before a more generous service. I will see it as a ground for pride. I will conquer my own disappointment, though I dread theirs. But I am troubled by their persuading their father to pour out the family money on them, money not meant for their own purposes. They are not the same sons there."

"People have to persuade people to pour out money on them. It is never meant for their own purposes, and persuasion is the only thing. Now is this the truth coming?"

"It is Matthew and Camilla!" broke out Harriet. "It is Camilla

219

as a wife for Matthew! I cannot bear it, Rachel. I cannot suffer it to be. She will take him into the wide and easy way that ends in darkness. She is taking him now. My son, my son!"

"Matthew is as easily led as Godfrey, is he? You have got them into the way of being led. You did that, and then you left them."

"It was not by my own will that I left them," said Harriet. "And as to that, Rachel, I hope I can say, 'God's will be done'."

"It sounds unnatural from you; and your exceptions are so arbitrary."

"I will gather myself together," said Harriet. "I will gird on my armour; I will stand up to the fray. I will fight my husband and children, my best beloved. That is what I have before me."

"Is it worth it, apart from the sound of it? Of course it is for that."

"I know you are trying to save me. But I do not shrink from the sacrifice."

"Then it is not a sacrifice for you. It is unnatural not to shrink from sacrifice for other people, but things must not be shirked because they go against the grain."

"You are only trying to save me."

"Why 'only'? Why should I not put you first? You are first to me, and you are evidently first to yourself."

"No, I am not," said Harriet.

"Well, God's will be done, or rather your will be done, Harriet. You seemed to think the first should hardly happen so often."

Chapter XX

"Well! so you are here, harriet," said Dufferin. Why are you running away from home by yourself so soon? I could have come to you."

"I can say what I have to better when I am here."

"I know you stick at nothing then. What do you want this time?"

"Nothing for myself," said Harriet.

"I am glad of that. You would hardly ask for what you did before, for anyone else."

"Antony, why did you let Camilla and Matthew come together?"

"Because Camilla liked Matthew better than me. There was nothing I was out for for myself in that."

"Why were you drawn to her yourself?" said Harriet, seeking light on Camilla's character.

"Well, well, things were in a tangle for her, and I might as well have had her as any other. I get rather lonely by myself at times."

"Did you feel her giving you up for Matthew?"

"No, she knew that didn't matter to me. Matthew is giving her the whole of himself, a thing I could never do. She is right to take him. I owe her no grudge there."

"She has not a good character," said Harriet.

"No?" said Dufferin, consideringly. "No, perhaps she has not. She can't ever get what she wants, and that hasn't been any help to her."

"What does she want?" said Harriet.

"A lot of men and a lot of money and a lot of everything that can be touched and used. It is a disadvantage to want so much."

"Ernest Bellamy cannot give Griselda any more than he gave her."

"No; but I suppose you don't think of Griselda as you do of her."

"Would Camilla be content if she had what she wanted?"

"Yes, I think so, but she can't have it, that I can see."

"I feel she is not a good woman," repeated Harriet.

"Yes, so you have said. And perhaps she is not; it is true that she is not. But I like her better than a lot of the good ones, and so do you."

"Why did you not keep to her?" said Harriet.

"To save Matthew?" said Dufferin, smiling. "Why should I keep to her, if she was no use? Because she would not keep to me, I tell you. She wanted Matthew, and Matthew wanted her a great deal more. And remember this about Matthew, Harriet. He is his mother's son. To be thwarted in his real desires won't do for him, any more than it did for you."

"Does he see her when he comes here to work?"

"Of course he does. What do you suppose he comes for? What you have come for, to get what he wants, because Camilla is round the corner. You would not ask that if you did not know."

"Antony, you take these things so lightly. In so many things you are careless, as I can judge. And yet in spite of it all I respect and trust you. I feel as if they are in your hands, to be saved from each other, Camilla and my son, whom I have wept and prayed over, whom I have brought up in the straight and narrow way."

"Yes, you have done that. Straight enough; and narrow enough too. I believe Camilla is taken with the straightness; she hasn't quite so little in common with you. But they are neither of them in my hands. Camilla is in her own hands, and Matthew is in Camilla's. There is danger that he may lose her if he does not marry her soon. I use the word 'danger', Harriet; it is the word I mean. And now I have a word to say to you. By weeping and praying over Matthew you are rushing to your own doom. Stop weeping and praying. Your prayers are not answered, are they? And people don't shed tears for you."

"No, they do not," said Harriet, standing with her eyes down.

"And better for them that they shouldn't. That is why they don't. Go back to them, and learn what is good for yourself, as they have learnt it."

"Antony," said Harriet, "does it strike you that my husband and children have less feeling for me than is given to most wives and mothers?"

"No, I should think more feeling; and you know I tell you the truth. But people don't feel as much as you want them to. Even you yourself—and you are a woman of very deep feeling, Harriet—want to have things your own way. Look back at this talk, and see that is what you have wanted. Go home and understand that other people want it too. Matthew is your son in many things. When you feel you don't understand him, examine into your own heart, and you will find the explanation there."

Harriet overtook Gregory, walking up the drive towards the house, and getting out of the carriage at the door, waited for him to join her.

223

"Where have you been, my son?" she asked, in her old manner.

"To see my old ladies," said Gregory, smiling at his mother.

"Gregory, my dear," said Harriet, "will you do something for me?"

Godfrey, who was coming out into the porch, stopped short, and he and his son stood with their eyes on Harriet's face.

"Gregory," said Harriet, "I can only just say it," and indeed she used a faltering tone. "I meant to come home and find you all without a fault, and I do find you so in yourselves, my dear. But I have to say this for your own sake, just this word. It would be wiser not to spend so much time with a woman so much older than yourself. A gulf of forty years cannot be bridged. I know how good to you Mrs. Calkin has been during my illness, and your mother is the first of those who are grateful to her. We will ask her here; you know we all respect and like her; and so you will often be with her. But give up this going to see her by yourself."

"I couldn't do such a startling and selfish thing. It is I who have to be grateful to her, not anyone else. It is evidently only I who am grateful, and that is natural. And you do not respect and like her, Mother. She gets nothing out of coming here. Of course I cannot stop going to visit her all at once."

"Then do it gradually, darling. You are right that that would be better."

"Yes, I think your mother is wise there, Gregory," said Godfrey, speaking as if this one minor point in the family situation might be criticised. "I think perhaps that little matter could be adjusted. And in that case you will adjust it. We will leave it to your own good sense and judgment, my dear boy."

Harriet went silently into the house, and Matthew, who had

been strolling on the gravel in apparent calm, came up to his father.

"Well, so it has begun. I saw it beginning."

"Matthew, I am at a loss to understand you," said Godfrey, his voice seeming to be adapted for his wife's hearing, though she was out of earshot. "If you mean that your mother is going to allow herself to fall back into the ways that were the result of nervous illness, I consider it pessimistic and unworthy. The little point about Gregory is one by itself, as you and he very well know."

"You are not much at a loss," said Matthew. "And you don't know as much as I do about Mother to-day."

"Matthew, we will not continue this conversation."

"Mrs. Christy is coming to dinner," said Matthew. "Camilla told her to come on after the working party. It is time she and Mother met on their new footing. You might break it to Mother, as you are so confident of her compliant spirit."

"Indeed I will break it to her, tell her of it, if you wish. And indeed I am confident of her compliant spirit. That is the word that fits the case. She will be delighted, as you know, to dispense her hospitality to a friend. There is something in your attitude that perplexes me, Matthew."

"You are fortunate," said Matthew.

Harriet came into the drawing-room, kind and cheerful, noticed Griselda's face, and at once came up to her.

"Why, be happy, my darling. You are not afraid of your mother, are you? If you only knew, there is no one you need be less afraid of. It is not there that your danger lies, my sweet."

"Why, Harriet, whatever are you putting into the child's head?" said Godfrey. "She is in no danger surely. Now there is Mrs. Christy, Camilla's mother! What a good thing it is when

225

people are on the time!"

"Dear Lady Haslam, now I shall be myself in my fullest sense. I have felt that a part of me has been wanting, and a part that is very essential. That dear boy, Matthew, arranged with my girl that I should consummate my relation with you. She says she is marrying to be your daughter-in-law, and I believe it has an element of truth. She and Matthew will make such an excellent pair, the one so much the complement of the other. It might truly be said that between them they make the perfect human type. And Matthew's thoughtfulness for me makes me really inclined to say, 'Winter is the mother-nurse of spring, lovely for her daughter's sake.'"

"There is no need to say it, Mrs. Christy; it goes without saying," said Godfrey.

"Now you are flattering me too, Sir Godfrey," said Mrs. Christy, more suitably than appeared, as this was Godfrey's intention. "I shall quite forget to visualise myself in the correct way."

"Do, Mrs. Christy, do," begged her host. "I ask you to do that while you are with us to-night. So you are inclined to be taken with our boy Matthew, are you?"

"Sir Godfrey, it is such a credit to him to work with such enthusiasm. Of all the things that are a confirmation of the dignity of effort, that stands out supreme. I say to Camilla, when she claims the whole of his attention, 'Would you have a drone for a husband, a mere idle aristocrat and eldest son? I know you would not.'"

"Do you think Camilla will settle down to a quiet life with Matthew?" said Harriet. "He will be a poor man for many years, if he holds to the work he has chosen."

"She asks nothing better than to spend her days with the man

226

of her choice, and be his lieutenant in every enterprise. Matthew counteracts so much that she regrets in herself, her tendency to be a woman among men, if you know what I mean. Her very gifts have led her astray. So many of her failings might be a source of pride."

"And will be to Matthew," said Godfrey.

"They are already," said Matthew.

"Well said, Matthew. Spoken like a man," said his father.

"Will she find it unsettling to have Ernest and Antony living so near?" said Harriet, using a remorseless tone.

"When she is through with a man, she is through! I get into the way of using her phrases. Whatever comes my way, I find myself becoming the mistress of it. I should make a better use of my aptitude. My girl pours out all her mind to me. I know she has taken for granted a monopoly of masculine attention. But I can't dispute that people have given her cause."

"I agree with you, Mrs. Christy," cried Godfrey. "Camilla is a girl whom any man would make a bee-line for at once. I can't understand why only one of these boys has fallen for her. Why, I have felt her spell myself. My eye is with Matthew's in the matter. I am not such a fogey that I am blind to a thing like that."

"I hardly think you can be interesting Mrs. Christy," said Harriet.

Godfrey gave a glance at his wife, put two fingers into his waistcoat pocket, and looked at the portraits on the walls.

"Has Camilla any convictions or interests that give her a definite hold on life?" said Harriet.

"I feel it was hard on the poor girl to be a clergyman's wife. She is not like dear Griselda here, so eminently suited for it. And how well you put things, Lady Haslam! With such precision and ease and force. Camilla will rate the atmosphere of your family

227

at its true worth, with its mental tone, its unforced interest in matters of the mind. She has the greatest respect for higher things. You must have noticed that."

"Yes, I have noticed it," said Harriet.

"Harriet, my dear, Camilla is one of us," said Godfrey, taking his fingers from his pocket and glancing at a coin between them, as if he had wished to confirm something concerning it. "We take her as she is, as we take each other. Mrs. Christy is not demanding from us an account of Matthew's opinions. And I'll warrant the young scamp has few enough at the moment. I know the sort of thing that ferments in his brain. It is not hidden from his father. Ah, I am not such a stranger to these scientific fellows as some of them might think. I didn't have time while you were away to get much further with him. That is, I thought it best to let those things lie fallow. But there isn't a pin to choose between Matthew and Camilla in the matter of opinions."

"I believe that is so," said Harriet.

"My dear girl, the true opinions are the most important things in life. If things are not right at rock bottom, we cannot build on the top. But making people feel that too much of a good thing is a bad thing defeats your purpose. I know how it has been with myself. I mean, we all bear and forbear with each other."

"You do your part, my dear," said his wife, and turned to give a direction to Buttermere.

"Mother, you are looking very tired this evening," said Gregory.

"Harriet, you are!" cried Godfrey. "You are looking as you used to look. We can't have any of that again. Now what is it that has taken it out of you?"

"Nothing, Godfrey; I did not sleep last night."

"You did not sleep?" said her husband. "Well, that is upon us already! Go to bed, and take one of those sleeping tablets the doctor gave you. We will nip this in the bud; we won't give it another chance to rise up and threaten us. Go this moment. Mrs. Christy will understand. Don't wait even to say good-night. But good-night, my own girl. I won't come in to see you, for fear I break your sleeping mood. You will tell me in the morning that you have had a good night."

"Matthew, will you come with me for a moment?" said Harriet, moving slowly to the door. "I want to say a word to you."

"Go. Go at once," said Godfrey, with a veiled but peremptory look at his son. "Go up and soothe your mother by whatever method is in your power. Nothing else would be behaving like a man. There is a great responsibility on you. Go and do what you can."

Matthew followed his mother upstairs and was drawn by her into her room.

"Matthew," she said, standing with her hand on his shoulder and her eyes looking up into his face, "I want you to do something for me; not a great thing, dear; I would not ask that. I don't ask you to give up your work, or to give up your marriage; I know you cannot give up. I don't mean that any of us can; I am not saying anything to hurt. I only mean that I would not ask much of you. I just want you to put off your marriage for a few months, for your mother's sake, that she may have a little space of light before the clouds gather. I don't mean that my illness is coming again; I don't think it will come yet. And if it were, I would not use that to persuade you. I would not do what is not fair, while I am myself. I think you know I would not then. But I ask you simply, and as myself, to do this thing for me. I feel I can ask you, because I have seen your eyes on me to-night, and I have said to myself: 'My son does not love me, not my eldest son. And it is my fault, because mothers can easily be loved by their sons. So I can ask this from him, because I cannot lose his love, or lessen it. I have not put it in him.' And so I ask it of you, my dear."

"Mother, what a way to talk!" said Matthew. "Indeed your illness is not coming again. You could not be more at the height of your powers. Your speech was worth taking down. You may use it again. It was only I who heard it. My eyes show all this to you, when all my eyes are for Camilla at the moment, and if anyone knows that, it is you! I might tell you what your eyes show to me, and you would not have an answer. Now take one of your sleeping tablets; I think I should take two; I have put them out on this table. And the marriage shall not happen until you sanction it. Camilla can get what she wants from this family, from you. She will have you as a friend before me as a husband. I daresay that will be the end."

Harriet stood with her eyes searching her son's.

He kissed her and left her, and turned from the door and gave her the smile that should safeguard for both of them this memory.

Chapter XXI

Godfrey came out of his wife's room with a rapid, agitated step, and his tones sounded through the house, hushed and urgent. Voices answered him and footsteps followed, and the house in a moment quivered with suspense and foreboding.

The young people, waiting for prayers in the dining-room, looked at each other. Even Matthew, who was reading in an easy chair, raised his eyes.

"Whatever is it?" said Jermyn.

"Father is coming into the hall," said Gregory.

Griselda opened the door and intercepted her father.

"There, there, my dear child," he said in a hasty, colourless tone, without coming to a pause. "Go back to the dining-room and keep your brothers there. Shut the door and stay in there together. Do that for your father."

"Whatever does it mean?" said Jermyn.

"Perhaps one of the servants is ill," said Matthew, turning a page.

"It is something more than that," said Gregory. "Is it Mother?"

"She is always better when she sleeps late," said Matthew.

"Hark!" said Griselda. "Father is sending a message."

Jermyn went to the door and opened it, in a single, silent movement.

"Ask him to come actually this instant! Say that I fear the very worst. I hardly know what words I speak. Tell him that I shall be deeply grateful." Their father's voice had a tone they had never heard.

"It is Mother!" said Gregory, and ran into the hall.

"Gregory, my boy, go back at once," said Godfrey, coming forward with his hand upraised and a tone of command and warning. "Gregory, I adjure you to return to the dining-room. Griselda, get him to obey me. Your father asks it of you, Gregory. I forbid you to go a step farther."

Gregory was hastening up the stairs, with Jermyn and Griselda following. Matthew came slowly after them, his book in his hand, and paused to speak to his father.

"It is nothing to do with Mother, is it?"

"It is your mother, my boy," said Godfrey with a groan in his voice, standing with his limbs trembling.

Matthew went on, and Godfrey remained by himself, sunk too far in his own feelings for further effort.

A boy's cry came from the landing above, and the father clenched his hands.

"Mother is dead! She is lying in her bed, dead! Mother is dead, Griselda, Father!"

Godfrey stood still and slowly lifted his head.

Jermyn's voice joined his brother's, and there was a sound of Griselda weeping. Godfrey turned and walked up the stairs, in lifeless instinct to do what was before him.

He stood with his children at his wife's side, while Gregory and Griselda wept, and Jermyn and Matthew kept their eyes on the bed, where Harriet lay as if in sleep.

"My dear children, it is on us now. It has come this time. We are alone now. This time we are really alone."

"How did it happen!" said Jermyn. "Was she ill in her sleep?"

"She must have been," said Matthew. "It seems that it must have been her heart. But I didn't know there was anything wrong with it."

"It would have been an easy death, wouldn't it?" said Gregory.

"Yes, quite unconscious," said Matthew.

"Yes, it was an easy way to go. She has left us easily," said Godfrey. "May we all go in the same way, all of us here."

"She didn't suffer at all?" said Griselda, with a wild look at the bed.

"No, no, my darling. No," said Godfrey. "Look at her peaceful face."

Griselda threw herself into her father's arms, and he caressed her as if unconsciously.

"We can't all stay here for ever," said Matthew.

"Dufferin will be here very soon," said Jermyn.

"Yes, yes, Dufferin will be here. Then we shall know," said Godfrey, as if this gave a touch of hope.

"We had better go down to breakfast," said Matthew.

"I don't know about that, my boy."

"We shall do no good by starving," said Matthew.

"No, that is true," said Godfrey, and turned and led the way from the room. "If we could, how willingly we would do it!"

"To save Mother," said Gregory, with an unnatural note of mirth.

"You know the truth, Buttermere?" said Jermyn.

"Yes, sir. You will have to keep up your strength," said Buttermere, as though the approach to the table needed some justification.

233

"We have a great deal before us," said Godfrey. "You will share our sorrow in a measure, Buttermere."

Buttermere gave his master a rapid glance, seeming new to the idea that he shared the family fortunes.

"We dare not face what is before us."

"You will have to accommodate yourselves again, Sir Godfrey."

"It passes me how it could have happened," said Matthew.

"'In the midst of life we are in death,'" said his father.

"But we are not," said Matthew. "That is not true. There must be some cause."

"Well, we shall know in a few minutes," said Jermyn.

"Could she have done what she tried to do before?" said Griselda.

"Oh, no, no, my dear," said Godfrey, and was silent.

Jermyn and Gregory looked at Matthew.

"Of course it crossed my mind," said Matthew. "How could it not?"

"But how could she have come by what was needed?" said Gregory.

"We don't know that she did come by it. There may be some other explanation. It is idle to speculate," said Matthew.

"She hasn't been near Dufferin's house since she came home," said Jermyn.

"She was there yesterday," said Matthew. "Dufferin told me himself. She waited for him in his own room, and had a talk with him afterwards. You remember she came home late from her drive. She didn't say a word of anything of the kind. But she was alone in his room for an hour."

"Would anything of that sort be about? Wouldn't it be put away?" said Gregory.

"Oh yes, I daresay it would; no doubt it would," said Matthew. "Dufferin might have such things in his room, but under lock and key. I daresay she did not get it; of course she did not. There wasn't any there that I know of. But this makes one think of any solution, and it is hard to see another. But there must be one. There is Dufferin's bell."

Godfrey rose and went into the hall, signing to his children to remain. He and Dufferin exchanged a word, and their steps were heard on the stairs.

"Well, I am not going to be kept here," said Matthew. "I have as much right there as either of them. I will come and tell you as soon as there is anything to be told."

"We somehow feel there is still hope," said Jermyn.

"We are still before the verdict," said Gregory.

"Nothing can make any difference," said Griselda.

"No, but Mother may not have felt as wretched as that," said Gregory.

"She couldn't have. She would have shown it. She is in her way a transparent person," said Jermyn, revealing his unchanged image of his mother.

Gregory went into the hall and looked upstairs. Godfrey and Matthew were standing on the landing, silent, and Harriet's door was closed. Presently Matthew came to them.

"Yes, Griselda was right," he said. "Dufferin thinks that is what it was. He is all but sure. It will be found out for certain later. She must have got it when she went to see him. She evidently knew his room better than he thought. She waited there for some time. We shall never know if she went with that purpose, or if the thought came to her while she was there."

"But how did she feel before she did it? What made her do it?" said Griselda.

235

"She could not have been herself," said Matthew. "Her searching for it points to that. It was not like her in a natural mood. That sort of secretive skill is sometimes symptomatic."

"It would be simply necessary. Open blundering would never work," said Jermyn.

"Oh well, whatever it is," said Matthew in a weary tone. He turned to the window, and his sister took his arm. He did not repulse her, but stood as if sunk in his thoughts.

Godfrey and Dufferin came on to the silence.

"I must go back to see if there are any of certain tablets gone," said Dufferin. "Don't be more troubled than you must. She suffered nothing; it was the same as dying in her sleep. Matthew can come with me, and be a witness about the amount that is missing. It is better than doing nothing here, though the rest of you must do your best with it. I am afraid it is clear how it was, though the bottle with the tablets will be a proof. In some manner or another she must have known my ways. The cupboard was locked, and the keys were in a drawer across the room. But after all it was possible enough for a reasoning and observing person. The thing that will be said, that she was temporarily insane, ought often to be the opposite."

"Will it all have to come out?" said Jermyn.

"Yes, it will; we can't help that," said Dufferin. "It is all but out now. But it will do no harm to anyone. It won't be different from other things of its kind. It isn't anything to dwell upon. You have none of you done anything wrong. Keep that in mind, and have an eye on your sister. Matthew and I will be back when we can. You must remain in the house, and answer any questions with the simple truth. The next few days will soon pass."

"Can't anything be done to keep it secret?" asked Griselda.

"No, my darling. I asked that," said her father. "It seems it has to be faced. We have that before us. It is a cruel thing that your mother cannot even pass from us in peace. I for one shall never feel ashamed of anything she has done. I shall feel to her simply as my beloved and loving wife, and my children's devoted mother."

"She didn't seem so unlike herself yesterday," said Griselda.

"I suppose she saw her life suddenly before her again, and felt she could not face it," said Gregory.

"She must have felt that, my boy," said Godfrey miserably. "But I didn't guess it. I didn't know what my wife went through on the last day she lived, the last of our thousands together. She didn't tell me, though she always knew of anything that I suffered. She didn't tell even Gregory. She went through it by herself."

"Matthew looks very ill," said Gregory. "I did not know people showed signs of shock so suddenly. From his eyes he might have known the truth all night. He is very like Mother."

"Ah, he is very like her, I fear," said his father. "I fear it for his own sake, because of what he may suffer. For myself I feel I have her left to me in one of her children. It is only in them that I can have her now."

Matthew returned very soon. Dufferin had seen his need to relax, and undertaken himself what had to be done. The young man entered with a lifeless step, and answered questions in an empty tone.

"Yes, there was a tablet missing out of a bottle with three. The things on the shelf were a little out of place. The keys were not returned to quite the same position. It is clear enough."

He sat down and put his hands on his knees, leaning forward over them.

"My dear boy!" cried Godfrey, hastening towards him. "It has been too much for you, having it all piled on you like this. You have had to face the most. You are your mother's son. Your extra knowledge does not arm you against that. You shall get it off your mind, if you have to burden mine in doing it. Ah, what is it, Buttermere? Matthew, here is a better doctor that I can be to you!"

Matthew had raised his eyes with the look of an animal afraid, but the next moment sprang to his feet. Camilla rushed past him, and flung herself on Godfrey's breast.

"Oh, dear Sir Godfrey, it is too impossible to bear! I loved her better than I ever loved anyone. I wanted so to belong to her; I was counting the days. I admired her more than any human being in the world. I wish she had known; I never had a chance to tell her. And Matthew with your eyes like hers! I couldn't love you for anything better than that. I will give you the love I was keeping for her. She would have liked you to have it. No, she wouldn't, the poor, anxious one! Well, I will be the woman she would have wished. Sir Godfrey, I will be the wife for Matthew his mother would have chosen."

"I have no fears on that score, Camilla. My wife would not have had them either, if she had had time to know you. And now I am going to put Matthew into your care. He needs it as much as he will ever need it."

"My poor dear boy, I will tend you as if I were already your wife, as if I had never been anyone else's. Your room is upstairs on the second floor. You see I display a wife's knowledge. We will go up together hand in hand. That is her room, isn't it? Let us stop just one minute. She is lying in there. May I just go in and look at her? I must see her once again. I saw her so much too seldom while she was alive. I never made the most of her. She looks wonderful, Matthew, young and innocent, and with such a peace on her dear, powerful face. I wish I were her kind of woman. I wish I could try to be."

Camilla broke off, for Matthew was leaning against the door, cowering away from the bed.

"What is it, dearest? There is nothing to be afraid of? Of course it is your mother, and even for a doctor that is different. But it is only the shell, the beautiful casket where the spirit has flown. They won't have a postmortem, will they? I couldn't bear for her to be spoiled. Don't let them have it, if you can help it. You want to go upstairs? We have left the door ajar. It must not be seen like that. I will go back and shut it. There is no need for quite such haste. Oh, close it gently, Matthew. Poor lamb, you are not yourself. You are bound to be restless until the next few days are over. I shall be so glad for you when they are, though for myself I can't wish her to be put away out of sight. Will your father get over this, do you think?"

"Yes, after the few days," said Matthew.

"Talk like yourself, my darling. Don't be bitter. You may feel it the most, but other people are suffering."

"You need not pity them. It is only I who need your pity."

"What about Gregory?"

"Pity him least of all. Thinking about Mother will always be pleasant for him, going over his life with her from the first moment to the last."

"And for you, when you are equal to it."

"Don't talk to me about my life with her from the first moment to the last, the last!" cried Matthew, sitting on his bed and raising his hands to his head.

"You are very wrought up, Matthew. I shan't like to leave you alone. The news was sent to Lady Hardisty as well as to us. Do you suppose she will be coming to you? I should go with an easier mind."

239

"She won't do for me instead of you," said Matthew.

"For all that I hope she will come. It is no kindness to you for me to stay. I always do sick people more harm than good; they suffer more and not less because of me. I couldn't bear to do you harm just now. I should always look back on it."

"You can't bear to do anything for me just now. I shall always look back on it too," said Matthew.

It was later in the day when Rachel came. She looked worn and altered, but her voice was her own.

"Godfrey, I am so ashamed of not coming at once. I know that people with deep feelings go about just as usual, only with an older look and a smile that is different. But an older look would not do for me; perhaps it would not be possible. And I was so startled by Harriet's meeting with success, when it is not in mortals to command it, and they may do more, deserve it. Of course she became immortal by doing what she did, and she did deserve success the second time. She couldn't do more than try twice. And she may have been in an imperious mood when she commanded success."

"Ah, Rachel, I am really widowed now. My children are really orphans."

"And I am really without a woman friend, and it is an established disgrace to be without friends of your own sex. You have the dignity of sorrow, not its disgrace."

"Indeed no," said Godfrey. "Indeed we have no disgrace! If anyone uses that word to me in connection with my wife, I shall rise up and confute him. But, Rachel, why did she not tell me? All those days we were together. And we were on our old footing. Believe me, we were. And she did that without a word. Why did she want to leave me?"

"I don't know, Godfrey; you say she didn't tell you. And it

wouldn't have been kind of her to tell any of us that. I think she behaved wonderfully. We must idealise her, as people always do their dead. We need not have remorse for not doing it while she was alive, because she could hardly have done it to us, as you suggest. I hope the people at the inquest will do it. I have noticed they do when they can."

"Ah, we have all that before us," said Godfrey. "It can't last for ever; that is one thing. It will all pass as in a dream now."

Chapter XXII

It passed as Godfrey said. With sureness and convention matters came to their end, the verdict of suicide while temporarily insane. Harriet's former attempt on her own life, her recent mental illness, her visit to Dufferin's house, the disturbance of his closet and keys, the tablet missing of the kind that had caused her death—nothing was wanting to the chain, and events moved swiftly to her burial.

Bellamy rose to the occasion with feeling as real as his dramatic gift. Godfrey stood pale and withdrawn at his wife's grave. Matthew was behind him, stooping and shaken, with Camilla weeping at his side. Agatha caught a glimpse of Gregory's face, and showed a contraction of her own that was not compassion. Sir Percy and Dufferin stood with Harriet's family, and the rest of the mourners were gathered a little apart. When the party for the house had driven away, the same group formed at a distance from the church.

Agatha broke the silence in a quiet, measured tone. "We must feel it an oppressive ending to a valuable life, this sudden vanishing in shock and violence. It seems that our passing should be a thing of dignity and peace. It is indeed a heavy trial for her family."

242

"There can't be any doubt of that, can there?" said Polly, pressing forward.

Agatha gave her a gentle look, and glanced at Mellicent in unspoken comment on the youthful presence.

"There couldn't be anything worse," said Polly.

"There couldn't," said Agatha kindly. "That is what I said, isn't it?"

"What I feel is, that it will make such a terrible blank in all our lives," said Mrs. Christy, coming to the front of the group. "I shall feel it myself with peculiar force, and not only because of the actual connection that was merely the coping-stone of our intercourse."

"There must be the difference for ourselves in the miss we feel for different people," said Agatha, with reminiscence and resignation.

"It is a good thing that Sir Godfrey and his family have some experience of managing alone," said Geraldine.

"Do you know, I think that makes it all the sadder?" said Agatha. "To look back on the time when they did without her, that was to culminate in their coming together, and to feel that this time the self-sought separation must have no end! To my mind that gives a peculiarly tragic flavour."

"It must to everyone," said Polly.

"I wonder if they feel very much about her taking her life herself," said Geraldine, beginning in a carrying voice and dropping it at the last words. "Of course it was brought in as insanity, but that in itself is not a thing people welcome in the family."

"What I should be concerned about, is how poor Lady Haslam felt before she worked herself up to do it," said Agatha, with a touch of open grimness. "That is what would be on my mind, if I were anyone near to her."

"What seems to me is, that we ought to be so careful lest we do poor Lady Haslam an injustice," said Mrs. Christy, looking flushed and disturbed. "I am not biased by any personal feeling, even though I felt myself almost of her family circle. I feel simply that it is such a tragic thing that that large spirit was under a cloud, and had to grope about for its own release. To me everything else is swallowed up in the dignity of its suffering."

"Mrs. Christy," said Dominic in a downright tone, "you could not more fitly express what is in all our hearts."

"Well, I think any aptness may be an echo from Lady Haslam herself," said Mrs. Christy, her tone steadying. "There was about her such a peculiar literary felicity. So often there fell from her the happy phrase, the sudden flash of cultured memory, that I think something may remain behind and colour any thoughts and words that relate to her. I really feel that may be the case."

"That is a feeling, Mrs. Christy, that has anyhow essential force."

"I thought I saw such sorrow in the eyes of her children," said Agatha, with full and womanly concession, "especially I think in those of Matthew, the eldest son. I can imagine the indissoluble thing between him and his mother. I often think the eldest son takes the place of the only son, the special place. Of course for the younger ones it is possible to do more in the way of compensation. It was rather wistfulness and bewilderment and a longing to lean on an older spirit, that I saw in those young faces."

Dominic's attitude could only yield before this light thrown upon hidden truth.

"Gregory is the one who was most dependent on his mother," said Polly.

244

"Most dependent. Yes," said Agatha, with impartial and interested weighing of the phrase. "That is a very good expression. Dependent on her, for advice, for understanding, for guidance through some of the intricate mazes of youth." She smiled at Polly to give her her part in these words. "But not so much involved in the something that can only be given by a mother to a son, that is given perhaps in full measure to the eldest or only son. Now I should never try to take a mother's place to either of those."

"Let us go on to the Haslams', and see if Mater is there," said Polly to her sister.

"It is a good thing she is not here," said Mellicent.

"Is it?" said Polly, as if she had thought the opposite.

"Will you say to Gregory for me, that I hope he will come to tea this afternoon?" said Agatha, stepping towards them. "I think it will hardly be a breach of convention for him to come to me."

"We will give the message most certainly," said Mellicent.

"Then I think we can count upon him," said Agatha, returning to the group with an unconscious air of purpose.

"Do people always stand about and argue after funerals?" asked Polly, proceeding on her sister's arm.

"Probably some people," said Mellicent.

"Oh, yes, I see," said Polly. "Mater will be with the Haslams, won't she?"

Rachel had sat with Griselda during the service, and came to the door to meet the men on their return.

"Godfrey, you carry yourself very becomingly as the foremost person in people's thoughts. I hope Percy watched you and took a lesson, as he will so soon have to do the same. His practice can't do everything for him. I have been reading in the papers all about Harriet, and I think the accounts are satisfactory and do her justice. Several of them commented on her skill and forethought. She really chose a simple method, but that makes it all the nicer of the papers. You all look very well in funeral clothes, quite your best. I am glad the Press people were there to photograph you, and that Percy did not have to be included."

"Shall I be in the photograph?" said Polly from the doorway.

"I hope not, my child," said her stepmother.

"I hadn't any real black of my own," Polly exclaimed.

"My dear, to think it belongs to someone!"

"So you were with us, little Polly?" said Godfrey.

"Yes. I hadn't ever been to a funeral," said Polly with an open and startled gaze.

"And do you feel inclined to make a habit of it?" said Gregory.

"No. I think they ought to have different kinds of funerals for different people."

"So they ought," said Gregory, approaching her. "You must see about it, Polly."

"Mrs. Calkin wants you to go to tea this afternoon," said Polly, bound in duty to deliver this startling statement.

"And will you come with me, Polly, or shall I have to go by myself?"

"I think she wanted you by yourself."

"You must go with quiet self-restraint," said Rachel. "You must forget my example of behaving as if my own feelings were important, so uncivilised and like the people in the Bible. Sackcloth and ashes are too ill-behaved. I will begin showing self-restraint at once. Gregory may give Geraldine my love."

"You don't really like any of them, do you?" said Gregory.

"Well, it is foolish to dislike Agatha for having been married, and Geraldine for not having been, especially when you resent

246

being despised for both yourself. That is what they are disliked for. I don't dislike them for those reasons at all."

"I am afraid of the old one," said Polly.

Gregory turned on her interested eyes.

"My darling, that doesn't sound enough like the Bible, and really it is too like it," said Rachel. "I always say you are just like my own child. But you are far too young to go to a funeral. You have missed something in the spirit."

Chapter XXIII

Agatha did not follow her custom of coming to the door to welcome Gregory, but waited at her fireside while he approached.

"This is not the first time I have received you in this trouble. I know you understand that I will do anything that is in me to make it easier for you. Happily you are young enough for compensation."

"I wish I could get at Mother's feelings," said Gregory, taking his place at her feet, and speaking as if he knew he might open his mind. "She tried to tell me the first time, and I suppose this was something like it, but she herself didn't seem at all the same. I feel that if I could realise how she felt, I should be more at rest."

"Isn't that a little too like your mother?" said Agatha, stroking his hair.

"That is the first thing we shall aim at now," said Gregory.

"In some things, yes, indeed," said Agatha, "but there are others in which she would be the last person to wish you to follow her."

"The one thing at the end she didn't recommend the first time, but she seems to have thought better even of that. She was quite herself the last day and night, really more natural than when she first came home." A shadow of condemnation crossed Agatha's face. "On the whole she believed she had no child on her own plane. She must have known she had not."

"Don't you think," said Agatha softly, "that you are at a time when we are apt to take pronounced, even exaggerated views of what we have lost? I can remember doing it myself, in those of my sorrows that could bear the light thrown upon them."

"I feel as if I were taking the right view for the first time. I don't know though that that is fair to myself; I think I always took it. But I wonder if Mother knew that I did."

"I think that whatever we feel honestly always comes through. I am sure we need not be in any doubt about that. What we do not feel honestly, what we only imagine or wish we felt, will separate itself in the end; and we shall be glad to feel it sorted out, and to lay it aside, knowing that we want only sincerity between ourselves and our dear one. I think I can tell you that for certain."

"Did you find that when your husband died?" said Gregory.

"Oh, that is a different loss," said Agatha, drawing herself back. "That is a loss we do not compare to any but itself, the loss unique, isolated, supreme. I did not mean that when I spoke about my sorrows; I thought I gave a hint of that. I hope you will never have to face it. That is generally the woman's lot."

"No one knows the difference it makes, when someone has died by her own will."

"Ah, that is what you have to face alone. That is where your experience has its own isolation," said Agatha, seeming to grant the advantage here. "There is the darkness, the hint of tragedy, the shadow of feeling that we must condemn. But in a way, does it not soften the trouble"—she bent down and just looked into his face— "that she left you by her own choice? That she had no will to live to be thwarted? Would not that have been a harder thing? You are spared that."

"That is the worst of it," said Gregory, with tears under his words. "She had nothing; she felt she had nothing. Her own courage was all she had. It gave way, and it meant the end."

"That is how I should wish my son to feel about me," said Agatha, as though struck by this realisation, "if I could be in the same place. We will imagine it for a moment for your sake. Of course he would know I could not choose that way out. It is not quite what we all call courage. But if I were not as I am, and could do the same, I should wish him to feel as you do."

"Would you dare to do it?" said Gregory.

"It is not a question of daring to do it," said Agatha, lifting her head. "It is a question rather of daring not to do it. Ah, I remember when my husband died. It did take some daring."

"Are you speaking honestly?" said Gregory.

"What did you say?" said Agatha.

"I said, 'Are you speaking honestly?'"

"It is of no good to ask a question if you are not sure about that. The answer would mean nothing."

"I never think those answers do mean anything. You are right that it was a useless question. I know we all give the answers. I should not have said the things that lead to them. Of course my trouble should stay where it is."

"Surely not, when you are talking to an old friend. If I have made you feel that, I have failed you. That is how we must put it."

"No, you have been too forbearing. The person does not exist who would not fail me at the moment. I make too much demand. Rachel will be killed amongst us all."

"Lady Hardisty is staying with you?" said Agatha.

"Yes, for a few days. Sir Percy is utterly kind to us."

"She is a very charming woman," said Agatha.

"Who is?" said Geraldine, entering the room with her sister. "Of the many women in the neighbourhood who is your choice?"

"Charm is rarer than women," said Kate.

"That is the point," said Geraldine.

"Lady Hardisty," said Agatha in an easy, open tone.

"Yes, she is charming. I should say brilliant is more her word," said Geraldine.

"Fortunate creature, to offer such a choice of words!" said Kate. "She undoubtedly does offer it. I was going to say clever."

"She is certainly an effective talker," said Agatha, moving with a soft rustle to the tea-table. "It gives one quite a thrill to see her come in and sight her victim. We are certainly indebted to her for a good deal of enlivening though perhaps we ought not always to enjoy it as we do."

"I did not know she made victims," said Geraldine.

"Didn't you? Oh, yes," said Agatha.

"Another gift," said Kate. "But I had not observed it. Her humour strikes me as so kind."

"True humour is always kind," said Agatha. "And Lady Hardisty is not without the knowledge of it. By no means. But she takes a pleasure sometimes in getting her shafts home. Oh yes, she does. Haven't you been struck by it? Oh yes."

"I believe I have noticed her getting them in at you, Agatha," said Geraldine.

"Well, it is no wonder if I have perceived it then," said Agatha, laughing and looking round, as she stooped to offer something to Kate. "I don't think it is anything to be surprised at, if it has not escaped me."

"You poor thing!" said Geraldine. "Ought we to have come

to your rescue? I don't remember more than half noticing it."

"I don't remember noticing it at all," said Agatha, laughing again, and motioning Gregory to keep his seat. "But it is no wonder, if it was so, that something came home. It would have been the last thing she was out for, to fail of that. I am glad I saved her effort from being quite wasted."

"Even though your perceptions were rather dim," said Geraldine.

"Yes, well, it is a thing I am hardly prepared for," said Agatha, standing up and speaking with deliberate frankness. "It is a thing I should never do myself, and that does not predispose me to think it likely that anyone else should do it. But if I have afforded any satisfaction, I am delighted."

"Rather a sardonic kind of delight," said Geraldine.

"No," said Agatha consideringly. "No, I do not think so. I should honestly have no objection to being the target for a little innocent fun, or the excuse for it, if you like. I think there is nothing we should rightly object to in that position."

"Then I should wrongly object," said Geraldine. "Nobody would dare to use me for such purposes. It is no wonder Lady Hardisty settles on you. Perhaps she would not do it if she knew you."

"I am sure she would intend nothing that was really ill-natured or malicious," said Agatha, glancing at Gregory. "I think I found her shafts rather flattering than otherwise, though she did not intend them to be so. Missiles often hit the mark better when they are not aimed."

"I thought you had not noticed them!" said Geraldine.

"I must be going. Thank you very much for putting up with me. I said I would be home early," said Gregory.

"Now what I think you want, is a succession of long nights," said Agatha. "You take my advice and see that you get them. If I were coming with you I should not leave it in your hands."

"Poor boy, he was very silent," said Kate. "I am sure I don't wonder."

"I wonder he came," said Geraldine. "I should have felt too self-conscious in my sensitive youth."

"Oh, he had plenty to say when he first came in, before he had an audience," said Agatha. "That might have made him self-conscious; I daresay it did. He came to get it all off his mind, I think."

"What did he say?" said Geraldine.

"Oh, we had the whole gambit to run through," said Agatha, standing with a pitying, tolerant smile. "I was not spared any of it. The poor boy felt he had to tell someone, I suppose. Well, I am only too glad that I could be of any relief to him."

"You were alone in being up to that," said Kate.

"I think there is not much in it," said Agatha. "I think it was only that he wanted just the life-stamp, that drew out his boyish confidences, without making him feel there was anything unnatural in his pouring them forth. That was all it was, I believe."

"You can hardly regard it as not enough," said Kate.

"Well, whatever it is, I am glad to feel he won't have to go home and face the rarefied atmosphere of Lady Hardisty, without the memory of something a little more human to leaven it with," said Agatha, suddenly seeming to thrust out her words. "I can just imagine him working himself up to greet her. And I think it is so hard on him at this point of his young experience."

Gregory met Rachel without making any effort on her behalf, and she began to speak herself.

"Gregory, Ernest and Griselda are in the library, and I can hear Griselda crying. And it is not the sort of crying that goes with to-day. She left that off when she heard he was coming. What is the good of his stopping one kind to start another? Can he be saying anything out of his own head about your mother?"

"What makes you think that? Have you been listening at the door?"

"I could not go quite up to the door. Buttermere might have come along."

"I should have been inclined to go in and interrupt them."

"But they would have known I had been listening, and I should not have heard the rest. I thought Ernest was wearing his own religious look when he came in."

Bellamy had arrived and greeted his betrothed, unaware of his betrayal of himself.

"We are to have a time to ourselves, we two! That is perfect of everyone who has planned it. People always are perfect in times of stress, and they must have been especially so to you. This is what my heart was crying out for. I felt I could bear no one but you to-day. I am a little drained out after the service. I put the whole of myself into it. Did anyone tell you about it? I had almost thought you would be there, as I was to give the address. I had half hoped it would comfort you. I thought of you in every word I wrote."

"I shall like to read it some time," Griselda said.

"You could not get an impression from my few rough notes. I jot down a word, and then get into the pulpit, and out it comes with a rush. I just want a hieroglyphic to start me off."

"Ernest, what made Mother go away alone and do it, go away alone? What did she feel when she did it, all by herself? All by herself, poor Mother, poor Mother, by herself!"

"Oh, come, come now," said Bellamy, "you must think of me, my Grisel. I cannot bear too much. You have not taken the strongest man for a husband: you must have a care for the man you have chosen. I have lived these last days in thought of you. I have thrown the whole of myself into my words of your mother, weighed every syllable I uttered, to give her only respect and compassion at this time which is a trial of our own strength. You know very little has gone well with me in my life; and now into this vista of hope and light there is come this shadow of darkness, the hint of hanging of the head; and it is getting to be much. You must remember I am a man and weak, and you are a woman and strong."

"Your share in this is nothing to mine," said Griselda, lifting her eyes. "It is my family who has had a tragedy, not yours. You make me feel how apart our lives are. Of course all lives must be. There is nothing to hang the head over in my mother's being ill and helpless, unless for people who are used to hanging the head."

"Ah, who is to be used to it, and who is not? It is not I who would say. Even her helplessness will be thrown at us. Family taints and what not will be bandied about our heads. But I am not to be the first to swirl the whispers about you. My part will be to stand on guard."

"It has all come to me beforehand through you," said Griselda, breathing deeply.

"Did not I tell you what my part would be? My whimperings were to throw my true self up in relief. Tell me you guessed their purpose. I am such a play-actor that I like the light and shade. Come, you are learning to know me. You must learn. Think how I have learned to know you."

Griselda stood with her head down, and Rachel and Gregory found it the moment to enter the room.

"Lady Hardisty, Griselda has been trying to quarrel with me, and making such a gallant effort that she has almost succeeded. She cannot get used to my posing ways, and cannot teach me not to bring them out before her. But you will let me stay to dinner, and be one of the family, and her heart will be softened when she sees me making a personal sacrifice, and pronouncing grace as if it were a difficult and important duty."

"Yes, yes, my boy, stay and be with us on this first evening of our new life," said Godfrey, crossing the room with a progressively widening step. "It still seems it can't be much of a life to us; but we may pull up and get going as we did before, as my dear wife would wish. Now, do you know, here is a thing to be told! If there is any one of her children who feels this, it is Matthew. He is simply laid on the ground by it, he of all of them! I hadn't an inkling he cared for his mother so much. It shows how blind we can be. Well, now the thing is, he is not coming down to dinner. He is to remain alone in his room. My heart rose and sank at the same time. I would give a good deal if his mother could have realised how he felt for her. There doesn't seem any point in it now. Of course there is more point in it than ever. She looks down on us and knows more about us than we know ourselves, and for any mortal frailty makes more excuse than we should dare to make."

"That will be a great advantage for you," said Rachel. "It is really very nice of Harriet. So many people in her place seem so different, from what people say, and expect too much. They are sometimes quite a strain. Making more excuse than we dare to make is superhuman, because all has been done that can be done. Of course Harriet is that now."

"Ah, yes, we shall appreciate our wife and mother as never before," said Godfrey.

Chapter XXIV

Mrs. Christy, sitting at a business interview with Dominic Spong, perceived from her window the sight familiar to her of a young man anxiously awaiting admission at her door.

"Now, Matthew, it is a long time since you paid a visit to your future mother-in-law. It is a good thing that my love does not alter when it alteration finds, that in that respect I am at one with the poet. Now if I come to the door I must not shirk what the duty involves. You will have a woman quite without false pride for your wife's mother. 'Be proud of what you can do, not of what you can't,' is my motto. 'Thank you,' I say, 'my dignity is safe.' Not that practical matters take the whole of my attention. I have come from quite an abstruse discussion with Mr. Spong. My money matters make no very great demand, but he always accuses me of having quite a man's mind. It is a most unfeminine thing to plead guilty to, but I must take my stand where he places me."

"Can I see Camilla," said Matthew, in a quick, harsh voice.

"If you will adjust your position a little, Matthew," said Dominic from the background, his measured tone suggesting entertainment, "you will have no reason to find fault with the evidence of your senses."

Matthew turned and laid his hand on Camilla's arm.

"Any more than," proceeded Dominic, "your betrothed appeared to have to find it with that of hers, when her ears informed her of your arrival. I think, Mrs. Christy, that you and I will discover ourselves Monsieur and Madame de Trop, unless we remove ourselves from the threat of that position."

"We will give the lovers the back room to themselves, and continue our researches into my financial mysteries in the large one, Mr. Spong."

"I suspect that, in spite of our advantage in the matter of the room, they are at a time when they are more to be envied than we are," said Dominic in a moved tone, as he followed.

"You don't give any sign that supports Mr. Spong's suspicions, Matthew," said Camilla. "Your voice would break on a different note in touching on this moment. The sooner it passes, the sooner I shall leave behind my perilous youth. You and Gregory have the same tastes. Your father is the natural man, bless him. And I have left it farther behind than you. So give up glowering, and tell me why you have come to watch me keeping the home fires burning. Do you want to add to our romance by surveying me as the beggar-maid?"

Matthew stood with his eyes, sunken and bright from sleeplessness, fixed on her face.

"Matthew, don't frighten me by that pose. Don't begin to show me what you will be like when we are married. I warn you not to do it. It is dangerous."

Matthew stood silent.

"Matthew, do you hear me?"

"I hear you, Camilla. The question is, will you hear me? I have come to ask you one thing, and to have an answer, to know

258

if I am the one man in the world to you, as you are to me the one woman. That is what I will be. And I live in doubt, I sleep in doubt, or I should if I could sleep. I am tormented by too many things for rest. I ask to be at peace about that one."

"You ask too much," said Camilla. "Of course you are not the one man in the world to me. The world is too full of too many men for that, and I am the one woman to too many. The dear old world!" She sang the last words and clapped her hands.

"Has any one of them ever done anything for you?"

"Oh, yes, everything, all of them. Betrayed people, played their parents false, got into debt for me. Each one of them according to his lights."

"I suppose not one of them has put an end to his mother's life for you?"

"Put an end to his mother's life! What are you talking of? Of course not. What a question!"

"That is what I found you were worth."

"Matthew, you should not say things to coerce and scare me. It is a most unmanly way to behave. None of the others has done that. And it is in very bad taste to drag in your mother's misfortunes. If you helped to drive her to what she did by harping on me, when she did not like me for your wife, it was cowardly and wrong, when she had just returned from her illness; and I like you less for it; I do. And I believe you did. You worried her about me and drove her to it, and I shall always feel it was my fault that she died."

"It was your fault," said Matthew. "You made me feel that your love for me would stand very little, and she might have given it much to stand. You see it was your fault."

Camilla stood staring at him.

"You don't mean anything?" she said.

"I mean what I say."

"You don't mean you did it?"

"I mean I did it. I put the fatal tablet with those she took to make her sleep. I put it out for her with one of her own, that last night. I did it because of you, for fear she might take you from me. She was getting you into her power."

"Matthew, Matthew! My poor darling Matthew! My poor, helpless, driven boy! I will do all I can to make up to you. I will give myself to you, body and soul. You shall not have done it for nothing. And your poor, poor mother! We both loved her. We will go on loving her together. I will see it does not get on your mind. I will show you it was my fault. It was utterly mine. You shall never think it was yours. I will live to see that you can't."

"Hush! There is your mother coming," said Matthew, in a normal, gentle voice. "People must not hear. They must not know. It must never be found out. They would take me away from you."

"Camilla, why are you getting upset like this? We heard your voice through the wall. Matthew, you must be careful not to excite her. Poor children, this waiting time is a strain."

"Oh, all right, Mother, a last lover's scene. We are not going to break it off or never speak again or do anything agitating. We were only vowing eternal faithfulness, and sealing our vows with tears. Our sentiments were much to our credit, especially mine. You would have got a different idea of me, if you had heard. Yes, I certainly think I came out best."

"Well, I think Matthew must go now. And I shall be glad when your wedding day is fixed. Matthew's dear mother would not wish to stand in your way. You will go through your lives remembering her together."

"Stop, Matthew, or I shall scream. Yes, Matthew, go home

and arrange with your father for us to be made one. He is eager to have me for his daughter."

"I will fetch you for dinner to-morrow night," said Matthew. "I can call for you on my way home from my work.

"I don't think I want to see you in your own home again just yet, your home where I used to see your mother. And on your way home from your work, that is to end in keeping people alive! I am somehow getting a dislike to your work. I think meeting here is better. It is the man who ought to have the trouble of coming and going. Oh yes, I know you attend me to and from my door. I know it, I know it. I don't mean anything. I mean nothing, nothing. I only mean I prefer to see you here. We have had enough embracing for to-day. Do make way for me to take a step in front of me."

Camilla walked with an upright head into the other room, where Dominic sat at the table.

"Mother, don't stare at me; don't peer about as if you wanted to ferret something out. It is such an odious habit. What kind of thing do you think you can read in my eyes? I shouldn't show it, if there was anything there. Oh, oh, don't gaze at me like that."

"My dear, I am not gazing at you. There is nothing I want to ferret out. You must not take yourself so seriously. We don't want to probe your little secrets."

Camilla flung herself across the table, and buried her head in her arms.

"My child, what is it? I could tell there was something. I thought Matthew seemed very moody when I let him in. It is only that his mother's death has upset him. It was enough to unnerve him, its happening in that tragic way. Think what it must have been to him, when it was so much to you and me. You will come to see that the trouble is nothing."

261

"Oh, yes, it is nothing," said Camilla, in a strange, light, bitter tone. "It is not worth speaking about. I will not say anything about it. I will go on and keep it to myself, and lock it all up, and get older and older knowing it. And I can't do it, Mother. I can't hide it all in my own heart. Think what it must have been to him, you say, his mother's death! Think of that! Think of that!" She broke into alternate fits of tears and laughter, and Dominic rose to his feet.

"I do not know how much I am justified in taking upon myself. But I advocate that Mrs. Bellamy should unburden her mind."

"Oh, yes, advocate! Your lawyer's word!" said Camilla. "You won't get at Matthew. There is nothing you can prove against him. No one can know he did anything. And he couldn't help it if he did. He was goaded to it. And he did love her. Better than I love you, Mother, he loved his mother. And she forced him to it, without being able to help it, and he will carry it with him to his grave. And I could not help it; I would have given him up. If she had known it, I would have. I did not want him so much; I do not want him. It was not my fault, it was not. I could not help her not knowing. No, don't come near me." She raised her hand to ward off Dominic's approach. "You shan't use what I say against me, against us, against him. I don't mean anything I say. I am telling you I don't. So don't you think you will. Because you shan't, you shan't." She ended on a shriek.

"It can hardly be necessary to state, Mrs. Bellamy, that anything you may say, or may have said, will be treated in the strictest confidence."

"You won't do anything?" said Camilla, her eyes wavering behind her hair like a child's. "You will leave him alone? But of course you will. You haven't anything against him." She sat up and her voice changed. "I have not said anything against him. I

262

do not know anything. I was carried away by a fearful dream I had. Something he said reminded me of it."

There was a silence. Mrs. Christy stood with her eyes on her daughter, her features showing the quick working of her mind.

"I don't know what you mean, my child. No doubt it is a fancy, a dream, as you say. But with the feelings that led to such dreams, is it wise to marry? My daughter, do not make a mistake a second time."

"No, no, that is a settled thing, Mrs. Christy," said Dominic. "Whatever may be meant, or not be meant by Mrs. Bellamy's words, that emerges."

"Then shall I write to him?" said Camilla, with simple appeal. "I don't know what to say. It will drive him mad. But I can't help it; he will have to go mad; I believe he is mad already. He behaves as if he were mad; the things he said were mad; you see they were. And I can't be married to a madman. Poor boy, he gets it from his family. His mother could not have been herself to do what she did. They said she could not. I have my own life to think of. I can't do any good to her now. And it was what she wanted, that I should give up her son. She did not know it would drive him mad. I wish I could say it without half killing him, but I seem to have to destroy men; it seems to be my lot. If only people knew what I suffer in writing these mortal messages!"

She pushed back her hair, and took the pen and paper that Dominic put at her hand.

My poor, dear Matthew,

I don't know how to say it to you, but I must get it into words at once. You would hate my being what I am, and I can never be anything else. And I should hate your being what you are, what you told me you were, and you can never be anything else. There, I have got it down. I could not bear it and I

263

will not bear it. So do not make the fatal mistake of persuading me; I say a fatal mistake. If you do, I cannot tell you what revenge I might take. You know I might say anything in a storm; you know I have no control of myself. I wonder if you know me well enough to see that this is my last word. If you do not, I am sorry for you, for reasons that are enough to make me sorry. I will not see you until you are married. And take my advice, and never tell that other woman what you told me.

Yours as much as I can be,
Camilla.

Chapter XXV

This letter, posted by Dominic, was read by Matthew at the breakfast table in the morning. He had come down after a sleepless night, and almost leapt at the message in Camilla's hand. He read it through, and suddenly sat down, as if something had let him down from a height; and looking round the table, seemed to find himself speaking.

"Well, there is an end of it now. It doesn't matter any more. Anyone may know it. I may as well tell you myself. I am tired of this covering up with silence. And Camilla does not keep things to herself; she says she does not; she means to say it." He held out the letter, and his voice and gesture suddenly threw back to his childhood. "Mother did not take the tablet on purpose. She did not want to die. You all know that she had stopped wanting it. It was I who wanted her to die, for fear she should prevent my marrying Camilla. Camilla had begun to listen to her, and she would never have stopped listening. It would have been like Gregory. But Camilla will never marry me now. This has made her know she does not want to. I was always afraid of her finding it out. I never meant to tell her the truth, but something forced me to say it. It was not much good my doing any of it, was it? I

265

would rather people knew; it is not the sort of thing I like to carry by myself. I do not care for it somehow, knowing it all alone. I do not like it in the night, when I do not sleep."

"Matthew, Matthew, what are you saying? You do not know. It is a delusion that you have. You have felt it all too deeply," cried Godfrey, rising and going to his son. "It is nothing to do with you that your mother died. What are we all coming to, that you should have been brought to this? There, there, my poor child, your father understands."

"No, you do not understand yet," said Matthew, disengaging his arm. "You still think I did not do it, that Mother did it herself. But it was I who put the tablet there. I got it from Dufferin's room. It looked like the sleeping tablets. I shall have to tell you a great many times."

"Tell us just what you did," said Jermyn, coming to his brother. "What was it exactly that happened? If you tell me, it will help you to see that you did not do it."

"I put a poisonous tablet with the ones she had for sleeping," said Matthew, in a suddenly surly tone. "That is what I did, since you want to know exactly. And I gave it to her with one of the others, when I went to her room that last night. She asked me to put off my marriage, and I knew that would mean it would never happen, that Camilla would escape. That is simple enough, isn't it? The tablets looked very much the same."

"My boy, my boy!" said Godfrey.

"Then Mother did not want to die?" said Griselda, who had been sitting with her eyes on Matthew's face.

"No, she did not. She did not think of it. It was I who thought of it," said Matthew, falling back into his strange simplicity. "It was an easy thing to do. It worked just as I thought it out."

"My God!" said Godfrey, putting his hand to his eyes.

"He may have thought it out, or something like it, in his brain," said Gregory in a deliberate, quiet tone, "and then imagined himself doing it afterwards. These troubles have set our minds running on such things. That is what it must be."

"Now let us have an end of this," said Rachel. "Yes, that is what it is, of course. It simply goes without saying. Matthew must come upstairs and rest. This will not go out of his head until he sleeps. Jermyn, send a message to Antony to ask him to come this moment. It would save trouble to keep him in the house until this matter has stopped reverberating. Griselda, don't sit with your eyes on your brother like that. There is nothing to frighten you in his getting a delusion through sleeplessness and shock and love trouble all at once. Godfrey, come and take his other arm; he is not steady on his feet. You see, this is just an echo of Harriet."

"I am not going upstairs. I am not going to sleep," said Matthew, looking at Rachel with calm, obstinate eyes. "I do not sleep nowadays. And it is not worth while to get back into the way of sleeping. I shall not have much more time. I shall be glad to come to grips with it now. Dufferin will believe me, when I explain how I used his keys. He knows I understand what he had, and that Mother did not. And Jermyn believes me too." He gave a natural, cynical laugh. "I can see he does. He believed me easily. And I do not mind. I am glad it has all come to an end."

"Buttermere, can't you go out of the room? Must you keep meandering about, doing nothing?" said Godfrey. "Can't you learn when you can do something and when you can't?"

Buttermere vanished with more than his usual noiselessness.

"You are too late, Father. He had heard it all," said Matthew with another normal laugh. "We may trust Buttermere."

"Yes, yes, we may," said Godfrey, keeping his eyes on

267

Matthew's face, and forcing himself to talk in his usual manner. "Yes, you are right, Matthew. Do you begin to feel more yourself, my boy?"

"I am quite myself, Father."

Godfrey's eyes showed fear.

"I will go and tell Buttermere to be ready to let Dufferin in," said-Gregory, looking at Rachel. Rachel followed him into the hall.

"Gregory, Matthew has a delusion. You see that is what it must be, what of course it is. See that everyone knows it is that. He is like his mother, and may have inherited mental unsoundness from her, and the rush of troubles has been too much for his brain. Antony must be told just that when he comes into the house. Wait here for him, and say those words to him from me."

Gregory walked up and down the hall, adopting a sauntering step when Buttermere moved into sight. When Dufferin came, he repeated Rachel's words with his eyes on his face. Dufferin stood for a long moment, meeting the eyes, and hurried into the dining-room.

Godfrey took a step towards him, as if to protest and explain, but drew back and watched the meeting with Matthew with aloof, almost furtive eyes.

"Well, come upstairs with me, Matthew. You are my patient this morning, and will do what you are told. You know better than to waste my time."

Matthew rose and went with his friend, as if willing for his companionship, and the family stood in silence.

"Well, has Gregory told you?" said Matthew, when they reached his room. "I did it because there was nothing else to be done. She would have parted me from Camilla; it was in her mind. I had got to read her mind. And now I find it is of no good,

268

that it is worse. Camilla has given me up because of it." His tones hurried and stumbled and his eyes went wild. "You know Camilla was in this room with me that day Mother died, that day we knew she was dead? She sat here on this bed with me. You did not know that?" He pulled himself together and went on with a quiet smile. "I am the victim of my own plot, and I am anxious for the end to come as soon as it can. I want to get in advance of Camilla. She will never keep it to herself. She cannot carry a burden. I begin to see that many people could not. I can't get the others to believe me, but I think Jermyn does."

"You took the tablet from my cupboard?" said Dufferin.

"Yes, you must see that I did," said Matthew, his voice sounding tired. "You see that I must have. You know my mother did not understand what was there. She could not have recognised the tablets if she had found them. I thought it all out. I knew she had been in your room by herself, and what would be said after what she had done before. And you know she had lost her desire for death. You knew it all. I wondered you did not think of it at the time, especially when the point was raised of my being the last person to see her alive."

"You did, did you?" said Dufferin. "Well, of course it was plain to you. But it didn't strike anyone as a natural thing for you to do, even though you had your own ends to serve. I thought there must be some other explanation, and accepted the only one. But you are right that I see it now. You thought your mother's life a reasonable price to pay for your own safe happiness! And you think your father's and your sister's suffering a fair exchange for your own peaceful exit, now you have finished with things yourself! For a man of such a mind neither death nor any living death is a useful thing. You will find you have no fancy for death, except for your mother. Your thoughts will go to the way of escape, that come to you through her. You may as well depend on her to the end, since you have learned how to put her to your own use. You have had a delusion. You have over-deep feelings, inherited from her, and a precarious mental balance, also that heritage. And her first attempt on her life had preyed on your mind. And I am not saying that all those things did not do their part. That must help me to do what I can for you; I shall need the help. You must take shelter behind that falsehood, and spend your life in its cover. You have shown you are not the kind to come out."

"I did not know you were cruel," said Matthew.

"You have been kind, haven't you, in putting an end to your mother, when she had some dark years behind her, and the chance of some better ones ahead? Who knew that you were cruel in the way you are? I am not saying you did not suffer from her, but you would never have suffered death. It was your life that was in her mind. People who think of themselves to that extent don't want their years snatched from them. It was your mother who was to lose her years. You will do no more harm, Matthew. You will fall in with what is best for other people, and its being best for you will not prevent you. You are too like your mother. The tragedy got on your mind, and you fancied yourself the author of the thing that made too deep an impression. That is a possible thing; perhaps you knew that. Now get your head clear about the truth—the truth, Matthew. And I will turn your key and take it with me, and go and explain your case to your family, as I have explained it to you. That suits your own mind very well?"

"I don't really care," muttered Matthew.

"You have got away from the desire for justice. People don't want what they deserve, when they deserve so much. You can lie down and be ill. You are ill for that matter; you are in a very low state; that part needn't be acting. And the rest must get not to be. It is a great relief to you to be free from your burden. That is so even between ourselves. We shall never say a word of this again, if we live to be old men. Doors have ears. I saw Buttermere's face. And I see yours too. You have learnt your lesson. You haven't needed much teaching, and you will never need any more."

Dufferin locked the door and went downstairs, humming a snatch of song. He entered the dining-room and left the door ajar.

"Ah, the poor boy! We have got it over. He will never have the fancy again. It was as real to him as if it had been the truth. He faced it as truly as if he had it in his memory. And he behaved well." Dufferin, in his effort to encounter Godfrey's eyes, found himself echoing his speech.

"He did, Doctor," said Godfrey, coming forward with extended hand. "I thank you for the words. He is a hero. I thank you for establishing it. We all thank you for lifting this great weight off our minds. For we didn't know what to think. I confess I didn't. He might have done it in illness, just as he fancied he had done it in illness, the poor, overstrung lad! He is like his mother. If any one of her children is like her, it is he. And seeming to feel the least all the time! Ah, still waters run deep. Well, Rachel stood by us, and did not let her belief falter. She held up her heart and she held up ours. She knew the truth. She sensed it. Her woman's instinct led her right. Ah, that is the kind of thing to trust."

"Then Mother did want to die?" said Griselda.

"Yes, she did want to," said Dufferin. "We have to look at that. But it was only a moment, and not the moment we imagine. She would have had a sort of exaltation."

"My poor, heroic, erring wife!" said Godfrey.

"Godfrey, you know you are sure that Harriet hears everything," said Rachel.

"Is Matthew clear now that he was under a delusion?" said Jermyn.

"Yes, it is all over," said Dufferin. "I don't think it can come on him again, but I am going to keep a watch on him to-day. I will take in his meals myself, and have him under my eye. Buttermere is not the person to be about him, or about anyone in a nervous state. Don't interfere with me. I know what I am doing."

"We are too grateful, Doctor," said Godfrey. "But one of us will go upstairs with the meals."

"No. I said I knew what I was doing. He would rather have me. He will be himself to-morrow, if he gets some sleep."

"Dear, dear, this sleeplessness! It is a ghastly thing to have in a family. The poor boy gets it from his mother," said Godfrey. "Now one thing I know, it doesn't come from me. I have never been sleepless in my life; and since everything has been to pieces about us, I have been a dead man from midnight to morning. Well, Buttermere, we have good news about Mr. Matthew. We can call on you to congratulate us. He has thrown off the sad delusion that was troubling him. It is off his mind, and the world is clear before him. You know his engagement is broken off?"

Buttermere barely inclined his head.

"It was that that was too much, and nearly wrecked his reason. Ah, it nearly threw him on our hands a helpless—threw him helpless on our hands. We are at ease about him now."

"Yes, Sir Godfrey," said Buttermere.

"You don't think it has got about, do you? See that the report doesn't spread. It would not be fair on Mr. Matthew. We know how easily words set into a form."

"Not a syllable will pass my lips, Sir Godfrey."

"Oh well, it is hardly as bad as that. But we don't want it chattered about all over the place. You see the distinction?"

"I agree there is apt not to be any, Sir Godfrey."

"Well, keep your mouth tight shut then."

"That is what my words amounted to, Sir Godfrey."

"Well, suit your actions to your words."

"I have expressed the intention of taking the wiser course, Sir Godfrey."

"What do you mean?" almost shouted Godfrey. "Are you insinuating that there is anything against my son?"

"Insinuation is not in my line or my place, Sir Godfrey."

"You are right about the last," said Dufferin. "But talk in any way you like, or in the only way you can, only where we can hear you don't talk at all. And bring something on a tray for Mr. Matthew. He had no breakfast. Bring it now, and I will take it up myself."

"I am to be depended upon, sir."

"Do as you are told," said Dufferin.

"If you think it wiser, sir," said Buttermere, hastening his step a little as he left the room.

"Can we go on having him about?" said Griselda.

"Taking him seriously would be giving a wrong impression," said Jermyn.

"We can hardly expect him not to show his disappointment," said Rachel. "Think of being baulked of what you would like best in the world, when in sight of it!"

"We shall be ill if we discuss him, and we already have illness in the house," said Griselda.

Godfrey walked from the room as if he could not bear again to be unduly stirred.

Gregory sauntered up to Griselda with a kind expression.

"It is all over now," he said.

"Well, what does it matter what happened, when the choice is what it is?" said Jermyn. "It makes little difference which tragedy we have in the family."

"It makes all the difference," said Dufferin. "And you know which you have. I have told you. People too simple to set aside the sick words of a sick man must be taught."

"I saw it for myself. I have proved I am not simple," said Rachel. "Even Matthew did not imagine he was that, at the worst moment of his delusion. He saw himself behaving in quite a complicated way. He kept his self-respect through everything."

"We have simply to be ashamed that we have less deep feeling than he has," said Gregory. "It is too heartless of us not to think we did it."

"I see how his mind may have begun to work," said Jermyn.

"No, that is not fair, Jermyn," said Rachel. "You know quite well that he put the whole thing into your head. Be generous like your father. He makes no claim at all, though no one appreciates it as he does. You have brought the tray, Buttermere. What is your feeling about having put the tablet with the harmless ones? You must not bring forward a definite claim; the family must come first."

Buttermere looked over the tray in silence.

"Take this key, and carry up the tray, and put it down by Mr. Matthew, and come away as silent as you are now," said Dufferin.

"Yes, sir," said Buttermere, leaving the. room with an even tread and the tray motionless.

"You can deal with anybody, Rachel. You have passed the final test. Now all of you go to your several occupations. You must some of you have something you sometimes do. And Griselda would be the better for an hour by herself."

Griselda turned to Dufferin the moment they were alone.

"It all gets more and more, Antony. It is more than it ought to be, for Mother to have wanted to die, not to have wanted her life any more than that; and for Matthew to think he did it, to have that to suffer as well as his own disappointment. It was always dreadful to see him disappointed. And I can't bear not knowing if he did it. We shall never know. You know we shall never know. And it is worst of all, yes it is, for Father not to feel things more. That was all she had in her life, poor Mother, all she had, when she was a woman who needed so much! And Ernest will feel he is taking too much on himself in marrying me. He wants a wife who will give him support, not someone crushed and disgraced by a family like mine. And I will not marry a man who does not let me have my brothers. I would have even Matthew, even if he had done it. I have never cared for him as much as the others, but I am his sister now. And Ernest will despise him for having delusions. He thinks he is the only person in the world who must be weak. I can't be strong enough for him."

"Be yourself with him, and let him see that he has more than enough. If he doesn't want you as you are, strong or weak, with or without his kind of strength and weakness, tell him you feel the same to him. More than one of you may be undertaking too much."

"I know I must seem to have strange feelings about him."

"He could speak the simple truth about you. You see that he does speak what seems to him to be the truth. I think he does that about more things than most of us. I think he is an honest man, Griselda."

When Bellamy came in later, he wore a look of simple

exaltation. He shook hands with the men, and putting his arm round Griselda, faced them with kindling eyes.

"Haslam, I have come not in a spirit of bitterness or judgment. I have come to identify myself with Griselda's family, to be Matthew's brother and your son. I have come to help you to be simply courageous and straightforward in tragic circumstances. For who are we who should judge? Who am I? He is a man and my brother, my brother in more than one sense. Something was too strong. And how know we on what day or in what hour our own temptation may come, and find us not on the watch but sleeping?"

Griselda stood with her head bent, looking up at Bellamy from under her brows.

"Ernest, my boy," said Godfrey, standing with his hand held out, but not advancing, "we thank you for your generous attitude. We thank you as much as if we needed it. But happily we have not come to that; mercifully you do not find us in that pass. It emerges that Matthew's love and grief for his mother transcended what others felt, and left him shattered. So that this sad delusion took hold of him and laid him low. But his will has risen victorious and truth has triumphed. With our friend the doctor's help, he is established as sinning not at all, but greatly suffering."

"Is that proved?" said Bellamy, speaking before he thought.

"Yes, it is certain," said Dufferin. "A case of transferring something that has made a deep impression, to himself, as people unjustly accused of a crime have been known to fancy themselves the authors of it."

"Poor boy, poor boy!" said Bellamy.

"Yes, yes, you say the words," said Godfrey.

"I feel I stand reproved," said Bellamy. "I feel I should have

276

known Griselda's brother. But the tidings came to me as established by his own confession."

"Tidings! Established!" said Godfrey. "His own confession! The poor child only spoke of it this morning. I hope the true report will get about as fast. We will ask you to do your best in that matter for us, Ernest. And of course you couldn't know what to make of it all. We were baffled ourselves. The confession came, as you say, from his own lips. He thought it was a confession, poor, suffering boy! He is terribly like his mother, terribly for him, appealingly for us. My wife leaves one child who is her equal in feeling."

"The rest of us will soon have borne enough," said Jermyn.

"Ah, Haslam, it is a complex heritage for us. We shall need our qualities to bear our pride, and live under the sword of Damocles. You need have no fear for me. I shall not flinch. It is Griselda, wild and sorrowing and burdened, whom I love, as I shall never love another woman."

"If you think of me in that way, you do already love another woman. That is not the woman I am. It is too much for you, the prospect of our marriage. I wondered if it would be. I knew you well enough to wonder. And it is too much for me. I could not support you under the strain of my family life. We should both of us have more than we could bear."

"Griselda, I have already almost had that," said Bellamy, holding out his hands. "You see me as I am, an overwrought and tired man. I need the strength that you can give."

"I am never one for thinking a woman ought to give more than a man," said Griselda in a breathless tone. "I don't see that difference between women and men. I don't want to see it between my husband and myself. I don't feel I am such a strong woman. My mother knew I was not. I don't want to give out so much; I should get weary with so much giving. I don't care for the men who are weaker than women, and I am no good to the kind that are. I think you are right in your judgment of yourself. There had better be an end of everything between us. Mother was right. There is an end."

Griselda broke down, and Jermyn and Dufferin followed her from the room. Bellamy made a despairing gesture and looked at Godfrey.

"Well, I can't help it, my boy," said Godfrey.

"Well, can I?" said Bellamy. "Can I help it, Lady Hardisty?"

"Well, Griselda implied that you couldn't," said Rachel. "And she seemed to have thought about you. But I should say there couldn't be a better person than you to marry. I have often thought about you two, and always said that."

"Well, I will go home," said Bellamy, as if he expected to be gainsaid. "I will return to my lonely fireside. No, I will give up talking like Spong. I will become a man who need not have his fireside lonely. I will learn Griselda's lesson; I find no lesson beneath me; and I am not slow to learn. I will depend on you all to remain my friends."

"Well, the reformation came too late," said Rachel. "Only a moment, but I think Antony has taken advantage of it. I can go home to my lonely fireside too, and settle down with Percy and his memories. I have some memories of my own now. Well, Harriet always wanted Griselda to marry Antony."

"Well, I declare, I believe she did," said Godfrey. "She never said so, and I never thought of it. But I believe she did."

"Why, of course she did!" said Gregory.

"Must you be going, Rachel?" said Godfrey. "I hardly have the energy left to thank you. I have come to the end of my tether."

"That is wonderful of you," said Rachel. "Harriet's husband and eldest son do her the greatest credit. Jermyn shall see me into the hall; it is unassuming of him not to mind being able to. I can't say enough for Harriet's family in their different ways."

"I wanted to have a word with you," said Jermyn, "and not about anything you expect. Not about Griselda's fluctuations, or even about Matthew's rise in general esteem. About something that will explain my mistimed consciousness of self. Here is my book of poems that has just come out. I wish my mother had seen it. I did not dare to let Mellicent read them before they were published, but the majesty of print has begotten confidence. I want you to ask her to be ready to tell me her impression. I know I sound egotistic, but life has to go on."

"It does seem too unchecked of life," said Rachel, "but it is quite the opposite of you to wish your mother had seen the poems. Do you really want Mellicent to tell you her impression? Wouldn't it be better for her to tell you yours?"

"Very much better. But I hope she will do both."

"It is a thing we have tried to break her of," said Rachel. "But if you must encourage her!"

"Yes, I encourage her to the last point. Thank you so much," said Jermyn, walking away, as his father came rapidly towards Rachel, unmistakably struck by a thought.

"Rachel, is there anything between Jermyn and Mellicent?" he said in a sibilant whisper.

"Nothing between them. Something in Jermyn," said Rachel. "Percy and I shall never prove to people that Mellicent wants to be a spinster. It has a too impossible sound. We shall have to face the dishonour of having a daughter unsought. Mellicent has inherited nothing from Percy's early self."

Chapter XXVI

"We must all find this a trying and exacting occasion," said Agatha in a voice of fellow-feeling, as she welcomed her gathering flock. "To think that Lady Haslam founded our society, and was the life of it for so long—because I am the first to say she was the life of it at the beginning—and then that it twice has had to hold its way without her, as if her spirit were no longer its vital force! It almost seems that she has died two deaths, and each one a darker death than we shall be called upon to die."

"It is useful to know about our deaths," said Rachel. "We have to be so brave, to live with death in front of us, that you are right to give us any comfort you are certain of."

"Of course I cannot be certain," said Agatha simply. "I can only say what is, humanly speaking, true."

"I should have thought it was more than humanly speaking," said Rachel.

"It won't come just yet for any of us," said Geraldine, with a note of irritation.

"Won't it? You are an unusual family," said Rachel. "Now I can make definite plans."

"Have we any real proof about Lady Haslam's death?" said

Geraldine. "We are told that the boy had a delusion, but I don't see how we can feel an absolute certainty."

"We must not ask to have it absolute; we must do without that," said Agatha.

"We do need courage," said Rachel. "Death in front of us and curiosity with us!"

"I am not conscious of curiosity," said Agatha.

"No, of course you are not," said Rachel. "Neither can your sister be in her heart."

"I am personally convinced that the certainty is absolute," said Mrs. Christy, "simply because it is not in me to think that Lady Haslam passed on at the hand of the son, who was gifted in the nature of things with the family quality. The idea carried its own contradiction. And I wish to say that Camilla's giving up Matthew had nothing to do with his delusion, that she sees it a proof of his devotion and an honour to him. And I should take it as a kindness if no one would hint things against Lady Haslam's family in my hearing. I was so very sensible of the honour of her friendship."

"We cannot be held responsible for things that happened outside our own control," said Agatha kindly. "We all saw qualities to admire in Lady Haslam, and we may several of us say we had the honour of her friendship, or the advantage of it. I certainly can say it, and do say it with all my heart."

"We all have our favourites," said Kate, "and I suspect Mrs. Christy was one of Lady Haslam's. I was not one myself. Lady Haslam made the mistake of never singling me out at all."

"Well, I think she did single me out," said Agatha. "I can remember many instances, more really than I care to count, as such preference must involve corresponding omission for other people."

"I never notice whether people single me out or not,"

Geraldine interposed. "Any effort on my behalf is wasted."

"But I do not feel that a reason for anything but frankness in dealing with her memory," Agatha continued. "I should ask nothing but that for myself, and I make it a rule to give other people what I should ask for myself."

"Of course people with good characters ask very little for themselves," said Rachel.

"It is best for us all not to make exacting demands, either in life or the dealings we claim after it," said Agatha.

"I have not given Percy directions about those, though I shall so soon be dependent upon them. Though not just yet, you say. But he knows we must not speak evil of the dead. It must have been people like Percy who established it. Besides it has less effect than speaking evil of the living."

"I wonder what the poor boy's feelings are now, whatever the truth is," said Agatha. "My foremost feeling towards him is compassion."

"Our feelings must depend on the truth of course," said Kate.

"There must have been a strange relationship between him and his mother," said Agatha, "a relationship that no simply natural mother, certainly not myself, could understand. The mere fact of his believing in his own guilt points to it, to my mind. I cannot see that things can have been normal between them."

"Normality may not always be such a good thing," said Kate.

"Common is the commonplace," said Mrs. Christy with a gesture. "I vouch for it that there was nothing average or on the dead level between any of the family."

"I think the really pathetic figure is Sir Godfrey," said Agatha. "Whatever he feels the reality to be, he has tragedy added to the last desolation."

"It seems the part of friendship to do something to help," said

Mrs. Christy. "It means so much to me to know that my friends are a little better because of me."

"You should have me for a friend," said Rachel. "I can't tell you how much better I am because of you."

"Well, I have my department of help," said Agatha, "handed over to me, clean-cut and settled, the youngest boy. My charge will be to see that he does not suffer more than he must from his family's position; to make up to him, as far as is in me, for his tragic loss. I hope I am qualified to do it. For whether I am or not, he will look to me to accomplish it."

"My singled-out sister!" said Geraldine, looking round.

"Through no choice of mine. The choice is his. I have not had much say in the matter. It is just assumed that I am at his disposal; and indeed I am, if I can do any good. I think the most ticklish part of the business will be to convince him that I do not think less of him for this ghastly uncertainty, that I take him on his own merits, as a human being by himself. It must be so hard for a young man to put his mother aside, put her aside in spirit as an ideal, and turn elsewhere. I feel so for him in the adjustment. I hope I shall make it as easy as it can be made."

Agatha perceived that a silence was attending her words, and looked round to see Gregory standing at her side.

"We have been talking about you," she said, without a break in her tone. "I have been saying that you and I will have even more between us, now you are to be thrown on your own resources. Shall we arrange our next meeting?" She moved to put herself between Gregory and the onlookers.

"No, I don't think so just now. It is not quite the time for it, not until things are clear between us," said Gregory, in a voice that would be overheard as conversational. "I daresay you were not thinking of what you were saying, but if you were, I have let you make a mistake. You will allow me to put it right, as the mistake is mine. No one can take the place of my mother to me. You would have seen that, if it had not been for me. She will always be one by herself in my memory; not as an ideal; I do not want an ideal; simply as my mother and as what she was in herself and to me." He moved away as if his words had been casual, and looked in a friendly way at the other faces.

Agatha, after a moment of standing still, walked in a cheerful way to her work, and settled to it with some appearance of compunction. Looking up at Gregory, she saw the direction of his eyes, and presently rose and stepped out into the room.

"Now, you two young people!" she said, beckoning to Polly, and drawing her to Gregory by the hand. "You can go off and have a time by yourselves. We don't want to force our middle-aged point of view on you young things. I am sure I don't. You have let me see what you want from me too well. That is what I like from young people, a real understanding of what they want, so that I can give it to them. If I make mistakes, I never hold to them; I know what it is my aim to do in the world better than that."

She pushed them gently away, and turned to welcome Bellamy, with an air of transferring her interest.

"Mrs. Calkin, I have had reason to complain before of your partial ways. As you are the head of the meeting, you should be more gallant. I have been here several minutes, and you have not dreamed of telling me that I could go away with your sister Kate. You go on as usual, simply favouring Gregory."

Agatha looked from Bellamy to her sister, who had come up to her at his side.

"Are you two going to be married?" said Geraldine in a sudden, piercing tone.

"Yes, but I never have before, and Ernest has only once," said

284

Kate. "It is not a matter of forming bad habits. And I promise I never will again. It would not be fair for Ernest to promise that at his age."

"When you are old enough to be his mother!" cried Geraldine. "Women who are older than their husbands are always old enough to be their mothers. Seven years is quite enough for it."

"The juxtaposition shows up the difference," said Kate, smiling.

"And everybody helps to show it up," said Rachel. "But we will neither of us mind them, my dear."

"Oh, now, you two, I thought there was something going on," said Agatha, lifting her finger. "It is extraordinary how we can feel that something is happening, and not put words to it, and then realise we have grasped it in its nature all the time. I don't think I have been in any essential doubt, though I had a moment's superficial surprise. My state was one of fundamental preparation."

"I am not very preoccupied with these things," said Geraldine. "They don't seem to reach the fundamental part of me. But it is all the more interesting when it is a surprise. I feel in quite high spirits. I always think my friends marry simply for my entertainment."

"Then we are in favour with you," said Bellamy.

"I do congratulate you, Kate. I am so glad," said Gregory.

"Ah now, and you, Gregory!" said Agatha. "I don't think you will go on deceiving us much longer. You haven't deceived me for some time, though I own I thought you were still deceiving yourselves. I was not prepared to see it come up to the surface quite so soon. You have 'had' even me in a way."

"Well, Polly is not old enough to be Gregory's mother," said Geraldine.

"No, it will bring everything back to Percy," said Rachel.

"It is the commoner thing of the two," said Geraldine.

"Yes, nearly everything brings it back," said Rachel.

"Well, I suppose I ought to be pouring out sisterly congratulations," said Geraldine. "I don't know if it is a compliment to Kate to tell her I am glad to be rid of her. She is only going as far as the rectory. It hardly seems a proper marriage at all. I am not good at feminine response to these demands; I don't feel any answering chord is struck. I believe the people are right who say I ought to have been a man."

"That is very satisfying for you," said Rachel. "We are often at variance with people who tell us what we ought to have been. Percy cannot agree that he ought to have been a bachelor, and ought to have had a son. Percy would never agree to both. And Polly may not agree that she ought not to have been born."

"Well, now, I think we ought to be getting on with our work," said Agatha, spacing her words. "This is a working party, and I don't see why I should countenance its being used for anything else. Now settle down, all of you, and make up for lost time. And if you two men don't want to make yourselves useful, you can just go away. We don't want you here if you are going to be idle."

"I am not going to be. I am going to keep handing Kate her scissors," said Bellamy. "I know a great deal about ladies' sewing, and handing scissors saves a surprising amount of time. Needles and cotton are less elusive."

"Oh, we shall always be handed things now!" said Geraldine. "We shall have a man in the family."

"That sounds kind and hospitable," said Bellamy. "But I hope you will not try to make a man of me, Geraldine. Kate will explain to you that I have to be a clergyman."

286

"I have no particular partiality for manly men," said Geraldine. "They are rather crude creatures, I always think."

"Yes, so they are," said Bellamy, "more so than womanly women. Everyone is best in between."

"That is what I have always been accused of being," said Geraldine.

"Then there is already a family likeness between us," said Bellamy. "I am quite settled in my mind about you. But now there is a dreadful thing before me. There is a cause and just impediment. I shall have to call Mrs. Calkin Agatha."

"We will not expect you to come to that all at once," said Agatha, smiling at him as if from above. "I am a great many years older than you. I am not going to take up a position of being anything else. I shall expect you to regard me only as a very maternal sister-in-law."

"Agatha is said to be candid," said Mellicent, "but I wonder if she knows how candid she is."

"He will have to rise on the stepping-stone of me to higher things," said Geraldine. "He got as far as me quite easily. He is making the most remarkable progress."

"Mellicent, my dear, why have you stopped working for the poor?" said Rachel.

"Jermyn has come to call for me; I saw him out of the window."

"Jermyn, take her away before she leaves me anything more to alter," said Rachel. "Really this is not fit for the poor. I don't see how any unfortunate person could wear it, not anyone already unfortunate."

"It is plain and strong," said Mellicent.

"I hardly liked to put it into words, but it is, isn't it? We must not call the poor thriftless, and then treat them as if they were not. What is the good of knowing about them?"

287

"What do you think, Mellicent?" said Jermyn, accompanying her along the road.

"I thought the verses very interesting, some of them, especially those with the definite signs of early youth. Something seems to go in the later ones."

"Well, perhaps those are more in my real manner. What do you think of their quality?"

"I think they are by no means without a worth of their own."

"You think me a fool to have published?"

"No, I think you are fortunate. My father is poorer than yours. That is the difference between us there."

"Mellicent, I hope that some day I shall have the right to publish your work. I am helpless until my own can struggle into the light of itself."

"And shall I not also be at that stage by then?"

"You did not misunderstand me."

"No, you made yourself clear. Would you like it except in the way you have planned?"

"You can't think I should not be overjoyed if you were to get rapid success. We can never tell what work will come most promptly into its first, facile credit."

"You hold to your plan," said Mellicent. "Would you like a wife who was better than yourself on your own line?"

"Yes, if she really were better. But married people can't continue on the same line. To a man and a woman there must in the end be a man and a woman's life."

"Now I have not refused you," said Mellicent. "You have refused me."

"You have not written much lately, have you?" said Jermyn after a silence. "I should like to see the poems I have not seen."

"You have not seen most of them. I can send them if you like."

"I should like it indeed. But I must make it clear, that as you don't want men and women distinctions in these things, I must not see it a case for chivalry. If you don't want my opinion, don't ask for it."

"I have not asked for it," said Mellicent, laughing. "It is you who ask to form it. Of course it is not a case for chivalry. I shouldn't expect it from a man who had refused me."

"Well, you will send the poems to-night," said Jermyn, waving a farewell.

"What will you do, my dear?" said Rachel, coming out of Agatha's gate, where the two had parted.

"Send my poems to Jermyn."

"Has it been as bad as that? Must you really? Being cruel to be kind is such dreadful cruelty. Being cruel to be cruel is better."

"I think Jermyn takes it for that."

"Well, it might have been worse. You are still friends, then?"

"Yes," said Mellicent, smiling to herself.

"You refused his offer?" said her stepmother.

"No, he withdrew it."

"Oh yes, the poems," said Rachel. "Must you really be a spinster, even though people will never understand it?"

"People like you will understand it."

"But do you realise how uncommon I am? There are no people like me."

"I think I am like you in one small way. Your happiest years were your single ones."

"Well, a selfish life is lovely, darling," said Rachel. "It is awful to be of use."

Chapter XXVII

"**M**y dear boy, my heart aches at seeing you set off. I don't know when I have had a moment that gave me a lump in my throat like this. I could set the waterworks on like a woman, if I let go of myself. I don't make any bones about it."

"You don't, Father," said Matthew.

"You take your father's blessing with you," Godfrey continued, bringing his hand down on his son's shoulder, and appearing to be deterred by convention from embracing him. "And I don't need to say that your mother's goes with it. I am as convinced of that as that I am standing here. I can say no more."

"Matthew knows that if there was anything more, you would say it," said Griselda.

"You have gone the full length, Father," said Matthew.

"You will have to go over it all again when I set off to Cambridge," said Jermyn. "I can't be put off with a lesser portion."

"Oh, my dear boy, that is not quite the same," said Godfrey, with a lighter hand for his second son. "Matthew and I have been through so much together that it has made a bond between us. There is that between Matthew and his father. And Matthew was the first born to me and his mother."

"We are not disputing it, Father," said Matthew, going a step further.

"Ah, Matthew, the future before you; an old man myself," said Sir Percy. "I don't want you to think of an old man. I shall be thinking of you; you need not give a thought to it."

"Ah, thank you, my dear old friend," said Godfrey, just avoiding monotony in gesture. "Matthew's heart is too full for words this morning."

"Matthew comes in for more and more credit, and deserves it," said Jermyn.

"The rest of us might make a suitable response," said Gregory.

"If you think, he has always been the silent one," said Griselda.

"Good-bye, Grisel; good-bye, Father; good-bye, all. Thanks very much," said Matthew, passing to the carriage.

"Ah, good-bye, my dear boy!" said Godfrey, standing with his hand over his eyes. "Yes, there he goes, our eldest son. His mother's eyes are on him and all of us at the moment of our parting."

"I don't believe Harriet gives her attention to everyone but me like that," said Rachel.

"I am sure she does not, Rachel. Her eyes are on you as you take her place to her children," Godfrey assured her, walking with his back towards her into the house.

"Not as I go back to my own concerns?" said Rachel.

"Yes, yes, Rachel, we will go home," said her husband.

"I must learn not always to be here. Habits get so set in old age. Harriet must sometimes look down and see her place vacant for herself. I was quite superfluous this morning, with her doing everything. She must have been pleased with Matthew's departure. He hardly said a word, and his father did all he could to show him up."

"Ah, you miss Harriet, Rachel," said Sir Percy, for the first time since Harriet's death.

"Yes. I am almost falling into Godfrey's method of keeping her."

Godfrey went into the library and threw himself into a chair, to find his common solace in his own companionship.

"Well, well, a turning point, a parting of the ways. My wife gone, my boy Matthew gone, the other children off on their own lives. The last to come, the first to marry. Nothing but an old grandfather before long. I must depend on myself. That time comes to most of us sooner or later. I shan't find it as easy as I once should have. I had those months with the young ones alone; a good time, good children, good to their father. It isn't as if I were starting again, with the relief of taking the days for myself in peace. Yes, well, there are other things, but there is relief. I won't shirk looking at myself. If Harriet knows my heart, she knows that. There are not worse things in it than in other men's. Better, I shouldn't be surprised; I am an easy sort of fellow. Harriet didn't have trouble with me. She might have had, ageing so early, my poor girl. I should have been ashamed to let her have it." He sat up and his voice gained force. "I can say that for myself. If that is Buttermere sneaking into the room, he leaves the house this minute!"

Godfrey sprang to his feet and strode to the door, to receive Camilla into his arms.

"Dear Sir Godfrey, Matthew has left you? I had to come and say a word. I waited until he was gone, because I would not hurt him by seeing him. I wish I had done him less harm. If you ever speak to him of me, say that I wish I had done him only good. He will understand. But I could not help it. I can't help these things I do to men. Say that you understand me."

"My dear Camilla, my dear girl, I do indeed say it. You know I wished to have you for my daughter. And my wife would have come to wish it too. My heart rises up and tells me so. And I thank you for what you say about her. Your words are as balm to my soul. They cheer me as I set off on my lonely path, hardly seeing what is in front of me. I do not set myself up to be of account. I am content to live with little."

"You make me feel I have done more harm than I thought. I shall have no peace. I cannot bear you to waste the prime of your life. I always loved you better than Matthew."

"Did you, Camilla? Did you, my dear?" said Godfrey in a far-away tone.

"I did, I did. I can't go on with my life until you are going on with yours."

"Cannot you, Camilla?" said Godfrey, as if the appeal of this just came home.

"Say you will never be different."

"Well, well, I will say I will never be different to you, Camilla. It is something to you to know that, is it, my dear?"

"You take advantage of my betraying myself in a moment of emotion!" said Camilla, moving away and throwing on him a different eye.

"Well, your feeling in that way is something to me. It will be a spar for me to hold on to, as I flounder through my life, trying to do my best, trying to look forward, with little enough to give me courage. People do not see me as you do, Camilla. They leave me to go my own way, as they go theirs. They cast not a look to the right or the left."

"We all have our special ones," said Camilla, with her head down.

"And I am your special one, Camilla? I have always felt my

293

heart go out to my son's future wife. You have been dear as a daughter to me. I shall look always to see you, and have the support of your words. You are the only one who sees me as I am, as I see myself, and not as a husk left over, with the kernel gone. For my dear and loyal wife, Camilla, that gifted and devoted woman, is seen to have left me somehow emptied, bereft of something, drained by what I have had to give, and have given so willingly."

"I know you would give a great deal," murmured Camilla. "I can feel you would."

"Camilla, there is no limit to what I would pour out on a woman who granted me a little in return, who would spare a thought to the manner of man who walked through life at her side. I am not an old man, as the world reckons years; I am a man in my vigorous days, as is accounted the life of men. I am younger than I have been allowed to be in the past. I could give much."

"You are not the only one of us who could do that."

"I make no claim to be. I should not ask nothing, Camilla."

"I should be the last woman to want a man who did."

"I believe you would, Camilla. I believe I am a man who knows what is welcome to a woman, what is acceptable in her sight. I have had little chance to show the man I could be."

"Better late than never! Never too late to mend! Never too old to learn!" chanted Camilla, pirouetting across the room. "Don't escort me to the door. I will creep out with bowed head as I came."

Godfrey walked up and down the floor, and finding the space restricted, continued his steps into the hall, which Gregory and Polly were crossing on their way to the garden.

"Well, my Gregory and Polly! Well, my pretty pair! I can tell you I envy you, or I should in some people's place. I know what you are feeling. It only comes once, at whatever time of life it comes, what is carrying you on its force. Some people would say you were too young, as they would say I was too old. They are as wrong in one case as in the other. For we know not on what day nor in what hour it cometh, whether in the spring or the autumn, the later summer of life."

Chapter XXVIII

Dominic entered the Haslams' house with somehow stealthy steps, as if he would be glad to leave it with the ensuing interview past.

Godfrey came to greet him with an easiness rather than ease of manner, that recalled the days of Harriet's illness.

"Well, Spong, I think you find me in better heart. I feel more prepared to pick myself up and get on my way, than when you saw me last. It was a rough tumble. But we must not stay at a standstill because we have had a set-back. Life is not long enough for that."

"No, Sir Godfrey," said Dominic, allowing his eyes to waver from Godfrey's face, and not expressing satisfaction in his account. "I have taken the liberty of calling on you, in the hope that you may be disposed to give me some of your attention. I have sympathised with your disinclination to concentrate upon material matters, but I shall be from home for a few weeks in the immediate future, and should be concerned if you desired assistance when I was constrained to deny it. I shall not need to impose exacting demands at a time when your mind is distracted by other claims."

"Yes, yes, let us get to it, Spong," said Godfrey, pulling up a chair for himself, and seeming to summon another by a glance, which Dominic supplemented. "Let us get it over. We have to set our minds in order, so that we can turn them to the next Chapter. For we shall have to act our part in it. We must not stay with our feet rooted in the past."

"No, well, Sir Godfrey," said Dominic, laying out some papers one by one, with his eyes upon them, "what I have to say concerns amongst others one point which, with your permission, we will turn to first, a slight one as regards comprehension and probably discussion. I have to state what it is likely you already know, what I make no doubt you already know, and disclose as a matter of formality." Dominic seemed to find each syllable useful in postponing the nominal utterance. "You are doubtless aware that your wife left you in control of the larger part of the income deriving from her estate, on the condition that, and for as long as, you remain her widower. Failing this, the money reverts, in proportions which she has laid down, to her children." Dominic, having accomplished the form, remained with his eyes on the table.

"What?" said Godfrey. "What are you saying? I had no idea of it at all, not an inkling! There must be some mistake. The income falls to me only if I remain a widower? If I marry, I am to have none of it at all? I could not keep up the place. I could not live here without my wife's fortune. We apportioned it out together for the different purposes. She took as much interest in the estate as I did myself, more interest. So this was why you slipped out of reading the will on the day of the funeral! You could not expose me in this position. And I hadn't a suspicion of it, and haven't given a thought to the will since. I happen to be a trustful person where those near me are concerned. What a condition! I should not have believed it. I don't give it credit for a moment."

"That is the stipulation," said Dominic, with the faintest possible tremor of his face.

"Well, let me see," said Godfrey, holding out his hand.

Dominic yielded a copy of the will.

"Oh, ah, well," said Godfrey, turning it over, not invited by the opening legal phrase. "Yes, well, I will take your word for it, Spong. It must be as you say. But it appears to me an unbelievable thing."

"You will understand, Sir Godfrey, that Lady Haslam did not solicit my advice, that I was merely the recipient of her instructions. I had no thought but that you and she were of one mind regarding this as other matters."

"Oh, well, yes, no doubt," said Godfrey. "There it is then. I shall have to make up my mind to it. I am tied up. There is an end of the good things of life for me; they are out of my reach. Unless I give up the good things I have. That is a fair way of putting it, I grant. Well, I suppose my wife thought it would be my pleasure to live in the past. I believe many people find it so, you among them, Spong. But everyone is not the same."

"No, that cannot be," said Dominic, a flush suddenly suffusing his face. "But for that very reason, Sir Godfrey, it was incumbent upon me not to leave you in ignorance of your position, an ignorance which I admit had been suggested to me as not impossible."

"Yes, well, I must pick myself up," said Godfrey. "I have a good deal of a life before me. I must not let myself sink to the level of bitterness. I must hold myself above that, above rancour against a poor, dead woman who was after all my wife, with whom I spent many happy years. I must learn not to ask much for myself, not to set my own claims high. After all, my life is in the past. She was life for me. It was the reaction from all my troubles that made me set it in the future. My wife knew me, Spong. She knew my temper, that does rebound. That poor, weak, suffering woman, who had hardly strength to continue her own life, who had not strength to continue it, had thought to give to the man who should have cared for her to keep him anchored where his heart was. Anyone might have had me, Spong; I might have been the prey of any woman. My very reaction would have flung me wide of any mark. I am grateful to my wife for divining my true heart. Hand-in-hand she and I made that will, as if we had made it together. And I daresay we did make it together; I daresay we spoke of it. You know I was never one for remembering much about these things. She was always there to take them off me. And she cares for me still. She leaves me what was hers, for my pleasure as long as I live, my dear, generous wife, provided that I remain faithful to her memory, so that we can go on our way essentially one. It is my young people who are having their romance, my Griselda and Gregory. In thinking of them, and identifying myself with them, I let my thoughts run on in the same groove. It was as if I imagined them deprived of their income, if they should marry, poor young things! I was quite put about by setting myself in their place. Well, Spong, I have to say to you that I thank you for your help, and for any help you gave to my wife in this matter and any other. Unless it was I myself in this one; I can't call it to mind. Well, we have the work to do, that she has left, in bequeathing to me her worldly all. I must recall what she said to me, just as I recalled what we did together, either in letter or spirit, just now. We shall have to get to it before long."

"That will devolve upon us in the near future. I had thought,

Sir Godfrey, I own I had gathered from your initial manner of expressing yourself, that you were surprised, perhaps even taken aback, by the conditions of the will. I am relieved to hear from you that that is not the case."

"Oh, no; yes. That is as I have told you, Spong."

"Yes, yes," said Dominic. "Yes indeed, Sir Godfrey. And now we can proceed to a general discussion, if you are so minded, or we can postpone grappling with general problems to a future occasion. I am leaving home for a short time upon matters connected with my own life, that I need not bring to your atten- tion." Dominic put his finger-tips together and looked at them, but Godfrey did not ask to have the matters so brought. "But on my return I shall be prepared to give my mind with you to what demands it."

"Yes, yes, Spong, that will be best. To tell you the truth, I am so wrapped up in my two young ones' fortunes, and my poor Matthew's troubles, and my personal bereavement, that I am hardly up to business at the moment. I might go off again at a tangent, and talk as if I were another man, and put you in doubt what to make of me. I still feel very uncertain and rooted up. Ah, it leaves one in a sort of fever. We will let it stand over for the present. And thank you, Spong, thank you. You will have some tea?"

The volume of Godfrey's thanks seemed vaguely to cover something beyond what was ostensible.

"No, I thank you, I will not, Sir Godfrey," said Dominic, with satisfaction in the positive refusal. "I have another appointment to keep. In fact, a friend is waiting for me at your gates; and I am proposing to hurry to her, as the sex indicated by my pronoun commands my haste."

Godfrey shook hands and turned and strode to the

drawing-room, which was peopled as usual by his family and friends.

"Well, well, that is over. I have had to see Spong, and square myself for the future. It is of no good to shirk, but I shall miss Harriet. I needn't say that, but I shall miss her in all these dealings with Spong. I can't bring myself to face Spong in her spirit; I can't manage him as she did. There is something about Spong." Godfrey gave a fillip with his fingers. "I can't say what it is; it is something I can't put a name to, that I haven't any fancy for. It is no matter, as he didn't show it to Harriet. Harriet was not a person who invited that kind of thing. I don't expect him to look on me in the same light; I don't do it myself. Well, Harriet has had her own way; she has, my girl! She made her will as it took her fancy, and I am glad she did. I am to have everything for my life, apart from the legacies to the sons and daughter; and then it is to go to the children, hers and mine. And I am to remain her widower; I am to do that. If I marry again, I lose every fraction of a farthing of what was hers!" He brought one hand down on the other, as if in satisfaction at the thoroughness of the condition. "Those are the terms. She would have her husband. And I am glad she would. I am exalted, I am flattered by it. It makes no difference to me. I don't want to marry again. I wouldn't insult her memory by speaking of it, if she had not put in the clause herself. But, would you believe it, Spong looked at me quite dubious out of the corner of his eye. I declare I could have let out at him, sitting there with his head on one side. Harriet had the touch with him. He tried to twist something I said—about Griselda and Gregory I believe it was, or said with them in mind—into an expression of resentment against my wife! I had a word to say to him then. I suppose he has never met couples with an understanding between them. I understand what was in my girl's mind, as well as if she had explained it to me. I daresay she did put it to me, only I have no memory for such things. That may be why I jumped at comprehension, that I was clear about it underneath. On the surface of course I had thought of the two of us going down into old age together. Not that I am getting near to that; I could wish I were, with Harriet gone from me. Well, Gregory, I hope you will have as much in your married life as I had in mine. That is your father's wish for you."

"It must be, Godfrey," said Rachel. "No one could do more than have a wife who admired him enough to think that other people would too, and actually put the feeling on record. So few people will reveal appreciation. I am quite up in arms about Percy and his first wife. She might have done better by him, even though she had not the illustration of him that we have. Harriet always comes out wonderfully."

"But I don't understand Mother's reasons for doing it," said Gregory.

"Gregory, Gregory, no hint of criticism!" said his father, raising his hand.

"Do you understand?" said Rachel in an undertone to Dufferin. "Harriet told you more than she told me."

"It was because she knew that Godfrey would marry anyone, and could be himself with almost no one," said Dufferin. "The tragedy of their lives was that he was himself with her. She never ceased to save her family from themselves, and to do it in her own way."

"Yes, yes, well, a woman, you know. It is well enough for a woman to do it," said Sir Percy, as the result of reflection.

"Yes, yes, it is, Hardisty," said Godfrey. "If a man did it, I daresay I should think him the meanest skunk on earth. But a woman may do as she likes. And anyhow my Harriet may. My

Harriet might do as she would with me. Ah, she knew she might. And I am glad she knew it, even though she has made me a little conspicuous in some eyes. They are not the eyes that matter, and it is a small price to pay for her having her mind at peace. I pay it willingly. But I can't have Spong mouthing at me, and making out that I am an injured husband, and what not. I am not prepared to put up with that."

"I heard some rumour that Spong was engaged to be married," said Jermyn. "But I thought nothing of it. It didn't seem likely. But perhaps it is true, and that is why he felt for you in your bondage."

"Oh, well, bondage. Well, some people might call it that. Some men might feel it in that way; I am not among them. But it can't be true about Spong. Spong is as safe as old Time. He wouldn't be a man a woman would fall for. It surprises me that a woman did once. To do him justice he is faithful to that woman's memory. That is the best thing about Spong. That always enhances our opinion of a man. But there wasn't any need to make conditions about him. His wife could spare herself the trouble, and no doubt did. And that is why he thought he had a look-in on me, when really the look-in was on the other side."

"The announcement of Mr. Spong's engagement is in the local weekly paper, Sir Godfrey," said Buttermere shaking out the teacloth. "It is out this afternoon, and there is a copy procured as is customary for the servants' hall."

"Oh, is that so indeed? Is it to anyone particular?" said Godfrey.

"Who is it, Buttermere?" said Jermyn.

"I will procure the paper, sir," said Buttermere.

"Let us guess," said Gregory. "I guess Mrs. Christy. I know Spong has been hanging about her house lately."

303

"Yes, it might be. But it is disloyal of you not to guess Geraldine," said Rachel.

"I guess Geraldine," said Polly.

"That is right, my dear," said Rachel.

"Not Mellicent?" said Godfrey.

"No, of course not, Haslam," said Sir Percy.

"Well, well, it must be someone," said Godfrey. "No one is likely, you know."

"Mrs. Calkin?" said Griselda.

"Well, I don't know why not," said Jermyn.

"I declare I expect it is Mrs. Calkin," said Godfrey. "No one is too old for Spong. I guess Agatha Calkin. Now we shall see if I am right."

Buttermere proffered the paper and left the room.

"Well now, let us see," said Godfrey, turning at random to a page and looking down it. "Oh, all right, Rachel, take it from me then. Well, you tell us all in a minute who it is."

"Yes, I will. Births, marriages, deaths!" said Rachel. "Oh, pull yourselves together! I could so easily have guessed it, and now I shall never have the credit. It is Camilla!"

"Oh, it can't be. I know for a fact that it can't be," said Godfrey. "I can tell you for certain that there is a mistake."

"We could all have done that," said Jermyn. "But it has not prevented it. It is a good thing Matthew is not here."

"Yes, yes, it is, the poor boy!" said Godfrey, after a pause. "Well, that is what old Spong had up his sleeve! Well, to me it is a disgusting thing for a girl to marry a middle-aged man. I shan't be able to get it out of my head. Spong is nearly my age. I should not have believed it. This does away with the redeeming point of Spong. I am quite pulled up by the thought of my poor Matthew's feelings."

"I should think he will feel less about her than he has yet," said Griselda.

"Yes, yes, he will, Griselda," said her father in a tone of realisation. "You say the truth. If anything could cure a man of infatuation, it would be a thing of this kind. I can say that for certain. Well, it may be for the best. She is tied up now, and no one can come to grief over her. Enough people have come to it, and there might have been more. For if any woman could make a man feel she was the one woman in the world for him, I declare it was that girl. I can put myself in Matthew's shoes as if I were standing in them."

"She always gave you a high place," said Gregory.

"Well, I believe she did," said Godfrey. "I believe she thought I wasn't so little of a man, not quite to be put on one side with a woman like herself. But what beats me, is how she can have fallen for Spong. For if there is a man more different in every way, who is more of an absolute contrast, who is less of what a woman might be supposed to want, you have to show him to me. I can't get at the bottom of it at all."

"He is very well off," said Dufferin. "His wife left him a fair fortune, and he has saved more than would enter the minds of ordinary spending men. A man is a man to Camilla, and he is a safe and sound fellow of his kind. Camilla always liked possessions better than people. It is for herself that she has to choose."

"Yes, yes, that is how it is," said Godfrey. "It shows how people are right when they impose conditions. Harriet had right on her side. I even felt it when she hinted to me that she would like to make the restriction, poor girl! I was glad to be saved from myself. I was glad she wanted to be tied to me. Why are you staring at me, Rachel? You are all eyes. It was a tribute, after all the years we had lived together as man and wife."

"It was a most fitting tribute," said Rachel. "But you have had quite enough credit for it, Godfrey."

"What amuses me," said Godfrey, "well, I don't mean it amuses me; what I take satisfaction in, is that Harriet has had everything turn out as she wished. Matthew is off to London to pursue his profession, and Jermyn to Cambridge for the same sort of thing, and Griselda is quit of her parson, and Gregory of the old dames, and I myself am laid up high and dry! I mean she got in her say about me as well. It is some compensation for being out of things, for passing on before, to see your wisdom bearing fruit. For it all followed on in a manner. Not that she needs compensation where she is now. It is we who need that."

"Harriet was always a fortunate woman," said Rachel.

A NOTE ON THE AUTHOR

Ivy Compton-Burnett was born in Middlesex in 1884. Compton-Burnett was encouraged by her liberal and unorthodox father, homeopath Dr Burnett, to prepare to read classics at London university (neither Oxford nor Cambridge gave degrees to women at this time). She had dearly loved her father, who died without warning from a heart attack in 1901 when she was sixteen. Her closest brother died three years later, and Ivy Compton-Burnett went on to lose three more of her younger siblings and her mother by the time she was 35, something she could hardly bear to speak about, but constantly explored in her novels.

Compton-Burnett published twenty novels, the first while she was in her twenties, in 1911. However, the first of her works to use her mature and startlingly original style was published when she was forty, in 1925. Compton-Burnett's fiction deals with domestic situations in large households which, to all intents and purposes, invariably seem Edwardian. The description of human weaknesses and foibles of all sorts pervades her work, and the family that emerges from each of her novels must be seen as dysfunctional in one way or another.

She was named a Dame Commander of the British Empire in 1967, two years before her death in 1969.

S
H
M

50
18

32